THE DOUBLE DELIGHT COMPLETE COLLECTION

ROMANCE IN NYC: DOUBLE DELIGHT

ANGEL DEVLIN

SOLD

DOUBLE DELIGHT BOOK ONE

CHAPTER ONE

Tiffany

Monday evenings were 'girls' night' in our apartment in Dyker Heights, Brooklyn. All three of us worked as realtors for a Brooklyn real estate company and we worked damn hard. So Mondays were downtime, complete with pizza and beer. There was me, Kayla and Haley. Our Monday nights were for sharing stories about work and to catch up on our—currently nightmarish—love lives. None of us were having much luck on the romantic front.

"Please can we not watch a movie with a sexy leading man tonight, because I swear my pussy will combust and it won't be a pretty sight," Kayla moaned. At twenty-four, Kayla was tall and slim, with pale skin, and long wavy red hair. She was stunning but attracted to men who were dicks. She hadn't had a date for at least two weeks and it was killing her.

"That bad, huh?" I asked.

"Yeah, I might go visit Daniel. While I'm there, I can see if there are any hot men currently hanging around Long Island." Kayla's stepfather lived on Long Island. Her mother—a serial cheater—had moved on long ago and had lost touch with her daughter. Kayla hadn't stayed at Daniel Scott's much, but out of all her many stepfathers he had been the only one to be a pretty decent man and he had always said there was a room for her at his home, even after her mother's departure. She visited rarely, but felt she owed it to him to check in. Guilt from her mother screwing him out of a lot of his cash no doubt.

"Well, I have a date tomorrow night. I think this might be the one," Haley said.

Kayla and I groaned simultaneously. Haley was a born romantic and every date she had, she thought would be her Prince Charming. Instead, they ended up being the Princes of Darkness. Petite, with long, straight, dark-brown hair, and an ass a Kardashian would envy, Haley was soft spoken and quite innocent. She'd only had one lover—a long term sweetheart—and when he had left her after college she had been devastated. She had felt he was her one, and we were sure she believed that one day he would actually come back for her.

"God, dating sucks," I proclaimed. "I had another loser send me a message through the company email today."

"Ugh, creep." Kayla said with a smirk on her face.

It happened a lot at Green's Real Estate. Our photographs were on the web page under Agents, along with our direct line and email address. Usually, it was a breathy phone call asking whether I was wearing panties, but today's had been an actual email.

I brought it up on my cell. "Listen to this," I told my friends, then I began to read it out loud.

TIFFANY,

Is this really you on your photograph? I guess I'll have to find out by meeting you. Right now, I'm looking at this headshot with my ten-inch dick in my hand. I'm imagining that my other hand is fisting your shoulder-length, blond hair; dragging your head downward toward my cock. Those green eyes are wide and begging for me to open your pouting lips and fill you with my girth. Your pink lipgloss is smeared over my cock while I push myself in and out of your hot mouth. You might try to hide your breasts under that baggy top, but I can tell you have huge tits begging for release. I'll suck on your nipples and then I'm going to stick my cock between those creamy mountains and fuck them until I come all over your face; your smeared pink gloss mixed with my creamy cum.

Speak soon, H.

"OH MY FUCKING GOD, WHAT A CREEP," Haley gasped. "Did you report it?"

"Nah, I get similar things at least once a week. Don't you?"

Haley shook her head. "No. I've never had a message like that."

"She doesn't have a photo posted, does she?" Kayla reminded me. "She's the sensible one."

"Well, I replied that I found his post offensive and not to contact me again."

"Really?" Kayla asked cocking an eyebrow. "I

think it's damn hot."

"You think everything's hot today. You need to go out and get laid."

"I do. I really do." She whined.

"Okay, Haley, get the pizza ordered. Kayla, go grab some beer from the fridge while I choose a movie. One with some ugly dudes and no sex scenes whatsoever."

"I think even an old wrinkled guy with warts would do it for me right now," Kayla moaned.

"Chick flick it is." I announced.

THAT NIGHT, with my stomach satisfyingly full of pizza, and feeling sated thanks to a couple beers, I quickly changed into my shorts and camisole and climbed under my duvet. I dreamed vividly about a man with short blond hair. I met him in a bar and he was someone I had known in the past. Years had passed, and I found him hot and attractive. He felt the same. I woke just after we had shared a panty melting kiss, with the promise of meeting again. A sigh escaped me. It had seemed so real and yet was a figment of my overactive imagination. My thighs clenched together. I didn't want it to end there. Fuck it! I'd carry it on in my half-awake thoughts.

．　．　．

I RETURN *to the bar and to the image of this blond-haired man. My lips back on his. His tongue invades my mouth, going deep and tangling with my own.*

"Want to get out of here?" He asks.

"Yes."

I pictured the frantic removal of clothing in his apartment and then my mind reverted to the email I received earlier. I tried to get my thoughts to take a different route, but they were relentless.

In my imagination I drop to my knees, taking the man's raging cock in my mouth. I'm so full, I have to stop myself from gagging. I cup his balls in my hand and lick around the tip of his swollen mushroom head, letting it slide in and out of my mouth. It makes a popping sound each time I let him free. He's frustrated and gripping my hair, forcing me to take him deeper in my throat. I suck hard and he groans, his pleasure evident on his face. He watches me, eyes alert as I continue to suck. He fucks my face hard until I feel his balls pull back, tightening, and then he fills me with his cum, emptying his load straight to the back of my throat. I swallow him down and lick my lips. He thanks me and wipes a thumb over my lip,

*smearing my pink lip gloss and droplets of his cum up
my cheek.*

"Beautiful." He says in a deep husky voice.

GODDAMN, I couldn't take any more of the
fantasy, so I shoved my hand down my shorts. I could
feel my engorged lips, slick with my juices, and I
pushed one finger, then another, into my pussy. I
pistoned them, imagining they were my fantasy
lover's cock. It took me over the edge and I tried to be
quiet—with my friends' rooms so near to my own—
but I had to let out a tumultuous scream as I shuddered with my orgasm. The sound was unmistakable.
I felt my cheeks flush. I pulled my legs together; the
aftershocks, smaller shudders, still coming. My
breath finally evened out, and I felt so relaxed, all the
tension having left my body. I turned over in bed to
finally try to get some sleep.

"I want whatever you're having." Kayla shouted
out from the adjacent room.

Fuck! I pretended I was snoring by making loud
noises as if I was innocent, but in reality my hand
went back between my legs, feeling how soaked I
was and how much I had dampened my shorts.

. . .

OUR APARTMENT HAD one open-plan area with a dining table to one corner, a small kitchen to another, and a living room that faced a large balconied patio window. To the back of the room was a long corridor where at the end were our three bedrooms and two bathrooms. The main tenant, Haley, had the room with the en-suite bathroom and patio window with a balcony, and Kayla and I shared the other bathroom. Walking past, I could hear the shower running and her singing. I wasn't a morning person, preferring to have coffee and breakfast before my own shower, so this worked out just fine. I poured a coffee from the pot and took a seat at the corner table, banging my mug down on the table top. Hot coffee sloshed out of the mug, scalding my hand.

"Fuck me, that's hot."

Kayla chose that moment to walk through, rubbing her hair with a towel. "Is that what you were saying last night in your fantasies, you dirty bitch?"

I blushed. "I don't know what you're talking about."

"If that's how you want to play it." She impersonated my loud orgasm noise. "That noise came from your room last night; you might want to check out what it was."

Haley turned to us from her position on the

couch, throwing her magazine down. "There's nothing wrong with masturbating. We all do it. Christ, I'd have seized up by now if I didn't."

"Haley!" We said in tandem. It was so unusual for Haley to say anything so bluntly.

"Well it's true. My B.O.B. is my other best friend apart from you two."

We all laughed.

Haley changed the subject, obviously done with any carnal conversation. "What's everyone up to today? Anything exciting?"

"I'm showing a client around a condo at Brighton Beach." I told them.

"Oh my god, I love it out there," Haley said, her hands clasped together. "Swap me so I can go visit."

"Not a chance with the commission I'll earn if I get him to purchase."

"It's a purchase, not a rental?" Kayla qualified.

"Sure is. A steal at $3.5m."

"*Jeez.*" Haley said. "Do you think between us we could buy a brick each?"

I chuckled. "So, my schedule is to meet the client at eleven, and I have nothing else going on because I centered my whole day around trying to get Mr. Carter of Carter Property Enterprises, to part with his cash." I swallowed the rest of my coffee and snatched Kayla's pop tart out of her hand. I took a bite and walked toward the shower. "Catch you guys later."

"Thanks for waiting to listen about my day," Kayla yelled out. "And for eating my breakfast."

I WAITED for Mr. Carter to show up in the lobby of the Brighton Condominium and Club. The lobby looked like it belonged to a luxury hotel: with reception, and a concierge, on first entering; and with a waiting area, plus a bar and restaurant set further back. The building had twenty-four-hour security, a gym, pools, and private beach access. I didn't want coffee breath when I met my client, so I sucked on a mint while I watched the doorway.

Two men entered the building at once. One was middle-aged, balding, and short. The other looked like a movie-star. I bet I knew which one was my client. Sure enough, the older one walked toward me. "Could you tell me, are you Miss Harris?"

"I am." I shook his hand. "It's a pleasure to meet you, Mr. Carter."

"Oh, no, sorry, you're mistaken." The gentleman said. "I'm Mr. Carter's driver. He's waiting for you in the bar." I turned around, following the man's pointed finger and my gaze was met by steely gray eyes from the movie-star man. "If you would like to go through to meet him, I'll go wait in the car."

I was intrigued. He couldn't introduce himself? I supposed he didn't know for sure it was me. Not everyone looked up my photo like the pervert. I stood up and brushed down my peach, knee-length skirt. My heels clacked on the marble floor as I made my way over to the bar.

"Mr. Carter?" I held out my hand.

"Miss Harris." He took my hand in his, holding it a fraction too long. I noted his hands were huge, his fingers had thick digits. His skin was as smooth as the marble floor under my feet. I took in his appearance: blond hair that was slicked back and came to midway down his neck and a chin covered by a touch of pale stubble. He was a man who worked out, had a medium-build, and I would put him at six foot two. He was dressed in a sharp business suit, but lacked a tie, and his white shirt had the two top buttons undone.

"I thought we would talk first before you showed me the condo. I like to know who I'm doing business with." He stated.

"That's fine." I nodded, removing my peach jacket, as it was becoming too warm for me in the bar. I watched his eyes follow my jacket, pausing for a fraction as my pale-blue blouse gaped at the front. Sometimes my large bust was entirely frustrating. I tried to keep my jacket on wherever possible and cover the girls up, but today was too warm and I gave up. I'd just have to put up with my chest being spoken to. It wouldn't be the first time. However, Mr. Carter's gaze quickly returned to my face, and that's where it stayed throughout the rest of our conversation, which made a refreshing change.

He ordered us two mineral waters. I didn't mind. I found a lot of these successful businessmen liked to do that. Displaying their egos as they took charge.

I explained about my background with Green's.

"So you have a lot of experience with rich businessmen then?" He asked, appraising me coolly.

"I'm one of Green's main realtors in high end real estate."

"Could I ask you something personal?" His finger skimmed around the top of his glass which emitted a whistling sound.

"Sure, though whether I'll answer or not depends on the question."

"Do you have rich businessmen bothering you all the time, thinking they can buy you as well as the property?"

My eyes narrowed. "No. They've never been anything but professional. They know should they be anything less, their reputation would be tarnished. Green's is a very friendly firm and we are all looked after. I have an alarm that rings straight to the office. Should anything unexpected happen, the cops would be on their ass before they'd have a chance to feel mine up."

"Good. I'd hate to think you had to put up with that," he answered. Mr. Carter smiled at me and it changed his whole appearance. His face looked years younger. I swore his eyes looked a warmer shade of gray, and his lips parted to show a row of pearly white teeth with one canine slightly twisted at the right-hand side of his front teeth. The fact that he had this slight imperfection pleased me. He was too perfect before. Now he seemed more human, just from that one flaw.

"Are you ready for me to show you the condo now?" I asked him.

"Absolutely. Lead the way." He said.

We took the elevator up to the eighth floor and I walked us to the apartment and opened the door.

"After you." I told him.

He walked inside.

The apartment opened into a spacious hallway

which resembled a mini version of the downstairs lobby with the marble floor. There were coat hooks, a coat rack, shoe racks and a sofa. I pushed and held open a further door which led into a vast open living area. There were windows to the front and right of the apartment that all overlooked the beach. The sunshine streamed in through the windows making the room glow and showing it to its best potential. The view was nothing less than stunning.

Mr. Carter turned to me. "Amazing view."

"Yes, it's something isn't it?"

He looked at me and there was a beat of hesitation before he replied, "Quite something."

The open living area housed a large kitchen which ran from where the windows ended on the right-hand side. It was dark wood and masculine. Not to my taste, but I hoped it appealed to his. I was led to believe this was a personal purchase as opposed to a business one. Quite a few clients purchased Brighton Beach condos and stayed there in the summer, commuting from their New York apartments. I showed him the bathroom next which was large, white, and functional.

I sang the praises of the separate large shower cubicle.

"It's just a bathroom. It's fine. Show me the master bedroom please, Miss Harris."

"Of course, right this way."

I opened the master bedroom door, and he walked through first, heading straight for the large window which gave him the same fabulous view of the beach. His gaze scanned the rest of the room: a simple wooden bed and matching bedroom furniture.

"What's your opinion of this room, Miss Harris, because I find it lacking."

I squirmed under his stare. "I agree, this room is quite basic given the luxury furnishings of the rest of the property; however, that may be something you could use to negotiate on price."

"Do you know what would improve this room?" He asked, passing me and walking toward the door.

I shook my head. "I wouldn't know your own interests, but I'm sure you would be able to hire an interior designer to bring to life any vision you had."

"What would improve this room..." He hesitated before switching the lock on the bedroom door. "Would be your naked body lying on that bed." His voice lowered to a husky whisper. A whisper suited for seduction.

I reached into my pocket for my alarm.

He held up his hand.

"I'm not going to attack you, Miss Harris."

My heart thudded in my chest. "Then why did you lock the door?"

"Just a precaution, so that no staff members accidentally interrupt us."

"Accidentally interrupt what? I'm showing you a condo." I snapped.

He walked toward me and whispered in my ear.

"Well it's up to you. You can reach past me and unlock it. I won't stop you."

I sighed. By now I should have kicked him in the balls and made my escape, so why hadn't I?

"Perhaps I should introduce myself properly, Tiffany." He smirked and held out his hand. "My name is Henry Carter, but you can call me H."

My eyes widened. Fuck! That email. It was him!

"So, Tiff... if I may be so bold as to call you that. Either you can leave, or you can lie on that bed and we'll do everything from my email and more. You decide. All I can say is that I wasn't lying when I said ten inches."

I swallowed, and my mouth went dry.

Should I stay, or should I go?

CHAPTER TWO

H

Some might say I was taking a huge risk with the game I was playing, but I didn't give a fuck. When you're rich, life could become extremely monotonous. When you had seen one luxury apartment, you had seen them all. I had assistants I sent out to do my property investment shit. But I looked at Green's web page and eye-fucked the photo of the luscious Tiffany Harris. I sent her an email from a non-traceable address, wondering how she would react. I tricked her landlord into letting one of my men in as a television repairman. Dumb fuck. He hid a camera in her room instead. It's so easy to hide one these days. I watched as she finger-fucked herself last night. She shouted out the word H as she came. Tiffany wanted me. She wanted the thrill of me. From what I had been able to find out, she'd had two semi-serious boyfriends in the past. Maybe they could fuck, but they wouldn't have been able to give her what I could. There's more in my plan for Tiff, but for now she stood in the bedroom, biting her lip, while she decided on her next move. It had better be towards the bed.

Tiffany

JESUS CHRIST! Why hadn't I left yet?

I'd tell you why. Because the man that stood before me looked like sex on a stick and he wanted to do dirty things to me.

Because I hadn't been fucked in over three months.

Because I kept picturing that email and the fact that although I told the others it creeped me out, the truth was it made me cream my panties.

Then there was last night and my feverish orgasm from a fantasy that started with a dream man and finished with thoughts of that very email.

He would do all of that with me?

Fuck my mouth with that cock.

Fuck my tits with his huge dick.

My nipples hardened. My breasts strained against my bra trying to make a break for freedom.

I stared up at H. He had that smirk on his face. He thought I was going to bolt.

"This is just between us, right? No one will know what happened in this room?"

"Correct, Miss Harris."

"I think you should stick with Tiff, if we're going to fuck, H." A sly grin pulled at my lips.

I placed my purse and my jacket on the dresser in the room. Then I stood in front of H and unbuttoned my blouse. He watched; his gaze a far cry from the man who smiled at me in the bar downstairs. He was completely predatory.

I pulled my blouse down my arms and discarded it to the floor. It was very hard to find a good fitting bra when you had tits that poured out over the top and the sides of the cups. I made a note to pay extra to get a proper fitted bra in case I ever found myself in a position like this again. H growled, and his hands were on me in a flash.

"Those fucking big titties. They're more than I ever imagined while I was jerking off." He pulled the straps down on either side and pulled my bra down at the front, so my boobs broke free, bouncing against my chest.

His mouth descended onto a nipple and he attempted to cup my breast in his hand. His hand might have been large and meaty, but it was no match for my breast. "Christ, I need two hands for one tit." He dropped one hand and grabbed one of my own and held it against his crotch. He was hard as a rock and I could feel he was about to punch through his own pants if his cock wasn't freed soon. I opened the button of his suit pants and then lowered the zip. It was a struggle against the size of his erection. As his pants came down, I pulled down his boxers and that enormous cock sprang free. Holy shit! There was no way that monster was going to fit in me. I had never seen anything like it in my life. My previous lovers had been average. A bead of pre-cum glistened on the end of his shaft and I ran my finger over it.

"Taste it." He demanded.

"You wanted me to smear it with the pink gloss,

did you not?" I put the droplet on my finger and smeared it onto my lip.

He grabbed my tits and pinched my nipples hard.

"That's for not doing as I asked. I asked you to taste me. I'll decide when your mouth gets coated with my cum, not you."

Oh, he liked to be in charge. Well, I was fine with that. I was feisty in real life, but in the bedroom, I could play a part.

He squeezed the end of his dick, so another droplet appeared. "Now, taste me." He demanded once again.

I swiped the bead of pre-cum with my finger and I sucked my finger into my mouth. My finger made a popping sound when I removed it.

"How do I taste?"

"Hmmm, like citrus and salt." I said breathily. "Like the best tequila flavored milkshake I ever tasted."

"Man milk. Nothing finer for you to drink."

I undid my bra at the back as the fastener was digging into me. I put my hand at the waistband of my skirt and looked to him for direction.

He nodded his consent at removing it. I stepped

out of my skirt, now left in only a lacy black thong and my black three-inch heels.

"Leave those on for now." He directed and then licked his lips.

I nodded.

"Now sit at the edge of the bed."

The chemistry between us was palpable. It had been since the minute we set eyes on each other in the bar. I licked my lips greedily. He was going to fuck me good I could tell. He was going to fuck me hard. I guessed I'd be leaving this room hardly able to walk and exhausted. Thank God, I had taken the rest of the day off! I would need a hot shower and my bed.

I positioned myself at the edge of the bed as he ordered. H stripped off the rest of his clothes, and Jesus was it a sight to behold! I hadn't been treated with such a display even when I had gone to see stripper shows. He removed his jacket first, folding it carefully and placing it over the back of a chair. H's every move was meticulous. His eyes fixed on mine as he unbuttoned his shirt. His hooded eyes impris-oned mine. He did it oh-so-slowly, revealing a rock-hard body with abs I could have bounced hammers off. The 'V' down to his groin made me stifle a moan.

"You like what you see?"

I nodded and licked my lips.

"Touch me. See if it feels as good as it looks."

He knelt between my legs and I ran my hands over the contours of his body. It did indeed feel like I had imagined it would. Taut. Smooth. I felt a drip of cum slide from my pussy out into the hem of my thong. I was soaking wet for him. He leaned over and blew on a nipple, making it peak even further under his ministrations. I could have hung his fucking jacket on it. Then he sucked it into his mouth, the warmth from his tongue contrasting with the cold air he blew before. I squirmed in place, desperate to have him take me, my walls already contracting with the thought of him there. He swapped to the other breast and sucked. Jesus, I could feel my pussy throb. I was so close to coming and he hadn't even touched me there yet.

He sat back, leaving me deprived. "This wasn't how my email started was it? If I recall, it started with you taking my cock in your mouth." He stood up with his dick in his hand. I swallowed. I would have to fit that in my mouth.

"Open wide, Tiff." He said, with a devilish grin that pulled at his lips.

I opened my mouth, and he pushed the tip of his cock in, pulling back out and repeating. In and out, in and out, teasing. I ran my tongue around the tip and up the underside, tasting his pre-cum again. I had to stretch my mouth wide for the girth. He pushed in a little deeper, then pulled back out, deeper again, then back out. The next time he pushed in, I sucked hard, and he groaned. He rammed his cock in as far as he could, right to the back of my throat, and I continued to suck as if my life depended on it. My jaw ached with the stretch and drool ran out the corner of my mouth. He collected it on his fingers and rubbed it into his dick. He positioned his hands behind my head and fisted one into my hair just like he said he would. "Make me come." He commanded.

I took over from his hand, holding his dick in my own hand. Wrapping my fist around the base of his shaft, I licked him from base to tip, swirling my tongue around his head. Then I took him back in my mouth. I remembered some advice I read in a magazine about doing shorter and longer sucks. H groaned and rocked himself in time with the sucks, realizing what I was doing. My jaw ached so much I was in pain, but I didn't care. It mixed with the pleasure. I looked up at H's face and his eyes were closed, his face showing he had given himself over to my mouth. Though I might be doing his bidding, right now it felt like I held all the power. I used the fingers of my spare hand to tease his balls, cupping them in my hand one at a time, stroking them and then running my fingernails down each one.

"Christ." He groaned.

H withdrew from my mouth and stroked the side of my face. "I'm not coming in your mouth today. I'm going to cum all over those gorgeous fucking tits."

He used his fist in my hair to pull me onto my feet. My legs felt unsteady. I was so goddamn horny.

"Lie back on the bed and hold your tits together, leaving me a channel for my cock."

I placed myself on the bed with my head on the pillows and did as he said. He knelt astride me and leaned over, removing the pillows from underneath my head and instead placing one under my chest so it was more pronounced than the rest of me. "Push them together now, that's right."

He pushed his dick between my large breasts and I held my boobs together as he began to move in and out. He slid in and out of the channel I had created for him a few times and then he stopped and withdrew. "Wait."

He walked over to his jacket pocket and withdrew a small bottle of massage oil and then he returned to sitting astride me. Loosening the bottle lid, he poured the oil into his hands; some of it splashed on my body giving me a hint of the cum that would shortly follow. He rubbed the oil between his hands and then rubbed it into my tits. They started to gleam as he massaged the oil in. My tits slipped out of his hands they were so greased up. "Right, where were we?" He asked.

I squished my boobs together again, and he rammed his dick between my breasts, getting faster and faster with each stroke. "One day you're going to titty fuck me from above and you will have to work for my cum in your face, but now I need to fucking finish. Clasp your hands together over the top of your tits."

I did as he ordered, and it meant my boobs were more under control for him. He thrusted between them, his pre-cum mixed with the massage oil, and it made him have a smooth journey back and forth.

His breath came in short, sharp bursts and I felt his body tighten. Then with one final massive thrust, he came in a spurt that landed partly on my neck and partly on my chin. I let go of my breasts, and he grabbed the middle of his cock, rubbing it with his hand and pushing out the last of his cum onto my chest. Then he put his fingers in it and scooping up a pile he rubbed it all over my lips. "Now that's what I was imagining. Your pretty, pink pouty lips covered in my cream. Now lick your lips."

I did as he asked. I felt hot and feverish and completely out of control. He dipped a finger, pushed my soaking wet thong aside and pushed his digit into me. I couldn't help myself. I moaned loudly, unaware of my surroundings for a moment as I lost myself in the feelings that were coursing through my pussy. I was so close to the edge and about to burst.

"Hmm, I think we'll leave it there," he said in a deep, playful voice.

My eyes widened in panic.

"Oh, if only you could see your desperate little face the way I can, baby girl. What do you want me to do to you?"

"I want you to fuck me."

"You want my ten inches stretching that tight little hole of yours?"

"Yes." I felt my pussy get wetter at the thought.

"Go stand by the window."

What?

"I- I can't do that. Someone could see us."

"That's what makes it even more exciting, kitten."

I walked over to the window. The view of the

beach was stunning, yet all I wanted to do was look at H and how his face hungered for me.

He stood behind me and I felt his cock, once again rock-hard, against my ass. He left me and dragged over the chair to the window.

"Put your left foot up on the chair."

I did, and my heel sank into the plush seat.

"I might damage the chair with my heel."

"Fuck, I hope so, or I'm doing something wrong."

I was slightly back from the window, so it was doubtful I could be seen, but the thought excited me. Who would believe the heeled realtor was on the eighth floor having her brains fucked out by her client?

Once again behind me, H put his gym-honed arms around my body and grabbed a firm hold of my breasts. "Got to make sure these babies don't escape my grip with them being all oiled up." He kneaded them with his hands, then let go to flick my nipples. Once again, his flicks connected the sensation in my nipple to a pulse between my legs. He stopped to pull my thong down and off my legs. From our reflection in the window I saw him sniff the crotch of the thong. "I'll be taking this with me to play with tonight." H threw them toward his own pile of clothing.

Grabbing his cock, already sheathed with a condom, he held it against my entrance. He slowly rubbed his thick head against my slit and I swear to God I almost came from that sensation alone.

"Are you ready for me, Tiff? I'm going to stretch you wide."

"Yes, please fuck me now. I'm so close."

With those words he thrust hard, his cock making my channel expand to fit him. Oh fuck, the feeling of fullness within me was incredible. Then he started to move. He thrust his cock in me. I rose on the balls of my feet with each thrust and then back down, my left heel sinking again into the chair cushion. He thrust even harder and faster and my walls relaxed further to accommodate him. I couldn't believe how easily my pussy had accepted his huge length. I caught sight of myself in the reflection from the window. My eyes were glazed. I was wanton with lust and looked like the star of a porn movie.

H fisted one hand around his girth and slammed into me as he brought his other hand around to the front of me and stroked my clit.

"Oh my fucking god, oh my fucking god. Yes, yes, please more."

"My name is H." He growled. "When you

demand an orgasm, you scream my name." He thrust again, his balls slamming into my ass.

"H, please, make me come." I panted, riding toward the edge.

He strummed my clit with his finger, hard and fast, matching his thrusts. It was too much for me. I couldn't take any more and started to peak. I soared and flew as I reached my conclusion and broke apart on his cock, tremors hitting me like an earthquake. His balls tightened and then a moment later he withdrew his cock and came all over my ass. I felt the warm spurts as they hit.

My breathing was ragged, and I needed to lie down. My legs gave way and H swept me up into his arms. He assessed the chair. "Look what you did." I cast my eyes down. There was a hole in the seat of the chair. Fuck. My client would go insane.

H laid me back down on the bed and then went into the bathroom. I heard him wash himself. He returned with two towels. One he had dampened, the other one dry. He wiped me down with the damp cloth and dried me with the other.

"How am I going to explain that these towels got used?"

"Do clients not usually use the bathroom?" H asked.

"No, they tend to use the facilities downstairs."

"I'll take care of it. Nothing money can't fix."

I was reminded of how I was a realtor and he was a successful businessman. I was just a plaything and would probably never see him again. I gave my thanks to fate or whatever gave me this experience that had shown me what sex could be like. Now I would never put up with an average fuck again.

We got dressed in silence. I put on my jacket and grabbed my purse.

"Could I ask you a question?" I asked quietly.

"Sure."

"Did you actually want to view the condo at all or was it all a set up to get into my panties?"

H picked up my thong and waved them in front of me. "These panties?" He asked as his lip curled into a grin, then he placed them in his pocket.

I bit my lip.

"No, I'm interested in the condo, though obviously I had imagined what might happen here. Turns out my imagination was lacking; the reality was much more pleasing."

I smiled. "I'm so glad I didn't disappoint."

"You certainly didn't, Miss Harris," he smiled, and I realized we were back to our professional business selves. "I would like to make an offer on the condo." He picked up the chair. "And you can explain that the strange gentleman making the offer took the chair he damaged with him and left a check for twenty thousand dollars in its place."

I gasped. That amount of money was obscene.

"I'm going to put this chair in my own bedroom in Manhattan and tonight when I drape my jacket across the back of it, I'll think of you grinding your heel into the seat as I ground my cock into your wet cunt."

He looked around the room.

"Well, though basic, this bedroom proved adequate for my needs. However, I'm sure I can get an interior designer to make the entire place my own."

"I'm sure you can."

"I'll be in touch, Miss Harris. Expect an email from me within the next few days."

"Okay," I nodded, and I held out my hand to shake his. "It was a pleasure to meet you, Mr. Carter."

"Oh, the pleasure was all mine. Please pay close attention to your emails. I'm very controlling about having my precise instructions followed."

"Duly noted, Mr. Carter."

"Just one thing before we leave." He turned to

me. A finger at his lip as if he was contemplating his next words. "Have you ever had two men at once?"

"What? *No, I have not.*" I snapped and turning on my heel, I walked out of the room, letting the door slam behind me, even though I was not allowed to leave a client in a property. Well, fuck it.

I heard his laughter behind me, fading as I moved further away.

CHAPTER THREE

Tiffany

I would have run to my car, except I wasn't sure if I would have remained standing due to the lack of energy after that marathon session. I had never had sex like that in my life. My feelings were so jumbled. I didn't know whether I'd had the most amazing time, or if I was just really pissed off with myself for submitting to H's seduction. Oh, who was I trying to kid? I'd had the time of my fucking life, literally. I could barely keep my eyes open, which wasn't great for my drive home. Also, my mind kept replaying what had just happened. I decided to stay behind the wheel for a moment. I closed my eyes and let my mind and body revisit the past hour or so.

Jeez, that body. He was so goddamn hard. If I had a garden, I'd like a statue of that body in it to look at every day. And his cock. Jesus Christ! I had never seen anything like that in my life.

But then he had to spoil it. Ask me if I had ever had a three-way. Two men at the same time. What fucking planet was that man on? I could hardly manage his huge cock, never mind juggle him and another guy at the same time. My traitorous core clenched at the fantasy as my thoughts ran rapidly through my mind. What did he mean? Like a taking turns kind of scenario, or one in my pussy and one in my ass? I felt myself grow wet again which wasn't great considering he kept my panties as some kind of trophy and my juices were going to run straight down my leg and onto my skirt. No more daydreaming, Tiff, I told myself. Well, at least until I got home.

The apartment was empty being that my two girl friends were busy showing properties. Thank god I wasn't competing with Kayla for our bathroom. I headed to my room and stripped off all my clothes. As I looked down, I realized that H had sucked a love-bite onto the side of my breast. I ran over it with my fingers. I carried fresh towels into the bathroom and decided to soak in the tub and began to run the bath. Before steam misted up the mirror, I turned and gazed at my reflection in it. Did I look any different? I felt more confident as a lover, like I actually knew more of what sex could be about. Totally losing myself in the moment. Complete abandon. I stroked between my legs with my fingers. I was sore from being stretched by that ten-inch monster. As I lowered myself into the tub, it stung slightly between my legs, but the heat from the bathwater worked on my muscles and soothed away any tension I had brought home with me. I placed my head back on my bath pillow and once again lost myself in thoughts of what had just happened. I stayed there until the water cooled and then dragged myself out of the tub. Wrapping my body in a huge towel and my hair in a small one, I returned to my room, where I quickly dried my hair and changed into some pajamas. I couldn't crawl under my duvet fast enough; my eyes were closing as I did it, and within minutes I was lost, sleeping away the exhaustion of a delightful fuck.

When I woke and checked my alarm clock it was five in the afternoon. Shit! I had slept for hours. Under my duvet was cozy and warm and I didn't feel like getting out, but I knew I should, or I would never sleep tonight. Sighing, I swung myself out of bed and after a quick bathroom trip, I wrapped a robe around myself and headed into the kitchen for a coffee. I couldn't be bothered to get dressed again. I had no plans for the night, so I would leave my pjs on. I wondered if anyone else picked their night outfit according to their mood? Often, I slept in shorts and a t-shirt, but sometimes comfy pjs were required. Especially when you had been given the orgasm of your life and it had wiped you out. I rubbed my jaw; it was ever so slightly achy. Unsurprising given the workout it had performed. I fired up my laptop at the table and checked my messages but there were no pervy messages from H. There were however business emails pertaining to the sale of the apartment and a celebratory email from my boss congratulating me on a job well done. Apparently, H had informed him that I was a consummate professional and a member of staff to be proud of. Huh? So maybe he didn't mean it when he said he would be in touch in that way? Perhaps I misinterpreted what he had said to me. Could I have misheard his two men comment? I couldn't help feeling disappointed about the fact he might not want a repeat performance. But I did know one thing. I would never chase a man. Been there done that and it had blown up in my face. One of my exes had stopped messaging me and I had discovered it was because his wife had taken his phone from him. Never again. If it was meant to be, he would get in touch with me. I slammed my laptop shut, annoyed with myself. Why was I making such a big deal out of a not-so-quick fuck? I'd had a good time. Hell, I'd had a great time. End of story. One for the memory banks on a hot evening flying solo.

I went over to the kitchen area and started prepping spaghetti for us all for our evening meal.

The girls came in just after seven and arrived within ten minutes of each other. Shoes and jackets were discarded around the room with sighs of relief that feet were no longer in heels. I handed them each a glass of wine and told them dinner would be ready in ten.

"You got home early?" Kayla asked.

"I got home hours ago. I made the sale and rewarded myself with the rest of the day off."

"So, what did you do all day? The apartment doesn't look any tidier." She joked.

"I slept. Today was exhausting."

"You might want to check in with your physician because if showing houses is making you so tired..." added Haley, "sounds like you might need a vitamin or two."

Kayla shook her head. "No, Haley. There's something she's not telling us. Look at her face. She has a little uplift at the corner of her mouth and she's flushed in the face. She only gets that when she has no idea whether to blurt out gossip or not. Spill, bitch."

"Oh look. Dinner's ready." I told them, trying not to laugh.

"Only a small portion for me. I'm meeting Malcolm tonight and don't expect me back," Haley said smiling.

"Malcolm from Green's? When did that happen?" I asked as I filled my plate.

"He asked me out on a date last week, but I needed to think about it. I wasn't totally sure about dating someone from the company. Anyway, today he brought me flowers, so I said I would meet him tonight for a drink."

Kayla and I met each other's gaze. Haley looked at both of us.

"It's not like that. He's really nice. Although I hope he's not too nice." She said with a devilish grin.

"Haley!" I said. "Are you hoping for a booty call tonight?"

She sighed. "It's been a while. It would be nice."

We took our seats around the table, and I finished off and refilled my glass of wine because I could see Kayla staring at me and knew it was only a matter of time before her twenty-questions started.

"So, how did the condo showing go? Did the client go for it?"

I nodded. "He did. He was very impressed with the place."

"So, who was he? Anyone we know?"

"His name is Henry Carter."

Kayla's eyes lit up. "Oh, he's hot. I've seen his photos in the papers. Totally loaded in the pants and in the wallet from what I have heard."

I blushed. She caught it.

"Oh my god, what are you not telling us? Spill!"

I took another gulp of my wine. "You know that disgusting email I read out to you?"

"The one with all the filthy things that man wanted to do to you, or you to him? Yes?"

"Well..."

"No!" Kayla's eyes widened. "It was him?"

I nodded. "Yup, Henry Carter is H."

"Holy shit! So, what happened? Did he come on to you? Lean in and kiss you? How did it play out?"

"She might not want to tell you, Kayla. She might want to keep it private, you know?" Haley said. "Though I hope not because we want all the juicy details." She pulled her chair closer to mine. Kayla laughed and did the same with her chair.

I sighed. Then I told them everything that happened from the moment I had met him in the bar to the moment I had left to get in my car.

"Holy fucking Christ. I think I'm going to have to go get my vibrator just from your verbal replay." Kayla said and then let out a laugh.

"I really hope I'm getting fucked tonight." Haley frowned.

"Ten inches? Ten fucking inches and wide too? Does he have a brother? Scratch that," Kayla smirked and then grabbed her laptop. "I'll check for myself."

"Kayla, eat the damn dinner I made for us. Haley's out tonight. We'll curl up on the sofa with the rest of the bottle of wine and do a full internet search."

"You're on."

"DO I LOOK ALL RIGHT?" Haley asked. I wished she was a bit more confident. She was so pretty, but always hid herself in tent-like dresses because she was embarrassed about her big ass. She was wearing a red dress that reached her knees and she did look nice. It suited her petite frame.

I checked out the back of it. "Easily unzipped and off. Yes, it passes."

She smiled. "That's why I chose it."

It was good to see her getting herself back on the dating scene. It had been a while and I think her confidence took a hit from her last boyfriend who had told her she was hopeless in bed because she refused to give him a blow job one night. Apparently, he wasn't all that great on the hygiene. Made me feel sick thinking about it.

"I'll lock the door behind you. Grab your purse," I told her.

As I opened the door, I saw a guy walk out of the apartment opposite ours. It had been vacant up until last week and this was the first time we had seen any hint of a new tenant. He stopped and stared at us.

And I'm very sure both of us stared back at him, because he was around six foot four, with short dark brown hair, shaved at the sides and longer on top. He had a very of-the-moment beard and mustache. He was wearing tight-fitting jeans, and a navy t-shirt that showed a sleeve of tattoos on his corded left arm. More tattoos poked out from around his neckline.

"Hey, neighbors. I was gonna come and introduce myself tomorrow, but I guess there's no time like the present. Unless you're in a rush?" He nodded toward Haley. It was at that point I realized I was standing there in my pjs and robe. Jesus, what a first impression.

"The elevator can wait a few minutes. Hey there, I'm Haley. Haley Martin." Haley held out her hand very formally, and he shook it.

"I'm Brandon. Brandon Bailey." They dropped hands and he turned to me and held his arm outstretched for a handshake.

I noted his long fingers. My mom used to call them piano fingers. I compared them to the meaty digits that were in me earlier. He stared at me. Christ, was he reading my mind? Then I realized I had left him holding his arm out while I daydreamed.

I shook his hand. "I'm Tiffany Harris, seeing that we're doing the formal thing with the handshakes and surnames and all."

He laughed, exposing a row of perfect white teeth. Fuck me, was he an actor or something?

"No, I'm not an actor." He smiled as the amusement washed over his face.

What the fuck? Had I said it out loud?

"Nothing as exciting as that. I'm a fitness instructor."

Haley received a text on her cell. "I have to run guys. My date has arrived."

"Good luck." I told her. "Hopefully we won't see you later."

"Fingers crossed," she yelled back.

"Right," I said to Brandon. Mr. Fitness Instructor.

Boy, I'd bet he could go for hours.

I chastise myself. Since earlier today I had been like some desperate horny housewife. "Well, I have to go. Things to do and all that."

"Yes, I was on my way to work."

I looked back at his jeans and t-shirt.

"Oh, I don't wear my gear there."

"I'm sorry. I'm being very rude. Ignore me, I've had a hard day. I'll be okay tomorrow after a good night's sleep."

"What do you do?" He asked.

"I'm a realtor for Green's."

"Bet you meet some interesting people in that line of work. I know I do in mine. We should share stories sometime over a coffee. A get-to-know-the-neighbor welcome coffee," he corrected, as my eyes widened and I stepped back.

"Tiff, what the fuck are you doing out there?" Kayla yelled from the room. I heard her footsteps pad closer to the door.

"Oh hey," she said to Brandon.

"This is the last roommate for you to meet." I said. "Kayla Jackson, meet Brandon Bailey."

"Fuck me, you're hot." She told him.

"Erm, thanks?" He chuckled.

"Kayla!" I scolded her.

"God, calm down. I'm just calling it like I see it. He's not my type. Sorry," she apologized. "I either like 'em young or a bit older. Come back and see if I'm single in about fifteen years, okay?"

I shook my head at her and mouthed 'I'm sorry' at Brandon.

"I found some interesting stuff on the internet search," she told me. "Don't be long."

"I am so sorry." I told Brandon. My face was flushed with the heat of my embarrassment. "I cannot believe what she just said to you. She gets worse."

"I hear worse at work, seriously. It's even more uncomfortable when they are interested. I have no problem with someone who isn't."

"Well, as a politer member of the household, a coffee would be very nice sometime. We can either have it here or we can come to you."

"Oh, don't bring the others." He said. "One's too shy and one's too bold. You. You're just right."

He winked and walked off down the corridor

toward the elevator and once again I ended up standing wide-eyed and speechless at the words from a man's mouth. Twice in one day. What were the odds?

I turned around and closing the door behind me with my foot, I clasped my robe over my chest and headed to the living room to find out what Kayla had discovered and got ready to drink a shit load of wine.

CHAPTER FOUR

Tiffany

I was daydreaming about my day's adventures while Kayla related boring pieces of information to me that she had read on the internet. He's rich. Blah. She couldn't find out anything about his private life, but he never showed up at business events with a woman on his arms.

"If he hadn't fucked you senseless, I would think he was fucking gay."

"Close the laptop now, I'm bored. Let's watch a movie."

"Oh, hang on, what's this? His name's on a

forum. Listen to this. "Henry Carter is the owner of a private members' club in New York called S. Members are not allowed to divulge what the club is about which makes it seem a little bit forbidden and naughty. If anyone can shed light on this, please let us know."

"And does anyone?" I asked.

"No." Kayla sighed.

"Well, there you go. More pointless hearsay."

"I want to go there."

"Well, you can't, can you? Because it's a private members' club which you're not invited to."

"I bet you could get us invited."

I turned to her. "Oh yeah? How do you work that out?"

"Call him. You have his number through work."

"I am not calling that man after what I did with him today. That would look needy."

"Tiff, you've been in bed all afternoon, so you aren't going to be in a rush to get to sleep. I'm bored of sitting and watching movies. Call him."

"No!" I told her. "Now I'm going to the bathroom. Go grab us some snacks and pick a movie."

I left the room. Sometimes Kayla could be a little too much. I hadn't processed what had happened today yet. I hoped to God Henry didn't report me to my employers. I started to feel nauseous. No, he wouldn't? I had received the praising email from my boss. He loved every minute of it and was the instigator after all.

I walked back in to see Kayla shutting my laptop, with a guilty expression plastered on her face.

"What have you done?" I snapped.

"Promise you won't get mad?"

"I'm already mad." I took my laptop out of her hands, opened it back up and tried to see what she had been doing. "Tell me now." I gave her my best narrowed eyed look that meant business.

"I only sent a little email."

Clicking through to my sent folder, I found Kayla had messaged Henry in response to his anonymous email of before.

I read it.

I WANT **to see the club.**

I'm intrigued.

I BREATHED A SIGH OF RELIEF. "Oh, thank fuck that's all you sent. I can live with that. I thought you were going to tell him I wanted his cock in my mouth or something."

"Well, I might have done that with a little more time, but you came back in the room too fast so I just hit send."

I shook my head. "Movie." I demanded.

She rolled her eyes and got up to choose one.

We had been watching *Deadpool* for twenty-seven minutes when there was a knock at the front door. Kayla pressed the pause button, and I dragged myself from the couch. I opened the door to find H's driver. He passed me a small square box. It was silver with a black ribbon.

"Mr. Carter asked that I wait outside for you for the next thirty minutes after you opened the box. I will leave it with you." He walked away and headed down the steps.

I closed the door and walked back into the living room, taking a seat back on the couch.

"What is it?" Kayla asked.

"It's from H."

I untied the ribbon and removed the box lid. Inside, the box was padded with black satin and on it laid a silver key with a black S on it. There was a card.

. . .

CAN'T HAVE **you left wanting.**

Come, see for yourself.

Matthew will drive you. Dress to impress.

KAYLA READ the message over my shoulder and squealed. "Yes! Sorry Ryan Reynolds, you're hot and all but we're going clubbing."

She dragged me off the couch. "Come on, we need to get ready."

I let her drag me toward my room. I couldn't help but be intrigued now too. I had heard of private members clubs before. Places only celebrities and the filthy rich attended. I wondered if this was one of them? They had to have somewhere to go where they wouldn't be annoyed by normal people, didn't they? Kayla was right. I wasn't the slightest bit tired. Though I irritated with her for what she had done, it was a night out. I looked through my closet. Dress to impress, right? I changed into a plain black silky bra that left no trace of lines and wriggled into a short glittery silver dress. I left panties out of the equation as they would cause a visible line in the dress. The dress had cap sleeves and a V-neck that showed a small amount of my large boobs. The tightness of the dress helped to hold my ample assets in place though it did nothing to hide them. I had bought the dress in a moment of madness, egged on by Kayla to stop hiding what I had. Tonight it was screaming at me to be worn. I wrapped a black pashmina around my shoulders just in case I found it too uncomfortable being under the gaze of others. I finished with black ankle boots that laced up my calves slightly. They had a four-inch heel.

I fixed my hair so that it was half up in a messy bun with the rest of it hanging around my face. Usually I would wear darker makeup in the evening and I stuck to a darker eye shadow, but kept the same pink lipgloss that H had smeared. I realized he wasn't forced to be there, but despite the sentence he left me with, I couldn't help but hope I saw him again tonight. I picked up my purse and headed back to the living room to wait for Kayla.

A few minutes later she joined me. Her red hair was curled in ringlets and she wore a green shift dress, with fishnet tights and black five-inch heels, which made her just a fraction taller than me.

"Ready? Let's go and have some fun." She winked.

I locked the door behind us.

. . .

AS WE WALKED down the stairs to head toward Matthew's limo, Brandon got out of a Hyundai Elantra. He whistled. "Ladies, you look mighty fine." He came around and bowed in front of us. "Where are you off to?"

"We're going to a VIP Members Club. Ssh. It's top secret. We'll explode if we give you any details. Don't wait up." Kayla winked and carried on walking to the limo.

"Well, have a nice evening." Brandon said.

"Thank you. I have no idea what to expect, but as long as there's music and alcohol, we should be fine." I smiled.

"Well, if it's not up to your standards, I have wine in my apartment." He said, smiling playfully. "Gorgeous women always welcome."

I laughed. "What a charmer. I'll see you around."

"You sure will."

I walked to the limo and nodded to Matthew and thanked him for waiting. I let him open the door to let me inside.

It took approximately twenty minutes to drive into Manhattan. Matthew turned onto East 57th Street and pulled up outside what looked like a residential building. There was some expensive real estate around here, with the skyscraper at 252 in high demand. The area was named 'Billionaires row' for a reason. Matthew handed the keys to an approaching valet and opened our doors. "Please, follow me."

He escorted us through double doors, opened by doormen dressed in smart gray suits. A very glamorous looking willowy brunette in a loose, royal-blue shift dress approached us.

Matthew spoke to her, "Could we have another silver key please, Ashley, and two chains?"

"Of course."

She went into a locked drawer underneath her desk and lifted out a key identical to the one I had. She threaded it onto a chain and then seeing the key in my hand, she passed it to Kayla.

Kayla got the idea and fixed it around her neck.

"May I?" Ashley took my key and repeated her actions. I placed the chain around my neck. The key fitted within the swell of my breasts, feeling cold against the heat from my body.

"I will leave you here," Matthew said. "When you are ready to leave, please let Ashley know you need transportation and she will take care of it."

"That's okay, we'll call a cab." I told him.

He shook his head. "Mr. Carter would want to make sure you were home safely. Please let Ashley phone one of our drivers to take you home."

"Okay." I agreed.

"Please go up in the elevator to the twenty-fourth floor. You will need to hold a key against the pad in the elevator." Ashley replied.

We thanked her and moved toward it.

The elevator doors opened. The space was large and had a black satin covered ceiling dotted with silver stars, like a beautiful night sky. I pressed the button for the twenty-fourth floor.

"I'm so excited I could piss my pants." Kayla squealed in delight.

I wished I felt the same. Instead I felt a sense of trepidation; like everyone here would be from money and we were going to look like fish out of water.

We walked across the lobby. The floor had the same pattern, black with silver stars, and doormen greeted us in front of two huge silver double doors. We had to remove our chains, so they could hold the keys up to a screen.

"First time?" One of the doormen asked. I assumed it showed up on his screen.

"Yes."

"Enjoy, and don't leave before midnight." I swore I saw a hint of a smirk at the edge of his mouth.

As we walked through the doors we gasped. The splendor of the place was incredible. There were bars at each edge of the room. A large dance floor was in the center of the room and there was a stage at one end where bands must play. Each black gloss table had a silver star in the center of it. The place was buzzing. Bottles of expensive champagne and wine were everywhere. All the men were in black tie and all the women dressed in the latest hot designers. I felt shabby in my silver dress. It looked good enough, but these women would know I wasn't dressed in designer clothes.

We headed to the bar where we both asked for a glass of white wine.

The barman—who Kayla was already flirting with—tilted his head at us. "First time here?"

"Yes," I stated, quite abruptly. "Is it really that obvious?"

He smiled, "Yes, because you asked for white wine when you have a silver key. No one likes asking for champagne on their first visit."

"I can't afford champagne." I told him. "I don't know if I'll be able to afford the wine yet."

Now the bartender's face was marred with

confusion. "You have a silver key membership. All drinks are included."

"Whoop," Kayla hollered. "In that case we'll have a bottle of Moet and two glasses, darling."

"Kayla!"

"What?" She gave a faux look of guilt. "We're here to enjoy ourselves. By the way, have you seen stud muffin yet?"

"No." I had looked for H ever since we walked in to the building, but he didn't seem to be here. I couldn't help feeling a little disappointed, but it was time to drink, dance, and enjoy ourselves as this membership was probably a one-time only thing and we needed a night to remember.

A SIREN WENT off at ten minutes to midnight, making us jump. The other members wore faces filled with emotions like trepidation and excitement. They passed knowing smiles and looks amongst each other. Kayla and I were totally confused. The atmosphere in the place had changed. Something was about to happen, and I guessed that the siren was the precursor.

An older gentleman with salt and pepper hair climbed the stairs to the stage and switched on the microphone. People moved closer to him, standing on the dance floor.

"What's happening?" Kayla asked.

I shrugged, not knowing myself. "Maybe there's a band coming on?"

The man spoke into the microphone. "Good evening, ladies and gentlemen. It's now time for the auction. Please welcome onto the stage William and Jesse."

"Auction?" I whispered at Kayla. "Goddamn rich people. Bet they're selling paintings or jewelry."

But when William and Jesse walked onto the stage, I realized I couldn't have been more wrong...

Tiffany

They were naked. Completely and utterly stark naked. Kayla almost choked on her drink. William was short and muscular with sleeves of tattoos and a buzz cut. His dick was soft. It looked average sized but quite thick. Jesse was tall and leaner though still ripped. His cock stood erect at about eight inches and appeared to have a small bend to it. They stood either side of the suited gentleman who didn't blink at the fact he was flanked by two naked men.

"Please gather your paddles. The auction is about to commence."

I realized that some people had paddles in their hands. They were silver stars on a stick with numbers across the star.

"What the hell is going on?" I asked Kayla.

"Fucked if I know. How do I get one of those paddle things? I want to bid if I get to win a date with one of those hunks."

We watched spellbound as people bid on the men until finally a woman won the auction with a bid of twenty thousand dollars.

"Thank you." The man said into the microphone. "The rooms will now open, and the main act will be on stage at one am."

"Well, well, well," Kayla said with a smirk on her face. "If I'm not mistaken, I'm guessing your Mr. Carter owns a sex club."

The lights came up and doormen opened several doors around the main room. The doors had looked like the rest of the paneling on the walls, which is why we hadn't noticed them before. People started to disappear through the doors.

"Oh my god." I said.

Kayla laughed. "I was so not expecting this. Shall we go look?"

"No." I clutched her arm. "What if they want us to join in? We don't know the rules here."

She sighed. "Yeah, you're right. Let's get another bottle of champagne and get ready for the main act at one."

A CURTAIN HAD BEEN DRAWN across the stage. At ten to one, the siren had gone off again and quite a few members made their way back from the rooms into the main bar area. It didn't take a genius to figure out that the messed-up hair, reddened faces and disheveled clothes meant that they had more than likely just fucked, or at least played around. At one am, some soft music began to play, and the curtain drew back to reveal a bed.

The woman who had won the auction, a slim woman who looked in her mid-forties, was lying on the bed. She was—like the men before her—completely naked. Her pert breasts were small, and she was displaying a completely shaved pussy. She was propped up on a pillow and pretending to read a book.

The music stopped, and William and Jesse walked onto the stage.

William took the book from the woman's hand and placed it on the floor. Then he took the hand that had clutched the book and placed it on his cock.

She stroked it until it grew. Jesse had been sitting at the end of the bed. He walked over, stood beside William, and getting the woman to sit up and perch on the side of the bed, he took her other hand and placed it on his cock.

I couldn't believe my eyes.

And for once in her life, I think Kayla was speechless too.

The woman pumped both cocks at the same time, looking to the guys for direction. They got her to lie back on the bed with her legs slightly apart. William sat at her head and made her take his cock in her mouth while Jesse held her ankles and plunged his mouth onto her clit. I watched as the woman bucked up off the bed in pleasure. As the cock left her mouth, loud moans began to escape from her. After coming through tongue-fucking, she was positioned on her knees on the bed. Jesse got behind her and unravelling a condom onto his cock, he held her by the hips and pushed his hard cock into her pussy. She screamed with pleasure. At the front of her, William sucked on one breast, then another, while his fingers played with her clit. The woman's head was back, lips apart, and she was moaning and wailing like a teenage girl seeing their rock idol in real life.

"This is so fucking hot." Kayla said, licking her lips.

To be honest, I had been so engrossed, I had forgotten she was there.

Both guys took turns fucking her and the performance ended with her swallowing Jesse's cum while William sprayed his across her tits.

The curtains closed, and the audience broke out in an ecstatic applause.

Coming back to my surroundings, I realized that I was soaking wet. Soaking wet and wearing no panties. I excused myself to go to the bathroom.

"There'll be more than you in there playing with yourself." Kayla said laughing.

"I'm not going to do that. Jesus, girl. I need a pee." I told her.

She took a sip of her champagne and winked at me.

As I made my way over to the bathroom, my phone vibrated in my purse. I picked it up, but waited until I had the light from the bathroom to help me read the message.

Mr. Carter: So, is the thought of two men still offensive to you?

Oh my God! He must be here!

I texted him back.

Tiffany: I guess that's for me to know and you to find out. But it's way past my bedtime now, and I'm leaving. Thank you for my key.

A moment later another beep indicated another text message.

Mr. Carter: Well you gave me a brand-new key today; it seemed only fair to return the favor. By the way, that's a life-time membership at the highest level for you and your friend. Let me know if Haley wishes to join.

Jesus. He knew the names of my friends. What else did he know about me?

I sat on the bathroom seat and changed his name on my phone over to H. It fit better. After today's events, I didn't think the formality of Mr. Carter suited anymore.

Leaving the bathroom, I grabbed Kayla, and we called it a night, accepting H's transport to take us home.

.   .   .

I GOT IN BED, but I couldn't sleep. Thoughts of the day and the night whirled around my mind. When H had mentioned two men, I had been appalled, and yet watching that woman tonight on the stage, I couldn't deny that I had been completely turned on. I pictured how one had fucked her pussy while another fucked her mouth. I assumed she wasn't into anal as they hadn't fucked her ass and pussy together. Between my legs, I started to feel wet with my daydreaming (or should that be nightdreaming?) and I grabbed one of my breasts as I remembered how one of the guys had took her breast in his mouth. In my imagination the scene changed to me lying on that bed and the man sucking on my breasts became H. Where the woman's breasts had been small and pert, H grabbed mine roughly, pushing and pulling on them and biting on my nipples. I pinched my nipples as I imagined his bite, remembering that one of my breasts had a love-bite on it from earlier that day.

Dream H moved his fingers down my body and trailed his middle finger to plunge in my wet pussy. I drenched his finger with my juices and moaned. Coming back to myself, I blushed as I realized I was in my room. I figured Kayla would be fast asleep by now, and Haley was already asleep in her room when we got back as we'd heard her soft snores, but I didn't want anyone hearing my moans and masturbation. I closed my eyes, mindful to keep as quiet as I could, and I plunged my fingers back into myself pretending it was H. But my fingers just weren't enough for this fantasy, and I found myself wanting, on the brink. I switched on my bedside light and opened one of the drawers in my nightstand I took out my dildo. It was purple and a close match to a real penis although harder in texture. It was seven inches so nowhere near H's massive cock, but it would do. I made a mental note to go to a sex store and buy a larger one. He had spoiled me with his large cock—average sized vibrators and dildos were not going to cut it now!

I turned off the light and got back under my duvet. With the dildo in my hand, I let my mind take me back to where I had left my fantasy. Now H was asking me to take his cock in my mouth. I shoved the dildo between my lips and tongued it, pretending he was begging me to fuck it. To get my fantasy to play out as the woman's scene had however, I needed another man. I had not found Jesse or William very attractive, so I didn't want them in my visual. I tried to imagine a mystery man, but my thoughts wouldn't play ball. Then he snuck in—Brandon. I felt my cheeks flush as thoughts of him joining us came into my mind and wouldn't leave. In my mind, Brandon had appeared from the edge of the room. He stalked over to me. He was dressed in a t-shirt and board shorts. His huge dick tented his shorts. He came closer and demanded that I pull them down. As I did, his cock sprang next to my face. He looked at H and communicating with their eyes, H removed his cock from my mouth and Brandon thrust his in.

"Suck me hard, bitch."

In reality, in my room, I felt my cum run down my leg, I was so turned on.

H moved himself between my legs and growled, "I'm going to fuck your pussy, while Brandon fucks your mouth, and you will love it."

I removed the dildo from my mouth and positioned it at my entrance. Oh, how I wished I had two dildos! I pistoned three fingers of my left hand and stuck them in my mouth while I held my dildo at the entrance of my pussy. Then I shoved the dildo hard inside myself, thrusting it in and out. It was hard to coordinate, but I tried to thrust my fingers in my mouth at the same time, imagining that both Brandon and H were fucking each hole at once. I came hard and I couldn't help but let out a cry as my body bucked. My orgasm had shaken my body, the force of it so intense. I had never come like that alone before. What had H unleashed in me? I laid back, the dildo abandoned at the side of me. Aftershocks shook my body and my heart thudded in my chest. I felt dizzy; that's how hard my orgasm had taken me. When I calmed down, I put my fingers to my pussy. I was soaked and used my shorts to mop between my legs. Then another thought came to me. I gathered some of the wetness from between my legs and smeared it over and in my asshole. Then I grabbed the dildo and nudged it at my entrance. I was an anal sex virgin and other than a past boyfriend sticking a digit in it once or twice, nothing had breached my puckered hole. Relaxing, I nudged the dildo, letting it push in a little, but it was no good. Though I was intrigued, my ass wasn't playing along. It stayed tight and unyielding. I could feel my eyes start to close, so I gave up and let sleep overtake my body. My alarm was set for six-thirty am and it was four am now. I was sure going to need that coffee in a couple hours, but with a last sigh, I decided it had been totally worth it.

CHAPTER SIX

Tiffany

I dragged myself into the living room at twenty-to-seven after allowing myself one snooze of the alarm clock. I knew that if I hadn't got out of bed at that point, I would have never gotten up that morning.

Haley snorted when she saw me, then she nodded her head toward Kayla, who was laid on the couch. "What on earth were you two doing that has you so dead this morning?"

"We went to a club, a sex club." Kayla blurted out, mumbling through the cushion her face was resting on.

"What?!" Haley gasped. Her face paled, and her eyes widened.

I sat at the table with my freshly poured coffee. "We looked up H on the net, and Kayla found out he owned a club. Long story short, we went. It seemed like a normal, but posh nightclub. Then at midnight it all changed. Rooms were opened, and there was an auction held to perform on the stage. A woman had a ménage with two guys in front of us all."

Haley's jaw drops. "For real?"

"Yep, and H gave us a free membership that included drinks, so we consumed far too much champagne and were so stunned and intrigued that we stayed to watch. Then we had even more alcohol while we tried to digest what we had just seen."

"Seriously, it was hot." Kayla mumbled. "We didn't see what happened in any of the side rooms, but you could take a wild guess looking at the people who left them."

"Oh, by the way, H texted me and said that you could have a membership if you wanted one too. Somehow he knows exactly who I live with."

"He texted you? When?" Kayla sat up on the couch looking more animated.

"Yes, just the once last night. Oh, and our memberships are lifetime. He asked me what I thought about the ménage. I think he's hoping I'll have a three-way with him."

"Would you?" Haley asked, then blushed. She really could be innocent sometimes. "I can't even get one lover, never mind two at once."

"Oh god, I forgot. How was your date with Malcolm last night? How did it go?" I asked.

"It didn't go. That was the problem. We had drinks and then we went back to his place. He couldn't get it up, and he blamed me. Said it had never happened to him before. Maybe it is me? He's not the first to suggest I'm hopeless in bed, is he? I think I need lessons. Maybe I'll go to that club and let people use me for practice."

Me and Kayla laughed at the same time. I was imagining Haley on the bed on stage saying 'just come fuck me'. As if! Kayla basically said what I was thinking.

"Haley, there is no way you would get on that stage. You would die of embarrassment."

"Well, maybe that's the whole point." She retorted with her hands on her hips. "I'm getting nowhere being this version of Haley. I might need to reinvent myself."

I got up from my seat and walked over to hug her. "Listen to me. You're perfect just the way you are. Don't even try to change yourself for other people. The guys you have been out with are straight up assholes. That's what you need to change. Choose a different kind of man."

She sighed. "Well now I have to face Malcolm today."

"If he gives you any grief, wave your pinkie finger at him and make it droop down. He'll shut his mouth real quick. No guy wants news of his lack of keeping an erection circulating round the staff and that's what he'll get if he's not careful." Kayla told her.

Haley smiled at Kayla. "Thanks for having my back."

"Anyway, back to you." Kayla's eyes were on me. "So, would you be up for a three-way with H?"

I squirmed on my seat. "Well, yesterday morning I was completely offended by the suggestion. But after last night, I'm not so sure. That woman seemed to be really enjoying herself. I have to admit I'm a little more open to the idea now."

"Well, you would certainly need to be open. Your mouth and your thighs." Kayla shot back with a wink. Then she burst out laughing.

"I guess like most women, I have been trying to get a guy who I could settle down with. The whole white picket fence and kids thing. Maybe before I look for that kind of a commitment, I should allow myself the opportunity to experiment if it comes my way."

"Won't be the only thing coming your way."

I groaned at her. "Please, stop. I haven't had enough sleep to put up with your humor."

"Go get ready, you two, and I'll make us more coffee to take in with us. I hope your schedules aren't too full today because I have a feeling you aren't going to be your usual sparkling selves. Go on, shoo. Tiff, you can use my bathroom to save time."

"Thank you, sweetheart. I'll be quick, and I'll leave it as I found it." I kissed her cheek and headed for the shower, hoping that a few minutes under the cold water would wake me up, although if the strong coffee hadn't worked it was seriously doubtful.

In the shower I once again noted the love-bite on my breast. I ran my fingers down it. I couldn't believe it had only happened yesterday. I thought about my schedule for today. It was going to be so boring in comparison! While I had drunk my coffee, I had checked my messages on the laptop but there was nothing from H. Maybe he would never contact me again, and I had just been a conquest? Maybe he only wanted me to contact him again if I was open to the idea of two men? I pushed the thought to the back of my mind. I needed to get out of the shower and get to work. Properties needed to be sold. As I thought of the word SOLD, I was back to the woman at the auction. To feel comfortable enough to bid for a slice of sexy action on a public stage? I couldn't imagine it, and with that, I blasted the shower onto cold to get my mind off sex and onto the day ahead.

THE REST of the week passed by quickly, with us all immersed in our work. I had to go in on Saturday too as I had so much work to do, but hey, it paid my bills. Sunday, I laid in bed until lunchtime and then spent the rest of the day just chilling around the apartment. On Sunday evening, there was a knock on the door. Kayla and Haley have gone to the movies, so I put my robe on and answered it. It was Brandon. Fuck me, I was in my robe again.

"I do get dressed, honestly." I laughed.

"I know, I saw you all dressed up the other night, remember?"

"Ah, that you did!"

"Well, I was checking in because despite my offering you coffee, you haven't taken me up on it. I sat in my apartment thinking I could either get really down about it and feel rejected, or I could come ask you again. So, would you like a coffee sometime?"

"I can do one better, Haley and Kayla are out. If you don't mind me being in my robe and pjs, I have wine that I'm willing to share?"

"Perfect." He smiled.

I stood back and let him in.

"Just kick your shoes off anywhere and excuse the mess. We work hard, play hard, but don't clean hard I'm afraid."

I watched Brandon look around the apartment. Thank goodness it was littered with magazines and nail polishes and not our underwear.

"I have two sisters. It reminds me of home."

I got the bottle of wine and two glasses and we got to know each other, chatting about our backgrounds and families. He was easy to talk to, and by the time a couple of hours had passed, I felt like I had known him for years. Of course, he was also easy on the eyes and as the wine had gone down, he had gotten sexier and sexier. I kept thinking of my fantasy from earlier in the week and blushed.

"Look at you, wine makes your face flush. You're all pink." Brandon leaned over and touched my cheek. "Your cheeks are burning!"

Of course, I blushed even more then.

"Stop tormenting me. You're making it worse."

"Hmmm, is it the wine, or are you enjoying my hot gym body? Is that it?"

I must have been almost a dark shade of red by now and I hid my face in my hands.

He grabbed my hands and moved them away. "Hey, I'm sorry. I was having a little fun. I don't handle wine well obviously, I'm used to beer. I hope I didn't offend you?"

"No, not at all." I laughed.

"What's funny?"

"Well, now I want to know if you do have a hot gym body, or if under those clothes you look like Mr. Bean."

He dropped his jaw in mock offence. "How dare you question my gym bod. Do you know how many women would love to spend the evening with it?"

"Sorry, I think you're going to have to show me."

What the fuck have I just said? What is wrong with me? I've become a fucking slut.

He lifted his sweater and tee and pulled them off over his head. I gasped in shock as tanned, taut skin was revealed. He had an eight pack. From his neck down over his pec at the left-hand side was a tattoo of a steampunk-style clock. His arms were threaded muscle, and he looked like he could lift me with just one of them. I stared down the sleeve of tattoos on his left arm: skulls, stars with writing in them, a series of interlocking gears. He was lean, but oh so solid. I reached over and ran my hands down his chest. He watched as I trailed my palms down him, all the way down to his lower abdomen and then back up.

He swallowed audibly. Then he caught my hand.

"Sorry." I shook my head. "It's the wine. I'm not usually like this. God, I'm so sorry. I don't want you to think the wrong thing."

"I think I'm in an apartment with a sexy as fuck woman and she just asked me to strip and touched my chest. I'm wondering whether to go and splash my face with cold water because I've got to be dreaming. Can I try something?" He asked.

I nodded. "Sure."

He sat on the couch at the side of me and leaned in. His mouth crashed on mine. Warmth seeped through my lips, and my mouth opened to accept his tongue. I tasted the wine on him. I kissed him back hard, and we launched into a frenzy of movement. My hands stroked his chest again. His hand slipped inside my robe and under my top, grasping one of my breasts.

"Jesus, your tits. Let me see them."

I opened my robe and pulled up my top, exposing my magnificent orbs in all their glory.

He pushed his head in between them and holding them at either side made groaning noises.

"Fuck, I'm going to come in my boxers from this alone."

He took a nipple in his mouth and sucked hard. Thank goodness, the love-bite from Monday had gone. I opened the button of his pants and lowered the zipper. He lifted himself to help me. I freed his cock and licked my lips. It had to be at least the same size as H's. It was huge! It was a little less wide than H's but was no less impressive.

"Fuck, you're huge."

"Eleven inches." He replied.

Eleven! My face must have looked worried. I'd had a hard time handling ten.

"Don't worry. I know what I'm doing with it and we'll manage."

He guided my hand to his cock, and I started to stroke him.

A loud laugh came from outside and I sprang back away from him.

"Oh God, the girls are back."

"Fuck!" Brandon grunted. He quickly pulled up

his pants, zipped them, and shucked on his t-shirt and sweater.

The only thing I had to do was let my top fall back down and pull my robe tighter. God, I was fucking horny. So horny I had lost track of time.

The girls let themselves into the apartment.

"Oh, private party going on here look." Kayla winked.

"I was just leaving." Brandon said, quickly standing up.

I followed him to the apartment door and opened it. "Do you want me to watch you walk to your apartment?"

"Yes please. I'm a hot man out on my own. You never know who's going to attack me."

I stroked his cock again through his pants. "Like that you mean?"

He groaned.

"Have dinner with me tomorrow night. I'm a good cook."

"You said a good cook, right?" I winked. "I didn't mishear you?"

He laughed. "And the rest. So take some vitamins and energy drinks because I can go for a long, long time."

"I was in when you said you were cooking. But

sorry, Monday is girls' night, so it will have to be Tuesday."

"I have classes Tuesday. Can you do Wednesday?"

"I can indeed."

"My balls are going to explode before then. Give me your cell," he demanded.

I passed it to him and he punched in his number.

"I'll text you tonight. I can't finish you off in person, but I can sext."

He leaned over and kissed me again. Then he headed the few steps to his own apartment.

"Later." He said and went in and closed the door.

He wasn't kidding when he said he could sext... I was a limp puddle in bed after ten minutes.

I was so looking forward to Wednesday evening!

CHAPTER SEVEN

Tiffany

He might have invited me to dinner, but hell we both knew it was mainly about dessert. I treated myself to some brand-new underwear. My bra was light pink with a black net overlay. On the inner and outer edges the overlay was floral and in the middle it was laced up with eyelets like on a bodice. It was unusual to find a bra to suit my huge breasts that also looked sexy, but I had pulled it off. I was wearing a matching thong. After staring at the closet for what seemed like hours wondering what to wear, I eventually settled for a button through shirt dress that could be tantalizingly removed.

I kept my hair down and a little messy and wore light, fresh looking makeup. I left off the gloss. It seemed disloyal to H somehow, which was crazy given he was a one-time fuck buddy.

I left the apartment with catcalls and jeers from Kayla (mainly) and Haley, then walked the few steps outside to Brandon's apartment door. I knocked and waited. He opened the door and the smell of some kind of sauce permeated the air, making my stomach rumble.

"Chicken in white wine sauce. Sound good?"

I put a fake look of dismay on my face. "Fuck, I should have told you. I'm a vegetarian."

His face fell. "Damn. I wanted to surprise you. Never mind, I'll order takeout instead."

"I'm joking, let me in." I said. "It smells delicious."

"You're going to get spanked for that, you tease," Brandon smiled and shook his head.

"I can categorically assure you that I eat meat." I said and winked, walking through to his living room.

I was expecting a typical bachelor pad with dark tones and a lack of accessories, but the apartment was decked out in neutrals and had green accents throughout, with soft furnishings. My surprise must have showed on my face.

"I rented it as it was. I haven't had the time to furnish it myself. The only thing I brought with me was some gym equipment," he said. I followed him down the corridor and he opened a bedroom door revealing a bench press, treadmill, and some weights. His apartment was a similar layout to ours except it had only two bedrooms. He told me that his room had an en-suite and there was a separate bathroom which was just like ours.

"I'll show you the bedroom later. Let's eat." He stated and ushered me into the kitchen.

AFTER FILLING OUR STOMACHS, we moved to the couch. Brandon put the rest of the bottle of red wine and my glass on the coffee table in front of me while he cracked open another bottle of beer. He pulled my legs over toward his knees and started to massage one of my feet. I had been in heels all day while showing properties and the feel of my toes being massaged felt amazing. I groaned in pleasure.

"Fuck, that noise you're making. Want to move into the bedroom and see how many more sounds I can get out of you?"

I nodded. "Yes, please."

We walked to his room. When he opened the door, it was again not what I expected. Unlike my own room, which was full of abandoned clothing, Brandon's room was completely tidy. He had a dark wood nightstand, the top drawer of which was slightly open and crooked.

"Come here," he coaxed.

I walked over to him in my bare feet.

"How tall are you?" I asked.

"Six foot three."

"Hmm, so tall." I said. "I'm five foot seven, you make me feel like I'm so tiny."

"You won't be thinking about our height in a minute."

I smiled. "Good."

He unfastened the first of the buttons on my shirt dress, then another.

"I don't have the patience for this," he groaned in frustration and with a yank he ripped my dress open from head to toe and buttons flew everywhere.

I gasped, both with the shock and the cool feeling as the air hit my skin.

"I'll buy you a new dress." He said as his eyes raked down my body. "Fuck, you're beautiful. I can't wait to be inside you."

My pussy instantly throbbed and became slick.

Brandon stalked toward me and fisted his hand into my hair. He claimed my mouth, sucking my top lip into his own mouth, then nibbling and biting. His facial hair scraped against my mouth and upper lip and I wondered how it would feel between my legs. I felt a jolt between my thighs.

The difference between Brandon and H became clear. Night and day. Brandon was focused on my pleasure, not his own. Oh, he wanted to come, but he was intending to wait until I'd had several orgasms myself first. He backed me onto the bed and pulled off my thong, situating himself between my thighs and licking up my slit. I bucked up off the bed as his lips wrapped around and sucked hard on my little nub. He brought every nerve to life.

"Oh, Christ."

My skin erupted in goose bumps as he teased my hard nub with his tongue and alternated this with probing my pussy. His stubble brushed against my folds, adding to the sensations. I grabbed the top of his head in my hands, pushing him closer to my core as I felt my first orgasm building. I fell apart over his face, shudders erupting from me.

"Fuck, Tiff, you came so hard. I could feel you shaking against my mouth."

He dove back down and feasted on my cum. When he raised his head again, his chin was glistening with my juices. He grabbed my head and kissed me, and I tasted myself on his tongue.

"You're sweet like fucking honey. I could taste you all day."

Next, he feasted on my breasts, removing my bra and sucking hard on each peak, while his fingers pinched my clit. I felt so fucking naughty as I bucked wildly against his hand.

"Bounce my tits around. Grab them, squeeze them." I begged.

He sat astride me and pushed one of my breasts upwards. "Have you ever licked your own tits?"

"No." I blushed. It seemed so wrong to even consider it.

"Do it now. I want to watch you. I want you to finger yourself while you suck and lick your own tits." He sat back on the bed.

I sat up and rested against his headboard. Then I moved myself onto my knees and spread my thighs apart. Grabbing my left breast in my left hand, I pushed it upwards toward my mouth, leaning my neck over and licking the pink bud. I could just reach my nipple with my tongue and I flicked it. Then I placed the fingers of my right hand into my wet pussy. My juices pooled down onto the sheets making a wet patch.

I took a look at Brandon. His cock was in his hand. It looked painfully distended. All purple and enormous. He slowly rubbed his hand back and forth against his shaft. I took in his washboard abs, and I closed my eyes and imagined it was Brandon on my breast.

"No. Open your eyes." He commanded. "I want you to know it's you licking yourself and playing with your pussy."

He must have read my mind.

So I did as requested. God, what did I look like to him? My knees splayed apart as I showed him my wet, pink snatch, complete with landing strip pubes. I pushed two fingers inside me while I used my thumb to flick across my bud. I feasted on my own tit making a noise that belonged in a porno. "Mmmm."

"Talk dirty to yourself."

I juggled my tits. "Come on, baby girl, lick your tit. Oh god, oh yes." I spoke to myself out loud, then took my breast back in my mouth and nuzzled it. Then continued my dirty talk. "Oh, your fucking juices are spilling all over my fingers. Fuck me, god yes, fuck me. I wanna come so bad."

I looked around his room and my eyes fixed on

something. "Can I get up off the bed and do something?"

"As long as it's hot and makes you come like a hurricane."

I moved over to the edge of his bed where there was a narrow bedpost. I sank my cunt on it and watched as the post disappeared inside me.

"Oh fuck. I'm never going to get that vision out of my mind." Brandon groaned.

I moved myself up and down on the post, flicking my clit at the same time.

"Oh fuck, I'm coming, I'm coming Brandon. I'm going to come so hard."

I bucked and shook over the post, then lifted myself off and lay across the bed. My chest heaved with my heavy breathing.

"Fuck, that was hot."

"It's your turn." I told him. "Do you want me to suck your cock?"

"No. I want it straight inside you, filling you to the hilt." He growled. Brandon leaned over to the partly opened drawer, and extracted a condom, quickly sheathing himself and then he plunged into me. I was so wet he slid straight in. I was so damn sensitive from my recent orgasm and I was on the edge after a minute then climaxed again. Brandon rested his cock against me for a moment while I recovered. Then he slowly began to slide in and out of me, going deeper with each thrust. He pushed my thighs further apart. The top of my thighs ached I was stretched so wide. He pushed my legs up so my knees were bent and held an ankle in each hand. "Are you ready for me? I'm going to fuck you until you can't walk straight."

I nodded eagerly. The truth was, I couldn't get enough of his cock and the orgasms he was giving me. I was insatiable and craved more.

He slammed inside my walls completely filling me.

"Oh God." I screamed.

He thrust further inside me and even harder. I came up off the bed he was so rough, yet I wanted more.

"Fuck me, fuck me harder with your massive cock."

"Yeah, baby, tell me what you want."

"I want to feel you cum. I want to feel your balls tighten and you erupt."

"Won't be long, baby. You're so tight. I can't last much longer."

He quickened his pace, thrusting in and out of me. I screamed, "Yes, yes, yes."

He grunted and groaned. "Oh fuck, fuck, your tight pussy." He tightened and then flooded the condom with his cum; a loud guttural cry escaped his mouth. He grabbed me and pulled me into his arms.

"That was amazing, baby girl. I've never had a fuck like that in my life."

Brandon slipped out of me and removed the condom and headed for the bathroom. I turned over and closed my eyes. A few minutes later, he slipped into the bed behind me and spooned himself around my back as we fell asleep.

I opened my eyes and saw the bedside clock. It was just past midnight. I felt Brandon's erect cock between my ass cheeks. He rubbed himself there.

"I've never done that." I whispered. "I don't think there's any way I could take your huge cock there."

"We can work up to it," he whispered back.

His arm that rested around my front, against my belly, started to move and his fingers once again trailed a path down to my pussy. In minutes I was soaking wet again. He smeared a finger in my juices and then moved his arm around to my rear. He placed his digit against my puckered hole. I tensed. "Relax. It's only my finger."

I breathed slowly and felt myself relax. He

rubbed my wetness against my asshole and then began to push his digit inside. At first, I felt myself clench around his finger, but then as I relaxed my breathing, my asshole relaxed and his finger pushed right in.

"See, you did it. How does it feel?" He asked me.

"Fine. I feel a little naughty having something in there. What does it feel like to you?"

"I can feel your ass walls, they're kind of spongy. I want my dick inside there sometime. I need you to know that. Can I try another finger?"

"Yes."

He took his finger out and then pushed two in. Again, my body accepted it without a problem. He pulled them out and pulled me, so I was on my back half resting against his hip. The fingers of his other hand splayed against my pussy and he strummed my clit, then dipped in and out of my channel. His hand was behind me and he pushed fingers into my asshole again. "Baby, you have three in there now. I'm going to fuck you with three fingers in your ass and three fingers in your wet pussy."

"Oh yes, please."

I bucked against him as he began his ministrations. He co-ordinated the thrusts, so they happened simultaneously. My ass felt full. His fingers felt deeper than the ones in my pussy. I thrust my hips up and down, taking in all the new sensations.

"You like it up your ass, don't you?"

"Yes."

I let my imagination fly and pictured H in my cunt and Brandon in my ass. I came hard within a minute of that fantasy.

"Oh, baby. I need to fuck you again."

He moved me on top, and I moved astride him and grabbed hold of his dick, sinking it inside me. It felt so good. Again, I was soaked, and my wetness dripped onto his stomach. He trailed his fingers in it and then pushed his fingers into my mouth. "Taste yourself. That's all for me." I sucked on his fingers and then when he slipped them out, I tipped my head back. I grasped hold of my tits and as I bounced up and down on his cock. Brandon pulled my hands away. "That is a sight to see, baby; those massive tits bouncing around right in front of my eyes. I feel like I'm in a porno movie."

I smiled thinking that I'd had the same thought earlier. My thighs were beginning to burn with the effort of bouncing up and down. I needed him to coach me at the gym as well as in bed. It was okay for him and his gym, sculptured body. Jesus, I couldn't remember the last time I'd had a workout like this!

He grabbed hold of my ass cheeks, holding them apart and groaned as I continued to move. This time I circled my hips a little, so I pivoted around on him.

"Oh yeah, keep doing that. God, yeah, just like that. Don't change a thing."

I felt the pressure of my orgasm building once again and I exploded, my pussy spurting out a large amount of liquid. Fuck, I must have pissed myself a little. I hoped he wasn't offended by water sports!

He pulled out his dick and sprayed his cum all over my tits. It ran down between my breasts and onto my stomach. Brandon grabbed my hips and moved me to one side, then he leaned over the bed and grabbed his t-shirt. He wiped off my stomach and breasts and then between my legs. After that he wiped his own cock, then leaned back against the bed, a massive, satisfied grin on his face.

"I'm so sorry," I apologized, looking guilty. "I've never wet myself before during sex. I must have lost complete control."

"Baby," he gathered me into his arms. "You didn't pee, you squirted. Not many women can do that. Have you heard of it?"

"Oh my god, I did? Yeah, I've heard of it, but didn't really know what it was. Are you sure I did?"

He kissed my forehead. "You did, and I am so fucking honored that it was your first time."

"I had lots of firsts today." I told him. "First time anything went up my ass too."

"I hoped you would be up for that." He said. "I have something I bought earlier. Can I give it to you and maybe take a photo? I have a Polaroid."

"I think you should show me what you bought first."

He opened his bedside drawer again and drew out a box. Then he removed the box lid and took out something shiny. I saw that he held a silver object in his hand. He covered one end of it up with his closed fingers, but the other end had a small silver ball visible.

"What is it?" I asked.

"It's a butt plug." He explained. "I'd really like to put it in you and take a photo."

"Oh, I- I'm not sure." I said. "I don't mind trying the plug, but I don't know about the photo."

"Just two. One for us both to remember tonight. I will just take a shot of your hole wearing it and you'll see a bit of your ass cheeks. No one will see it, and no one would know it was you if they did. Please? I want to jack off while looking at it."

"You mean you have the energy for more?" My eyes widened.

"When it comes to you, it would appear I can't stop." He answered.

"Okay." I told him. "For your eyes only."

He put the ball in front of my mouth and asked me to suck on it. "Lube it up baby."

I sucked on the cold metal. Then he withdrew it. "I'll just get some extra lube."

After a minute, I felt a cold wetness as his finger teased my puckered hole, slipping some of the lube inside me.

"Bend over on all fours." He requested, and I did so.

I felt the cold of the ball against my asshole and then he pushed it slowly in. Again, I felt full.

"God, it looks so beautiful. Stay there while I take the pics." He moved from the bed and I heard a door open, which I presumed was his closet. He got back on the bed and I heard the camera shutter twice.

He pulled out the butt plug and put it back in the box and back in his drawer. We waited for the photo to appear on the film. He put on a pair of low-rise lounge pants and I visited the bathroom to clean myself up and then quickly got dressed. I noted that

I'd have to hold my dress together with my hands between here and my own bedroom.

"Thank you for tonight. I hope it's the first of many dates." Brandon whispered as he moved himself against my body and kissed me. "I really like you, Tiff, and I thought that before the amazing, mind-blowing sex."

"I had a great time too, but now I'm exhausted and need my bed, or I won't be able to work tomorrow. Keeping me up late." I pretended to scold him.

"I think actually you kept me up," he winked.

He walked me out of his room and I headed toward the door, slipping my heels onto my feet before I left.

He pushed the photo into my hand after not letting me look at it before.

"Wait until you're in your bedroom on your own." He whispered.

"Okay."

We kissed again for a while in the doorway before I backed away from him with a groan. My lips felt swollen and I ached between my legs. "I have to go. I'll see you soon, okay?"

"Yes, we'll make another date. I'll message you."

I headed back to my own apartment.

When I got in, I breathed a sigh of relief when I

realized both Kayla and Haley were in their rooms, presumably asleep. I didn't want twenty-questions at this time in the morning and my legs could barely hold me up. Actually, I was too tired to even brush my teeth and put on pjs. I placed the photo down on my bedside table, shrugged out of my dress and climbed straight under the covers in just my undies. Then I picked up the photo.

It was indeed just a photo showing the cheeks of my ass and the butt plug in between. What I hadn't seen however—as it was covered by Brandon's clenched fingers—was the end of the plug had a jeweled embellishment. Shining out of my ass was a diamond encrusted silver star.

Fancy that! A silver star. I put it down to coincidence, dropped the photo into my top drawer, and placing my head on my pillow, I fell asleep in seconds.

CHAPTER EIGHT

<u>Tiffany</u>

I was in love.

No, I wasn't kidding.

I was seriously, head-over-heels in love with Brandon Bailey.

The only time we had spent apart for the last few months or so had been on my Monday girls nights, and when he had classes and gym sessions to run. Other than that, we had dated and fucked. It was sheer bliss. Who would have thought when the new neighbor moved in that he would become my guy!

Certainly not me. I had an extra bounce in my step which meant I was owning it at work too. My commissions were HUGE this month.

So, why was I still thinking of three-ways?

CHAPTER NINE

H
—

I watched her still.

She had no idea.

She was too busy falling in love.

It's what I wanted for her. Marriage, babies, the white picket fence.

I couldn't give her that.

Anything else she desired, yes.

But, not that.

That part of me would always belong to my wife.

I could love Tiffany, though it would hurt.

But I couldn't give her the world. I already gave that to someone else.

And now they were out of reach, and my everything was still with them.

CHAPTER TEN

Tiffany

Brandon was working, and the girls were both going out. I was going to S.

I wanted to visit the place on my own. No Kayla to distract me. No one to follow me around. I intended to observe tonight. I wanted to know what happened in those rooms and I definitely wanted to see tonight's show.

I changed into a black jumpsuit with a silver chain belt, and placed silver heels on my feet. The jumpsuit had a deep V at the front, so I made sure I was secured with tit-tape. The key would look like a carefully chosen accessory. I ordered a cab, and within the hour I was back inside the club, drinking a Bellini.

The auction tonight was different. The only thing to bid for was the stage itself. A couple won the bidding and once again at one am, we gathered around to watch the show.

The man, who I pictured to be in his early fifties, came out onto the stage dressed as an aristocrat. He wore a black suit with a waistcoat. He had on a white shirt with an upturned collar and a black tie. When his partner came on dressed in a long black dress with a white pinafore over, a frilly cap-like thing on her head, I guessed these two had a serious obsession with Downton Abbey.

"I've brought your tea, Sir."

"Thank you, Mary. You look chilled. Please, take a seat by the fire."

Mary looked toward the imaginary fire and knelt in front of it.

"I am so cold, Sir. You will catch your death outside, so be sure to wrap up warm should you venture out."

"You're so kind, Mary. Come here and sit beside me in my chair. It's much more comfortable than the floor."

Yeah, come here so I can stick my cock down your throat.

Mary walked over to her Master and tried to sit in the chair on the stage but there wasn't enough room. She ended up sitting on his knee.

"I apologize Mary, you're sitting atop me in this manner has made me hard. I hope you aren't offended. It is a sign of my attraction to you."

"I'm not offended at all, Sir. I'd be very honored if you'd let me see it. I've often wondered what one looks like."

"You've never seen a phallus, Mary?"

"No, Sir."

"Well, let me show you."

Sir dropped his trousers to the floor and kicked them away. Then he pulled down his briefs and freed his member. "You may touch it, Mary."

Mary grasped his cock and stroked her hand up and down it in a very practiced manner for someone who'd supposedly never seen one before. I looked around me. People were really getting into the scene, but it wasn't doing anything for me at all, yet I carried on watching.

She put her mouth around his cock and sucked, drinking every last drop of his cum.

"Mary."

"Yes, Sir?"

"I thought you hadn't seen a man's member before, but you seemed to know how to suck my cock very well."

Mary looked downward. "Sir, the truth is I have practiced with Thomas so I knew how to satisfy you if I ever got the chance; but I swear my virtue in intact and is only for you."

"Come here, Mary, and lay across my knees with your bottom in the air. You need to lift up your dress and remove any panties."

Mary did as she was told, and her ass stuck out toward the audience.

"Do you understand you need to be punished for tricking me?"

"Yes, Sir."

"Good."

He raised his hand and brought it down sharply on her ass, striking at her white flesh. I watched as it pinked up between his repeated strikes. In between each one he rubbed across the pink, mottled flesh. Mary groaned with each further slap to her behind. Sir stopped and placed his fingers between her thighs.

"You're saturated, Mary. Someone likes a good spanking, don't they?"

My own panties had now dampened. The idea of being 'punished' by someone, I realized, turned me the hell on.

Sir pulled off Mary's cap and undid her hair, so it reached her shoulders. He held it in his hand like a ponytail and dragged her to the bed by her hair. "I'm going to fuck you now, Mary, and if I find out you've lied about being a virgin, I will fuck your ass as well."

He penetrated her hard, thrusting with all his might and Mary screamed with delight, "More, Sir, more."

He stopped, withdrew, and removed his tie.

"Strip off all of your clothes, Mary."

She did so and stood in front of him.

He put his tie around her mouth. "You will be quiet. I do not wish to raise the attention of other members of this household. This shall be our little secret, Mary."

She nodded and opened her mouth for the tie to be fastened around her.

When she was gagged, he pushed her onto the bed face down and mounted her from behind where he gave her one of the hardest poundings I'd ever seen. You could see when she came because she twitched and then tried to move up the bed away from him, but he grabbed her by the waist and held her in place until he came. He then declared her a virgin by pretending he'd seen evidence of virgin blood.

The performance was over, and people started to applaud. I was dissatisfied and walked away toward the now open doors to the other rooms.

As I walked inside, a doorman nodded to me and indicated three bowls with wristbands. My brow creased, and I looked at him with a question in my eyes.

"Madam. White is for observers. Blue is for people who are partnered. The black with silver stars are for those who would like to be approached by others."

"Thank you." I told him, and I took a white wristband and put it on.

I walked down a corridor. It reminded me of exhibits in an aquarium. Large glass windows went the entire way down the right-hand side. Behind the glass there were rooms, sectioned off with partitions that could be opened or closed. It became apparent that there could be private sex play or an entire gang-bang behind these windows.

I continued to walk down the corridor glancing in at the action, seeking something I had yet to find. Then I saw what I had come for.

A woman laid on a bed. There were two men with her. The men were both masked and dressed in black long-sleeved t-shirts with just their bottom halves nude. This room had the sectioned off area pulled across. It was a scene only for the three of them plus observers. I stood behind others who were watching and peeked over a man's shoulder as I wasn't yet comfortable with openly watching the action before me. I don't know how long I watched but I saw everything. I didn't know how this woman remained able to continue.

One fucked her mouth while the other fucked her pussy.

One fucked her pussy while the other fucked her ass.

One fucked her ass while the other fucked her mouth.

She took both of them in her mouth.

She performed oral on one then the other, a long suck for each until they masturbated themselves and came on her face.

One fingered her pussy while the other sucked her breasts.

It never seemed to end.

I was dripping wet, my juices pooled in my panties, and I needed to come so damn hard. I'd had enough of being at the back and moved forward to watch as she once again got fucked in the pussy by one man while the other one laid across her face with his cock in her mouth. No one was watching me, all eyes on the scene in front of them, so I placed my purse across my pubic area, holding it with my left hand and my right hand disappeared under the purse, rubbing across my satin dress material. Why the hell hadn't I worn a dress slit to my thigh? I flicked my finger across my clit. I knew I would come in another couple of strokes. My eyes closed, and I bit on my top lip as my orgasm washed over me. I opened my eyes a moment later. What the hell was I doing? I looked quickly around me. No one had noticed thank God. I had lost my common sense. I looked back into the window. The fucking had finished and one of the men seemed to be staring straight at me. I looked behind me but there was no one there. The man removed his mask.

It was H.

I gasped and ran down the corridor, away from the rooms and out of the club. I grabbed a cab and rushed to the safety of my own home. All the way there I scolded myself for going there. I was in love with Brandon. Why had I felt the need to go to the club?

When I got home, I felt full of guilt. Brandon was all I needed. I didn't need a club, and I didn't need a ménage. There were ways around this. I sent him a text.

Tiff: You awake?

A text came back.

B: Can be??

Tiff: I'm coming over. Make some room.

Brandon had given me a spare key after a couple of weeks as I spent so much time there. I grabbed my dildo from my bedside drawer and left my apartment and let myself into Brandon's. I crossed the corridor and headed to his room. The light from the moon and street lamps cascaded through onto the bed and I disrobed and climbed under the duvet. He turned toward me and curled me into his arms. His warm front was against my cool back.

"You need warming up." He said in a sleepy voice.

"Sorry, to wake you." I whispered.

"Don't be. I wasn't sleeping well anyway. When you're not here, I don't. I miss you."

"I miss you too."

He propped his head up on his arm against the

pillow. "So, what have you been up to tonight that kept you out so late?"

"If I tell you, promise you won't be mad."

His posture stiffened.

"It's nothing bad." I stroked down his arm, and he relaxed.

"I visited that VIP club. The one I went to with Kayla that time. It's a sex club. I was curious, so tonight I went again. See, I wanted to go alone so I could see what happened. I hope you don't mind that I went. I didn't do anything, except watch."

I felt his erection pressed against my back.

"Well, I knew you liked being fucked, but I hadn't realized you liked to watch too."

"I'm not sure I do." I confessed honestly, turning around to face him. "The first scene didn't do it for me at all. It was watching someone being fucked in their asshole and their pussy that I liked. Also, the spanking turned me on. Anyway, I brought this with me." I placed my dildo in his hand. "I figured that maybe you could fuck me in one hole and use this for another, and I could get to experience how it felt for myself."

"God, I love you." Brandon groaned. Then his posture went rigid again as he realized what he had just said.

I stroked down his cheek, leaned in, and kissed him with all I had. "I love you too, Brandon. Now fuck me so hard I can't walk."

I guess some people who professed their love for each other would follow it with a dose of tender and gentle lovemaking. I found myself pushed further up the bed while Brandon feasted on my pussy.

"You're sopping wet. Is this how you left the club?"

"No. I washed between my legs when I got home, this is all for you." I panted.

My nipples were hard as pebbles. Brandon twisted and pinched them while feasting on me. I lifted my pelvis up to his face trying to get his tongue to sink deeper into my cleft. The feeling was amazing. My breasts heaved into his hands as I writhed beneath him. As I was on the cusp of coming, he moved away from me.

"No. Don't stop." I cried.

"I'm not stopping." He grunted. "Turn over."

He slapped my ass cheek. It stung, but it felt good and as he did it, it pushed my nub against the linens. I groaned.

"You enjoyed that, didn't you?" Brandon almost growled, his voice was so low and husky.

"Yes. Do it again."

"You need to learn your lesson." He strummed my clit, taking me to the edge again and then stopped.

"That's what happens to naughty women."

"I'll be good, I promise. Please, spank me again."

"I'm going to give you five strokes and you'd better not come."

I wasn't sure I could promise this, but I said it anyway.

"I promise."

"One." Slap.

"Two." Spank.

"Three." Thwack.

"Four." Slap.

"Five." Spank

"Oh my God. I'm so close."

Brandon stuck his fingers in my mouth. "Suck on all your juices. I need you to calm down a bit, otherwise the finale won't be as good as I want it to be."

I sucked like a good girl.

"Now play with my cock. Get me ready for you."

He came to sit further up the bed. I moved myself so that I could stroke his shaft and pump him. Then I brought him over to my mouth and sucked and swirled on his immense cock.

"Christ, I can't wait any longer."

He turned me back, so I faced the bedcovers and dragged me up onto all fours, doggy style. He grabbed the dildo. Rubbing his hands through my wetness, he smeared my cum over and around my asshole and then he opened his tube of lube and had me dripping. He positioned himself at my rear entrance and pushed in.

I pushed back against him, relaxing so my puckered hole relaxed to accept his girth.

He pushed in more and we got a rhythm going until he was fucking my tight ass with long strokes.

Then he reached underneath me and pushed the dildo into my cunt.

I felt so full from his cock and the dildo. He pushed the dildo in to match his thrusts. I lifted one of my hands off the bed and grabbed and pinched at my own nipples. I had never felt anything like it in my entire life. It was exhilarating having both holes fucked at once. I hungered for more, for the feel of an extra cock instead of the dildo. In my mind it was two men who were fucking me. I screamed out my orgasm as it claimed my entire body. My mind, body, and soul were flying through the air, and as I came down, I was so breathless I felt a small amount of panic that I had gone too far and might have half killed myself during sex. As I came back to myself, I felt Brandon tighten, and he came all over my ass cheek—the one he'd spanked—and I felt him rub his cum into my skin.

We didn't need any more words that night.

He gathered me up in his arms and we slept until his alarm went off.

H

I sent a text the next morning.

She needs more.

It took an hour, by which time I wondered if I was being ignored, but then a reply came back.

So much more. She's ready.

I called Green's and explained that there was a problem at the condo I was in the process of purchasing and that I would need Miss Harris to meet me, so we could solve it. They must have sent her a message right away.

Tiffany: There is no problem at that condo is there? What do you want?

H: I want to talk to you about something. It has to be in person.

Tiffany: I won't tell anyone what I saw at the club. I would be grateful if you would extend me the same courtesy.

H: The Club is entirely confidential. What happens in the club...

Tiffany: Stays in the club, right? Well, I was just curious about the rooms. I have a boyfriend. I'm happy.

H: I'm glad you're happy. I just need to talk to you about something. I promise I won't touch you.

Tiffany: Okay.

H: Unless you beg me to...

CHAPTER TWELVE

Tiffany

This time I made sure I was dressed in a dark black pant suit. I added ankle boots. Beneath the jacket of the suit, I had a pale pink blouse, but the jacket was wrap style and mostly covered me apart from a flash of pink at the neck. I straightened my hair and left it down, trying to look as conservative and professional as I could. I didn't want H thinking I was there for him to fuck again. I was with Brandon now.

As I entered the condo lobby, my mind flashed back to the time in the apartment. Why had he not wanted a repeat performance though? Had I not been good enough? Was that it? Why I was here? Because he wanted to give me some pointers, so I could satisfy Brandon better? Who the fuck knew. The best thing I could do was go to the apartment.

When I got to the correct floor and walked to the condo door, it was already unlocked. I walked through to the room and found H standing at the window. He was dressed in jeans and a tee. My heart leaped, and my pussy got wet. Traitorous heart. Traitorous core. He looked so much younger, dressed casually. He ran a hand through his blond hair.

"Tiffany. Thank you for coming." His voice was thick and husky.

I nodded. At a loss for words.

"So, I guess you're wondering why you're here?"

I swallowed, trying to make my throat wet enough to speak.

"Just tell me what you need, so I can go. I have a lot of work to do and then I'm meeting Brandon."

"Ah, yes. Mr. Bailey. The one you're in love with." H looked back out of the window. "But he's not enough, is he? Not on his own. You need more."

My eyes narrowed. "What are you talking about?"

"The club. Last night. I watched you watching

the three of us. I saw you make yourself come. You liked thinking of two men fucking you, didn't you?"

"No. I didn't do any such thing. You're imagining things."

"So why, when you got home, did you go to see Mr. Bailey and let him fuck you with his cock and a dildo to imagine what it's like then?"

My jaw dropped, my heart plummeted to the floor, and I stared at H.

"Are you spying on me? What the fuck is going on?"

"No." Brandon replied, as he walked out of the bedroom and came toward me. "I told him myself."

I stood stock still, rooted to the spot. How could Brandon be here at the apartment, in the same room as H? Oh my god, was it all a set up?

I placed a hand on my hip. "Someone better tell me what the fuck is going on here."

The men looked at each other.

"Do you know what? Forget it." I shouted, and I ran from the room. I couldn't wait for the elevator. I headed for the stairs and ran down them as fast as my heeled shoes would let me until I reached the foyer. As I moved toward the exit I was stopped by Matthew, H's driver.

"Miss Harris. Please, wait a moment."

"Matthew, I can't. I need to leave."

"I've got this now, Matthew, thank you."

I tilted my head back in frustration at H's voice. His strong hand was now on my arm and I was powerless to move unless I wanted to make a scene in front of the many guests in the lobby.

"Please, Tiffany. Come to the bar and let me explain. It's not what you think it is."

"So it's not a set up? You didn't put Brandon in that apartment?"

He sighed.

"That's what I thought." My eyes teared up. "I told him I loved him. What a fucking fool I am."

"No, you're not. Please, come to the bar."

I nodded and walked alongside him. To be honest, I felt so foolish and devastated I wanted to hide, and my legs felt like they wouldn't hold me up any longer.

"Two brandies please." H requested from the bartender. I didn't protest, instead I asked him to make it three.

I walked past H and found a dark corner of the bar area, where I took a seat. H sat down at the side of me. He was too close. His knee was alongside mine. The bartender brought over our drinks and placed them on the table. I drank one straight down, choking as the alcohol burned my throat and tears stung my eyes.

When I recovered myself, I narrowed my eyes at H. "I'm listening."

"It's no secret that I want you, Tiffany. However, I felt that maybe my attraction for you was too much."

"Too much for whom?"

"For me." H took a sip of his brandy.

"I lost my wife twelve years ago. A brain tumor. She was carrying our son at the time. I lost the love of my life and the family I should have had."

I covered my mouth with my hand, while I stared at the man at my side who was now slumped in his chair, looking down at his hands.

I took a moment to compose myself. "H, I'm so sorry."

He rubbed the heel of his palm on his chest and in a flat, monotone voice said, "I won't allow myself to commit again to a woman. Veronica was my life, my world, and that's the position where she will always stay." He drank the rest of his brandy and motioned for the bartender to bring another. "You had the right idea, to order more than one." A slight smile crossed his face. The man at my side then brought himself up to a straighter position and returned to the H I knew.

"So, I have sexual partners, but I have never loved anyone else. But then I met you."

"We only fucked once. You're staying true to your wife."

"That's just it though." He replied. "For the first time since I lost her, I wanted more."

I gasped.

"I do want more." He added. "Tiff, I want you in my bed on a regular basis. I want to take you to nice places. I want to love you."

I took a large swig of my brandy because for a moment I felt I might faint.

"But you would want more. You would want marriage. A family. I can't give you those things. So, I sent Brandon to live in the apartment."

I jolted in my seat.

He held up his hand. "Stay. Let me explain."

I sat while I waited for the words that I expected would tear my life apart.

"Brandon works at a gym I own. He was looking for a place to live. I asked him to flirt with you, maybe take you out a couple times. I wanted you to be distracted from our rendezvous in the condo. To have some fun. But then he told me he'd fallen in love with you. And I watched as you fell in love with him. I was happy to step back. He can give you what I can't."

I closed my eyes. My relationship with Brandon wasn't fake. Thank god for that. A deceitful start that I had to think about, but our love for each other was genuine. I could have cried with relief, but the man in front of me wasn't going to get to see my emotions for another man.

"Then, I watched you at the club. The first time, when you saw the auction and the ménage on stage you looked shocked. Then you came back by yourself and you watched me, though you didn't know I was under the mask. You got off on it, on seeing two men with one woman. You went home and took the dildo to Brandon. I had told him, if he was enough, I would walk away. Back right off. But if you craved more, I would step up."

"What do you mean?"

"You love Brandon. You can have a family life with Brandon. But we are willing to offer you more. Brandon is a good man and he sees that he is not enough for you sexually."

My mind tried its best to process his words and the fact they were true. It was devastating to hear the facts out loud, but yes, sexually I craved more. It might be that a one-time experience would be enough. I didn't know. But I desperately wanted to know how it felt to have two men at once.

"So, what now?" I asked.

"Now, Brandon comes down to talk to you. You can either leave with him, or..."

"We come back to the apartment."

H smiled. "It's been a pleasure to meet you, Tiffany Harris. I hope to see you again, but if not, I wish you all the best for your future." He lifted my hand, kissed the skin next to my knuckles and then rose from his seat and walked away.

What the fuck just happened? And, what did I do?

I FELT like a girl waiting for a blind date to show up. I was so nervous as I sat looking for Brandon. He walked around the corner and I saw his head rise searching for me. I waved to him and he smiled. I loved his smile. My stomach settled because of that reassuring smile.

"What are we drinking?" He asked.

"Brandy, but I've had two already."

"Third time lucky," he winked and motioned for a bartender.

When we had our drinks in front of us, Brandon took a deep breath. "I'm so sorry, Tiff, for not being completely honest with you. I wanted to tell you so many times about how I had been asked to flirt with you, but then I fell for you anyway."

"So, why didn't you?"

"Because I was scared you would walk away. Kick me to the curb. I didn't want that. I don't want that. Tiff, I want us to be together always. I want you to wear my ring and have my kids. Do you feel the same way? Or have I damaged us forever by taking a chance that you want more sexual freedom?"

"You haven't damaged us forever. It was a shock that's all. A shock that's still there but having the edges dulled by brandy."

"And I haven't scared you talking about commitment?"

"No. Because I feel the same way. When you know, you know, right?"

"Well, I'm glad you feel that way," he replied. Then he dropped to one knee and opened a box.

"Tiffany Harris. Please would you do me the honor of becoming my wife?"

My fingers splayed across my mouth and my body shook. "Oh my god. Oh my god. Yes." I squealed. He placed the ring on my finger—a diamond solitaire—and I jumped into his arms almost knocking him over.

"How did you know my ring size?"

"You sleep like the dead, Tiff. I measured it then."

I pushed him with my now diamond adorned hand. "It's a good thing you're gorgeous."

He pushed a piece of my hair back behind my ear. "There's no rush on a wedding, okay? Whenever you want. I know we have been only dating a few months."

"Excuse me."

We looked up, having forgotten that anyone else existed, to see the bartender standing beside us. "Sorry, but we saw the proposal and on behalf of the Brighton Condominium and Club, we would like to offer you our heartfelt congratulations."

We noticed there was a small crowd of people standing around us and as we took the bottle of champagne, they gave us an ovation.

"I think we should take this back to the room, don't you, Mrs. Bailey-to-be? That's if you're ready to have all your wildest desires met?"

I hesitated and sucked on the left side of my bottom lip.

"Tiffany, if you don't want to do this, you can say

no. I'll be happy to tell Henry to leave. If we start it and you've had enough, same thing. If we commit to this relationship, it's going to be once every two weeks, okay? At any point, you say the word and the arrangement is finished."

I nodded. "Okay. Listen, I want you to know that I find Henry attractive obviously, but I don't know him. I don't love him. I love you."

"Well, I'm comfortable enough with my manhood that you can like him a little bit." Brandon laughed. "Now take my hand, fiancée, and let's not keep the man waiting any longer or he'll think we left."

He led me to the elevator, and we went back up to the apartment.

When we walked back through the door, H was back looking out of the window and he turned to stare at us when we came through.

Brandon nodded to him. "We're ready."

I blushed. How did this work? I felt so dirty saying I would fuck two men at once.

H spotted my nervousness. "Tiffany, Brandon and I discussed how we would do this if you agreed, so all you have to do is let yourself go fully. We will lead you through the first time."

"Don't forget, you can stop this at any time." Brandon's voice was full of concern.

"All you need to remember, Tiffany, is that ultimately we're here to worship your body. This is all for you." H whispered. I glanced from Brandon to H and it became clear to me. They were here to meet my deepest, darkest desires and no one but these two knew about them. I felt the tension leave my shoulders. I undid my jacket and then my blouse and I threw them on the back of the couch. Finally, I took my shoes off my feet and shimmied out of my pants, so I was left in a light-pink sequined bra and a matching lacy G-string.

"Let's move it to the bedroom." H's voice was cultured and smooth.

My mouth dropped open when I walked in. Although he had yet to complete the sale, he had already changed the furniture. There was a huge king-sized bed in the room. H went to stand by the window and Brandon walked up to me. He leaned in and kissed me, capturing my tongue with his own. He slid a strap of my bra down my arm, then the other and backed me onto the bed. Once I was lying back with Brandon at one side of me, he pulled down my bra to reveal my huge tits and sucked on them. Then he turned to H. "There's plenty to share."

H joined us and knelt at the other side of me on the bed. He swirled his tongue around my nipple. My tits were being sucked on by two men at once. I swore my pussy would sing if it could. The sensations were almost too much for me to bear and I moaned and gasped and begged for more. They removed my bra and panties and their eyes explored every inch of me.

I expected to be treated like a sex slave, so I was surprised when instead I was almost worshipped by them. They trailed fingers over my skin, caressing every part of me. H grazed his fingertips across my clit and I arched upwards. Brandon showed me two of his fingers and then pushed them inside me. They fingered and played with me. At one point, H added a light tapping pressure to my bud, and it tormented me to the edge of an orgasm. I cried out for release. H moved over, and Brandon spread my legs apart, parted my folds and licked my pussy. H once again added his fingertips to my nub. They kept a steady rhythm until I surrendered my body to its crescendo and exploded all over their face and fingers. I opened my eyes, and a thrill went through me as I saw two men both by my pussy.

"You're too dressed." I complained. "Take all your clothes off."

They both smiled and walked to opposite ends of the room where they stripped. Jesus Christ. Two huge cocks. I might need vaginoplasty after this.

"Shuffle to the end of the bed, Tiff," Brandon said in a commanding voice.

I did as he asked. The men stood to each side of me.

"Suck our cocks." Brandon added.

I took Brandon's cock into my mouth and as I sucked on it, I grasped H's dick and began to pump it with my hand. Then I swapped. I did this for a long time, enjoying comparing one and then the other. I asked if I could hold them together and they nodded. I grasped them between my fists and stretched my mouth open as wide as I could to take in both cocks at once. The edges of my mouth felt as if they were going to rip apart, but I sucked for all I was worth, while I tickled up their shafts with my fingers. Drool ran down the sides of my mouth.

When they withdrew, my jaw ached.

"We're going to fuck you hard. Any preference as to who takes your pussy and who claims your ass?" Brandon asked.

"Surprise me." I said.

They asked me to kneel. Brandon came to the front of me. "As H has not yet experienced the delights of your asshole, I'm letting him play there first."

"How thoughtful." I giggled.

Brandon knelt in front of me and cupped my mound. "Ah, sopping wet as always. Ready and willing for my dick."

He pressed his girth against my cleft and pushed inside, filling me.

I groaned in response.

"You're dying to feel what it's like with two cocks inside you, aren't you?" Brandon added. "To see how it compares to my cock and the dildo."

H was at the side of us. He lubed up his pulsing shaft and then placed himself behind me. His dick nudged at my asshole.

"Relax. Make it easy for me."

He pushed forward, and his cock sank in me an inch at a time. I was stretched so much by Brandon's cock and now H's at the same time. This was not something I would want all the time—to some extent it was strange and uncomfortable—but I guessed like anything you had to get used to it. Then they both started to move. H had one hand holding my hip, and the other wrapped around my front and he pinched my nipple. Brandon had one hand on my hip and the other fingered my pussy.

"Are you okay Tiff?" H asked with concern. "Do you want us to stop?"

"Fuck no. Fuck me, please." I begged enjoying every thrust.

They picked up the pace, thrusting inside but being gentle. My pussy was soaked with my juices and I squirmed under Brandon's fingers as my orgasm built. I screamed so hard when I came that I was scared they were going to call security. H and Brandon pulled out and jacked themselves off to their own orgasms. They sprayed their cum all over my front and back. Brandon picked up a couple of towels from the end of the bed and threw one to H as he wiped himself and then me.

"We thought we would go gentle the first time. What did you think?"

I smiled and looked at them both with devotion. "That was amazing. I could never have estimated what two men at once felt like."

"Let's hit the shower." H said, "and then we can rest."

The water in the large walk-in shower cascaded down over our naked bodies. H grabbed a sponge and soaped it up. Once again, I was the filling between a Brandon and H sandwich. I was lathered up and my body washed while Brandon got the shampoo and washed and then conditioned my hair.

I noted that they were both rock hard again.

I dropped to my knees and took Brandon in my mouth. He groaned and tipped his head back. H stroked his shaft as he watched me give oral pleasure to Brandon. Brandon came into the stream of water and I watched his cum as it swirled away down the drain. He moved me nearer to H and nodded his head. H backed me against the wall and grabbing his cock, he thrust inside me. While he fucked me, I kept my eyes on Brandon. It was so fucking hot being fucked by one man while another watched. H's thrusts meant I was repeatedly jostled against the wall and I imagined someone watching us now, seeing what we had all been doing together and I begged Brandon, "Suck my clit."

He lowered himself to his knees and from the side of me he licked my clit, biting and sucking it. Against the plunging of H's cock, it was too much, and I came, squirting my juices all over Brandon's face and H's cock.

"Did you see that, H? Our little Princess likes to squirt."

"I did." He replied. "I'm very impressed."

I felt strangely proud, as if these were my

teachers and I was the star pupil. Maybe that was a role play idea for another time?!

H once again soaped up a sponge and washed between my legs and then his cock. Brandon also washed himself and then we stepped out and wrapped up in bath towels. We made our way over to the massive bed and once dried, we climbed under the duvet. I was cradled between two taut bodies and it was total bliss. I completely surrendered and fell asleep.

When I awoke, I saw that H was up and getting dressed.

"Hey," I said to him quietly.

"Hey." He nodded to the bedside table. "A key for you."

"But you haven't completed the sale yet."

"Money buys anything, Tiffany, and I have a lot of it."

He stroked my cheek. "I hope to see you again sometime." He picked up my hand and studied the ring. "It's beautiful. Congratulations. I hope you'll be very happy together."

"We will be." I told him.

He walked out of the bedroom door and I heard the click of the outside apartment door as he left. I curled back up to Brandon and fell back to sleep.

CHAPTER THIRTEEN

Tiffany

I kept everything that had just happened to myself until the Monday evening, though I was desperate to tell the girls about my new experiences. Kayla came home with Chinese food for us all and as usual we opened some wine. After the meal, at the point where we usually choose a movie, I finally filled them in on all my adventures.

"Oh my god. I am so jealous of you right now." Kayla pouted. "I didn't even know I wanted a ménage, but I do now."

Haley sighed. "I have enough trouble with one

man and one penis, never mind double the trouble. Are you sure it's not going to get messy, Tiff?"

"Well, we can only see what happens." I replied. "If Brandon starts to find it difficult, I'll stop it. My love for him is stronger than my need for an extra cock. They make plenty of realistic dildos these days."

"So why not do that?" Haley asked.

"Because it doesn't come with an amazing chest with rock hard abs." I smiled.

I hadn't worn my engagement ring yet, so I went into my purse. "I have something else to show you. Just a minute."

I brought my hand out when my sparkling diamond was in place.

"Oh my fucking god." Haley squealed.

"Haley Martin! Scrub your mouth." Kayla mocked. "Tiff, it's Brandon you're marrying right? Not both of them or just their cocks." She added.

"Yes," I rolled my eyes. "Brandon asked me to marry him and I said yes. I know it's fast, but we agreed we don't need to rush to get married, but hey, we're madly in love."

The girls flung their arms around me for a group hug.

"So, the other thing," I told them. "I'll be moving

out and into Brandon's apartment. The good news is I will only be a few steps away. We can still have our Mondays if that's okay with you?"

I looked at Haley. "I'll give you notice okay and pay whatever rent you need to cover the place while you find another tenant."

"Actually," Kayla interrupted. "I'm doing really well at work and if possible, could I pay Tiff's share and have her room? It will mean I get the bathroom to myself and I can use the extra bedroom as a walk-in closet.

"That would be great. I would be nervous to get a new tenant. What if we didn't like them?" Haley stated. "That's settled then."

We toasted my engagement and all the new arrangements, and then Kayla chose *Bride Wars* and spent the movie debating how much of a Bridezilla I would turn into.

CHAPTER FOURTEEN

One year later...

<u>Tiffany</u>

I WAS NOW Mrs. Brandon Bailey. Mrs. Tiffany Bailey. We had gotten married a few weeks earlier and had just returned from a honeymoon in the Caribbean.

Last night I had caught up with the girls. Haley's love life was unfortunately no better, and Kayla was getting ready to go visit her stepfather, as he said he needed to speak to her about her mom. Apparently, she had caused chaos again. Kayla joked about it all, but I could see it was getting her down.

For part of our engagement present, Kayla had given me her key to S. She said it was my place with H owning it, and she didn't ever want me looking over my shoulder if I visited, thinking she might be there watching me. Well, her actual words had been, 'If I saw you with your snatch out I'd vomit', but I learned to speak fluent Kayla a long time ago.

Of course we saw each other at work too, but we rarely got time to chat there, always out trying to earn more commission.

Anyway, tonight, Brandon and I had received a special invitation from H to the club. It was our wedding present from him. He had said we could dress however we liked because he had ordered costumes for us. I was already excited. We had been in our regular ménage for just over a year now and it worked beautifully, once every two weeks. H and I were extremely fond of each other. I would go so far as to say we loved each other, but we weren't *in* love. My confidence in the three-way had grown, and I thought H intended to capitalize on that tonight. We would see if I was right...

·   ·   ·

THE AUCTION WAS ABOUT to begin. The emcee took the microphone and explained that a private bid had been entered for this evening and so the stage was sold. Then a gentleman walked up to our table and asked us to follow him. We walked through a side door, down a hall, and into a room that resembled a fitting room in a store. There were shelves of different clothes, but looking at them closely, they were costumes of different kinds.

"If you could stay in here to change, Mrs. Bailey, your outfit for the evening is in the white box." He nodded toward a large, rectangular shaped white box which was wrapped in a black ribbon. "I will be back for you in about ten minutes, please enjoy the refreshments. Mr. Bailey, if you could follow me next door."

Brandon kissed me on the mouth. "I'll see you soon."

I took a drink and then lifted up the box. Walking over to the chaise longue in the corner of the room, I took a seat, then untied the bow and removed the lid. Carefully, I pulled back white tissue paper to reveal a black, wet-look PVC bustier and matching panties. There was also a pair of what must have been six-inch stilettos in black patent. I would be lucky if I could walk down the corridor in them.

H totally had a thing for sex with a woman in high heels. There was a note in the box asking for me to tie my hair back in a ponytail and a black band in the box to secure it. I walked over to a full-length mirror in the corner of the room. Having a fitness instructor husband agreed with me. My body was tanned from our honeymoon and toned from all the swimming we had done, plus the gym sessions I attended a couple times each week, hitching a ride in with the hubby. It was hard to stay away when the instructor was so hot!

Finally ready, I poured myself a glass of the champagne on ice, and nibbled on a couple of the strawberries on the silver platter at the side. I didn't intend to eat much here as I was waiting for my main course on the stage.

There was a knock at the door. "Mrs. Bailey, are you ready?"

"I am."

The gentleman came back in. To his credit he treated me as if I was fully dressed and asked me to follow him again. I thought we would be getting Brandon from his room as well, but we didn't. I walked very slowly and carefully down the corridor in the stupidly high heels and finally I was asked to climb a few steps to where there was a side door. Apparently, that would take me onto the stage.

"What about my husband?"

"The men are already on stage, Mrs. Bailey." He pointed to a hook at the side of the door. "When your performance is finished, I will be waiting here with this robe for you and will escort you to the aftercare room."

"Aftercare?"

"Yes, it has a shower, so you can freshen up. I will move your clothes there while you are on stage."

"Thank you...?"

"Mitchell, Mrs. Bailey. My apologies for not introducing myself earlier."

"Thank you, Mitchell. I'm Tiffany."

He held open the door for me and I walked onto the stage.

THE STAGE WAS BRIGHT, but the audience were in muted tones of darkness, with the bar backlit at the rear. I thought I would be overwhelmed at everyone watching, but it was hard to actually make out any of the faces. Anyway, I didn't care. This was what I had been asking for, for a month or so now. To make it onto the stage at S and perform in front of everyone. I had asked for a smorgasbord of my favorite fantasies and that was my present, our wedding present, from H.

On the stage was a bed. On the bed were red satin sheets, all the better to slip and slide across. The ultimate in a girl's wet dream, yet far too impractical to actually make it onto my bed at home. Lying on that bed was my husband. He had a leather mask across his eyes and was wearing a leather thong. Sitting on a chair at the left-hand side of the bed was H, dressed in a suit.

"You're late. Our entertainment was booked for midnight. What sort of a whore are you that doesn't keep to time? If you charge by the hour, you need to arrive on the hour." H barked.

"I'm so sorry. It won't happen again." I said in a quiet voice.

"Hmm, maybe we'll send you back. Unless you can state why we shouldn't?"

I had no clue as to what would happen on the stage, so I made it up as I went along. "Because I'll do anything."

"Anything? What do you think, B?" He turned to Brandon.

Brandon sat up and leered at my body.

"She's hot, let's keep her. I have an idea for later."

"Well, she must be punished for arriving late." H walked over to a drawer and brought out what appeared from the black fronds to be a flogger. I stared at his hand. The handle was glass and sparkled under the light. It was a dildo, a glass dildo. He handed the flogger to Brandon.

"Okay, we tossed a coin and B is the first to get to play with you. I'm going to sit back over here and watch. You'd better be worth it."

Brandon moved off the bed slowly and his eyes raked over my body like a predator. "Remove your panties." He commanded. "Then sit on the edge of the bed."

I walked over to the bed and dropped and stepped out of my panties. Brandon picked them up and threw them to H. "Something for you to play with while I play with her."

H lifted the panties up to his nose and sniffed the hem which I knew was already soaked with my juices. "She smells divine, as you'll know when you're tonguing her pussy."

Brandon knelt on the floor in front of me and pushed my thighs wide apart. He sat to one side so my glistening, wet core was on display to the crowd watching. "So wet," he growled. "But your punishment first."

He held the flogger in his right hand and gently whipped it over my pussy. It tickled, and my clit responded with a jolt like an electric shock. As he repeated the motion, I tried to arch my wet pussy up toward it.

"Keep your ass on the bed. If you do that again your punishment will only get worse." I was dying to know what that worse punishment would be, so I raised my hips up again.

Brandon stopped what he was doing, reached and grabbed my ponytail and dragged me onto my feet. "I warned you." Now lie across my knees.

I positioned myself so my ass was high in the air. Brandon brought the flogger down on my ass cheek but did it hard this time, so it stung. I whimpered. "Good girl, keep quiet and take your punishment." He smacked me another four times. I could feel heat radiating through my ass cheek.

"I think that's enough. Now it's time for my own pleasure. Lower my thong and suck my cock."

I dropped back onto my knees. Brandon stood in front of me. We were sideways on stage to the audience, so they could see our actions. Brandon's eleven-inch cock protruded hard as a rock and I took him into my mouth and expertly gave him head. I tongued the underside of his shaft, pumped the base with my hand and sucked hard. He fucked my mouth hard, holding my hair by my ponytail once more. My head bobbed up and down with the motions of the blow job he was receiving. "I'm going to come and you're going to swallow it all." His seed spilled into my mouth and I swallowed and then licked around my lips. He withdrew his cock and patted me on top of my head. "Well, you are a good girl after all. I think I may allow you to come now."

He picked the flogger back up and sitting back on the edge of the bed he put his fist on the bed so that the glass dildo was standing straight up. "You can do all the work. Fuck it."

I moved onto my knees on the bed, so I was positioned just over the dildo. Then I sank myself down onto it. It was cold, and it made me shiver as it entered my pussy. The combination of the cold and the fact it was so hard made my pussy clench around it. I could care less that I had an audience. All I searched for right then was my orgasm, because I was so fucking wet and horny.

"Do not close your eyes. Watch yourself fuck it." Brandon demanded.

My eyes looked down and I watched myself come up off the dildo. It was dripping with my cum. In fact, my cum pooled onto Brandon's hand as he held the base of the dildo. "Please may I touch my breasts?" I asked.

"You may."

I pushed a hand down the right cup of my bustier and I pinched and tweaked my nipple as I continued to fuck the dildo. My breath came out in short, sharp pants as I pumped up and down on the glass cock. "Oh, god, oooooooohhh." I jerked as my pussy pulsated. Brandon pulled the glass cock away and my legs buckled, and I sank onto the bed.

Brandon got up and walked over to H, handing him the glass dildo. "Your turn. I want to watch for a while."

H slowly moved out of the chair and slipped off his suit jacket. He stood in front of me, unbuttoned his shirt, removed it and tossed it on the floor. Then he demanded that I unfastened his pants and free his cock. He wasn't wearing underwear. Another giant cock was in front of me and I wanted to snack on it.

"Get on all fours on the bed so your ass is pointing at me," he ordered.

Now my puckered ass was on display to the whole audience.

"Time to introduce your new friend to another receptive hole."

He pushed the dildo into my tight asshole and

once I was relaxed around it, he thrust it firmly into my ass. God, it felt good. He fisted his cock with his free hand while he hammered my ass. I could hear the noise of him doing it. The noise stopped and my bustier was unfastened at the back. It fell off around my waist. My breasts swung like gigantic pendulums.

"I'm ready." H informed Brandon.

H removed the dildo and threw it onto the stage floor.

He grabbed my hand and pulled me with him toward the floor at the very front of the stage.

"So, B, what was your hot idea?" He asked.

"A spit-roast." He answered.

I was guided onto all fours and H positioned his cock in front of my mouth. Brandon was at my rear.

"We're all going to come together." H informed me.

I tried to imagine what this looked like to the audience. I was sideways, completely naked with my huge tits hanging down. When they fucked me they would swing around. I had one massive cock teasing my lips with pre-cum being rubbed into them and another was teasing the entrance of my pussy.

"Ready?" H asked Brandon.

"Yes."

And they entered me. With a tandem rhythm they worked their cocks in deeper. I deep throated H while my pussy gushed around my husband's cock. I felt my breasts, freed from their constraints, bouncing around. I looked up at H and he watched my breasts. Our performance was polished, and I yielded to the pleasure that coursed through my body. H was the first to reach his pinnacle. His balls retreated, his cock tightened, and he exploded all over my face. His hot, sticky cum ran down my cheeks and onto my chin. Then Brandon pinched my clit and that sent me over the edge. I shuddered around his dick as I felt his own cum spill inside me. A few moments later after we gained control, we all stood up and faced the stage. Cocks still dripped, and cum still ran down my chin and from my pussy. Our most intimate selves were on display in front of a hundred or so people. They broke out into applause. The lights rose, and I saw that so many of them were half dressed themselves. Fingers were in pussies; cocks were in mouths, pussies and asses. The doors opened at the edges of the club and patrons made their way over, ready to continue the party for many more hours.

But we were finished for now. Maybe forever. I didn't know. The arrangement had been a fantasy lived out, but now a reality was starting. Brandon and I were planning a family, and we had agreed we would finish on a high. H had just accepted our notice. He didn't think we would return to the scene afterward. He thought it was out of my system. H did say the door might be open if we came back later, but added that his own life was moving on and he was seeking fresh adventures.

Our finale then could not have been any finer, played out on the stage in front of a captive audience.

The curtains dropped. H took my hand, dropped a kiss there and walked away.

As I walked behind him, I was handed my robe and helped down so I didn't fall down the stairs, still in those goddamn heels. "Damn, woman, I thought I only had to carry you over the threshold, not down club hallways too." Brandon threw me over his shoulder and spanked my ass as we headed toward the aftercare room.

THE END

Double Delight continues with SUBMIT – Kayla's story.

Author note: You can read the continuation of H's story in *The Billionaire and the Virgin,* though for your ultimate reading experience finish the Double Delight series before moving onto the Billionaires.

SUBMIT

DOUBLE DELIGHT BOOK TWO

CHAPTER ONE

Kayla

It was time to visit Daniel, my stepfather. He had been messaging me for a couple weeks now, saying he needed to catch me up on some news from my mom. I had delayed visiting saying I needed to give notice to take vacation time from Green's, the realtors I worked for. He was bound to know I was bullshitting him; he had never been a dumbass. As I threw clothes into my suitcase, Haley, my roommate hovered in the doorway.

"I'll miss you, Kay. It's going to be so weird being on my own in the apartment."

"Hey, it's only two weeks, Haley. You can spend the time masturbating away as I won't be here to listen to any rude noises. You can have a good scream."

She rolled her eyes. Haley was used to my ways as we had lived together a while now. Up until a year ago, there had been three of us, but our other friend, Tiff, now lived next door with her husband, Brandon. I had taken over her share of the apartment, meaning I had two good-sized bedrooms and my own bathroom. We still saw Tiff every Monday when we had our girls night where we ate good food, watched a movie, and gossiped.

I had never told them much about my stepfather though. Or about my mom. They knew she had paraded me through a stream of stepdaddy's as she chased money. My mom couldn't live her life without wealth, and I had been an unfortunate incident for her. Her relationship—if you could call it that—with my father, had been the catalyst for all the drama that came after. He had left her penniless, and she had sworn it would never happen again.

Out of all my stepfather's, Daniel, who I had met when I was seventeen, had been the only decent one. The only one who had realized I existed, beyond being a hanger on. He had told me I always had a place at his home, and even after my mother had worked her way through most of his wealth and moved onto Chuck, the stepdad that came after, he still reminded me I could stay anytime. I had never fully worked out my mom's relationship with Daniel. They had never seemed hooked on each other like she had with some of them. Her public displays of affection with one or two had made me feel nauseous. Largely through my life, I had kept my head down and done the best I could with my educa-tion, given the fact I was never at one school for very long before she had us on the move again. Once I turned eighteen, she had moved on once more and this time she told me she was done raising me and I was on my own.

It wasn't the shock it could have been. Like I said, she had been absent most of my life anyway. I graduated and eventually started at Green's where I made my good friends and never looked back. I'd had a couple boyfriends but no one special. The girls were used to my cocky manner about guys, but to be truthful I was more talk and no action if you get me. I'd not had much experience, though I was no virgin. I was kind of jealous of my friend, Tiff. She had been enjoying a ménage for the last year. That woman walked around the whole time like she still had a cock up her pussy. I swear she always wore a shit-eating grin. Jealous, me? You better believe I was.

Anyhow, I couldn't put off visiting Daniel any longer as he had said my mom had been causing chaos again, and he needed to update me. I had hoped she wasn't hanging around for his money again as he had recently recovered his wealth, having had some of his art bought by a prestigious gallery. When I had first met him—when he and my mom hooked up—he was the owner of a string of tattoo parlors. He had secretly painted on canvas, using the talent that had drawn designs on clients, until he had finally got the guts up to show them to someone. They'd loved his work and taken a couple pictures to try in a gallery where they had been bought by a collector the same day. He now had a new profession, which was great because my mom had nearly caused him to go bankrupt with his tattoo business.

I hadn't stayed at Daniel's much. Instead, a schoolfriend's mom had practically let me move in there, knowing my background with my own mom. No, I hadn't stayed at Daniel's very often for a good reason.

I had always had a huge crush on my stepdad. There was no way I could have lived with him and my mom. If they had kissed, I would have wanted to punch something. I knew that was stupid. Girls got crushes all the time. But Daniel was something else. He was ten years younger than my mom and had been twenty-eight when I first met him—eleven years my senior. He had dark shaggy hair back then and the darkest eyes. When he smiled, he always looked sexy and goofy at the same time. His face all kinda crinkled up. He had these really plump cheeks when he smiled. I had always wanted to reach out and touch them. I was sure that whenever he spoke, heat rose in my cheeks. I guess that was when I had started to become the brash kind of Kayla because I hadn't wanted to appear all young and innocent around him. Thing was, I always felt he was trying to save me, you know? Always telling me I had a home with him, even after my mom almost ruined him. He had gotten this look in his eye like he hadn't wanted me to lose touch and even though I had tried to cut contact with him over the following years he had never given up. Still texted, called, sent me birthday and Christmas cards, and checks I never cashed. When I visited, I would do it on the way somewhere else and not stay long because I couldn't. Being too close to him killed me. But now I had to go, and he had told me I would need to stay awhile—at least a few days—so somehow, I would have to work through this crush I had. I was twenty-four now. It had been six years since my mom had hitched a ride with her next victim. I had never seen or heard from her again, yet now she had done something that affected Daniel and me once more.

Zipping up my case, I turned to the doorway. I had been so lost in thought, Haley had left. I'd spent some time with her before I drove to Daniel's. She was my best friend, and I was gonna miss her while I was gone.

The drive to Port Jeff was less than a couple hours which made my lack of visits there even lamer I guessed. I swung into the large driveway of Daniel's colonial. He was so lucky to have not lost this amazing property. His four bed, four bathroom home in Harbor Hills looked out over the waterfront and had its own private beach. I exited my car, leaving it in front of the double garage and walked to the front door where I rang the bell. After a couple minutes the door opened and Daniel stood there.

He looked as hot as ever and I felt my cheeks burn again. Why was I so goddamn sensitive around him? His face broke out into his signature smile and he stepped forward and embraced me in his arms. The heat from his body enveloped me. I didn't want to move, but he then outstretched those strong arms and looked me over.

"Hey there, Kayla. It's good to see you. You look well."

I half smiled at him, feeling uncomfortable.

"Shoot, ignore my manners leaving you out here on the porch. Come inside. You need help with your luggage?"

"Please. There's a case in the trunk."

"I'll grab that and then I'll park your car in the garage. We'll take your luggage to your room and then I'll fix us a drink, okay?"

"Okay," I replied.

I hovered in the hallway while I waited, taking in the vastness of the space. Every time I came here, the place took my breath away. He hadn't decorated the place and the realtor in me saw the potential of the property that had yet to be unleashed. The hall had a central staircase leading up to a landing from which all the other rooms veered off. It was a little old fashioned to me with its wooden moldings. It cried out for a modern makeover. If it were mine, it would be fabulous.

"Okay, let's get your things in your room." Daniel had reappeared with my case. I grabbed my duffel from the floor and followed him up the stairs.

This wasn't good. He was wearing jeans, and they hugged his ass as he climbed the stairs. I wanted to reach out and feel his ass cheeks, see if they were as peachy as they appeared. His biceps bulged as he carried my case up the stairs. I felt between my thighs get wet. For fuck's sake, he was only walking!

We headed a little way down the hall to my old room. He pushed open the door. It was exactly how I had left it, or rather, how my mom had decorated it. The room was ocean blue—everywhere. With its frilly curtains and bedding, it hurt my eyes to look at it. Daniel caught the grimace on my face.

"Maybe we could decorate while you're here? Make it more your own?"

"Maybe. Though I'm not planning on staying too long, you know. My life's back in Brooklyn and I need to return there as soon as I can."

Daniel nodded. He looked a little disappointed, and that made me feel bad.

"Though I guess it wouldn't hurt to do a little makeover, given the hideous paint colors in here."

"Great." Another smile broke out on his face. "It would be good to get the house looking a little more modern. I need to make the most of having a hot realtor in the house."

At that, my face burned so hard I thought I might need a fire extinguisher.

Daniel ran a hand through that still shaggy brown hair. "Christ, Kayla. I meant hot as in good at your job. Jesus, I'm an idiot."

"It's fine." I waved my hand in front of my face. "I knew what you meant, and I am really great at my job." I needed to get sassy Kayla back as soon as possible. That's how I was. Confident, and not afraid to speak my mind. "I've seen enough of this room for now. How about you fix me that drink and we sit out on the deck?"

"Sure," Daniel answered.

I needed him out of my bedroom.

We walked back down the stairs, entering the hallway and then walked off to the right, through his vast living room with its dark leather chairs and huge TV, and out into the back yard. There was an acre of lawn out there, complete with a heated swimming pool at the rear of the lawn and a pool house. I had spent a lot of time in the pool house when I had visited when my mom lived here. It had been a place to escape, with its comfy couches and two separate rooms, one with a queen bed, the other a bathroom. Right now, I could see it was all opened up. At the left hand side was the living room area with its large flatscreen television against the far wall. To the right was a kitchen with all mod cons. It was perfect for hot summer evenings, lazing by the pool and eating a barbeque. We had never done that there. We had never been enough of a family to eat together, never mind relax together.

"I know you always kinda liked staying out there." Daniel nodded towards the pool house. "But it's better for this trip that you stay in the house."

He excused himself to go fix the coffee, and I took a seat on the swing seat out on the decking. There were two separate seats on it, so I didn't have to sit too close to Daniel. He came out with two steaming hot mugs of coffee and placed each one on a side table at the side of the swing seat before taking his own seat.

"So, what's she done this time?" I cut to the chase. No point in waiting around to find out what chaos my mom had caused.

Daniel turned to me. "She's shacked up with a movie producer this time. They got married a month ago."

It was good to see my mom hadn't changed. Still after the men with untold riches and still keeping her only child out of her life. Not that I would have attended the wedding anyway, but hey, it would have been cool to know my own mom was getting hitched again.

"So how does that impact on us? Are they making a film about her life and they want us to star in it?" I joked.

Daniel sighed.

"Ah, nothing so amusing."

"Her husband has a son. By all accounts, he's always been a little rebellious. Excluded from school, that kind of thing. His mother died when he was eight. His father excused his behavior, right up until he met your mom."

"Figures."

"He threw him out just over two weeks ago. Parker—that's his name—went through your mom's belongings and found my address, so he headed here to find you. He thinks he can get you to reason with your mom. I've tried to explain, but he won't listen to me. I said I would invite you over and we could all talk. See if there was anything we could do. I said he needed to let you explain your relationship with your mom and that you hadn't had it easy yourself."

"So, where's the little brat so I can put him straight?"

Daniel's lips curved at the corners as if he knew something I didn't, which of course would be the case, seeing as he had already met this son who had been excluded from school.

"I told him to wait in his room. I'll call him now."

"Wait! In his room? He's living here?"

"Yeah. I felt bad for him. He has no one. So I told him he could stay here until he got back on his feet. I kinda think he needs a father figure."

I shook my head. "Daniel Scott's home for stray kids. You can't save us all, you know? Sometimes parents are just a waste of space."

"Yeah, my own was like that, so I guess it hits a nerve when I see it someplace else. Anyway, I'm thirty-five. I'm too young to be your dad or his dad. I know you always considered me as a stepfather, Kayla, but your mom and I were never married, so I wasn't really."

The door banged as Tom Hardy walked through it. Well, he looked like Tom: dark hair shaved close to his head, doe eyes and a wide pout to his mouth. Obviously some employee of Daniel's. He needed to watch his manners. He was acting like he owned the place.

"So sweet, listening to the old family reunion, so I thought I would come join in." He held out a muscled arm. This guy was stacked and seriously worked out. I figured he could lift me with just one of those arms.

Standing up, I took his hand, looking toward Daniel for clues, then back at the Tom Hardy lookalike.

"I'm Kayla."

"Aww, hello little... well... what should I call you? Your mommy is married to my daddy, so... stepsister?"

I stepped back. "What the heck?" I turned to Daniel. "This is Parker?"

I was expecting a boy recently excluded from school. This guy was not that young.

"Yes. Parker, meet Kayla. Kayla, Parker."

Parker grabbed my hand and shook it. A little too firmly. I felt uncomfortable as my first thought had been how sexy the hired help was. Now I found out he was kinda my stepbrother.

"I'm sorry," I said, flustered. "I was expecting someone a little younger."

"I'm twenty-one, so I'm not that old." He replied. "How about you?"

"Twenty-four."

"Well, now that those pleasantries are out of the way, I need you to come with me back to Los

Angeles to get your whore of a mother away from my father." He sneered.

I sighed. "If only life was that simple."

"Are you kidding me? It is that simple. We go back home. You tell my pop her history with men. He kicks her out. Job done."

"My mom hasn't wanted anything to do with me for the last six years, so if you think I would get anywhere near her, you're sadly mistaken."

"Well, you need to try. I'm on the outs here. She's bleeding him dry. That's my inheritance we're talking about."

"Oh, it's great to see that it's your pops you're missing." I sneered. "I've about had it with all you money-oriented bastards."

"You can't be doing too bad. Dan says you live in New York."

I narrowed my eyes at him. "I live in Brooklyn. I have a share in a rented apartment. I work round the goddamn clock to meet my rent. Don't come here playing the victim because it doesn't work with me. You want a nice life? Go out and earn one. I won't be helping you with your daddy issues."

I turned to Daniel. "Thanks for the coffee. I'm gonna head back up to my room and unpack. Maybe lie down for a bit. I'm feeling a headache coming on."

"Okay, Kayla." I could see in Daniel's gaze that he wanted to say more but couldn't.

"Well, I'm gonna hit the pool. I'm feeling a little heated." Parker walked off down the deck.

"I'm sorry, Kayla." Daniel's mouth was down-turned, his shoulders slumped.

"You have nothing to be sorry about," I reminded him. "I'm sorry that your relationship with my mom brought these problems to your door.

"We should talk about that sometime. My relationship with your mom."

"There's no need."

"I think there is, Kayla, because I doubt it was what you thought it was."

I nodded my head and walked back into the house. My head was already buzzing with meeting Parker and being reminded of my mom's behavior. I didn't need riddles from Daniel accompanying it.

CHAPTER TWO

Daniel

I had no clue how to handle this. Kayla had entered my life when she had been seventeen, supposedly as my stepdaughter, but hell, I had never felt that way about her. Her mom's clear mission to hook me for my money was apparent from the beginning and I wouldn't have stuck it out were it not for the tall, willowy redhead that hung behind her. She was beautiful but downbeat. I had figured she needed someone to look out for her, to believe in her. So I had kept her mom in money so I could give Kayla a home. Instead, I had ended up keeping an eye on her from a distance as she decided she preferred staying with a friend and her friend's mom rather than here. I tried not to take it too personally. Her relationship with her mom was complex. But the times I did see her, she was always awkward around me. As much as I had tried to show her I wasn't the same as the other stepfathers that had gone before me, she stayed distant. Once she had turned eighteen, I asked her mom to leave. Her mom moved on and Kayla was led to believe her mom had left me. There was no reason for me to keep in touch with Kayla at all, but I couldn't help myself.

When I'd opened the door to her today, I'd been mind blown. Her red hair was tousled, and the breeze had blown it across her face a little. I'd wanted to reach out and push it behind her ear. My dick had hardened as my gaze had taken in her pale-green sundress, with its thin straps resting over her freckled shoulders. Its loose cotton hung over that still slim silhouette and with the light behind her it had made the dress partially see-through, so the shape of her legs and the space between her thighs was clear as she stood there. My first thought had been to hug her—she was finally here. Then I'd realized Kayla wasn't the hugging type, so I'd just held her away from me. I'd made an excuse about getting her luggage so that I might hold the suitcase in front of my crotch. The last thing I'd wanted to do was to embarrass her. I knew she would have enough to contend with, in the fact she was going to have to meet Parker soon.

Then I'd showed her to her bedroom, even though she knew how to find it herself. It had been so long since she had visited, she was acting like a stranger. The room had been a mess, still in the paint that belonged to the nineties. I loved to paint, but unfortunately, it was on canvas rather than walls. Still, I'd suggested she might like to decorate it. Again, my conversation stemmed from the fact that as I had stood in the bedroom alongside her, all I wanted to do was push her down on the bedspread and lift that dress up so I could see her secret places.

And I'd called her a hot realtor. I'd wanted the ground to swallow me whole.

The worst thing though was her introduction to Parker. I knew Parker was a good-looking dude and there was no way I wanted them to hit it off in that way, so I'd encouraged the stepbrother talk. I figured though they weren't related, if she saw him in that kind of relationship, it would prevent anything from happening.

It was also the reason I had given Parker a home

here. He was a decent enough guy, though a little self-centered. But it gave me a reason to get Kayla into my home. I didn't want her to go rushing off to LA in search of her mother. Not that I thought for a moment she would anyway. But selfish or not, I wanted her here with me for a while. So I could spend time seeing her laugh, listening to her sass, and, admittedly so I could fantasize about nailing that sweet little body. I had wanted her for seven long years and if I had my way, she would be seeing me in a far different way to a stepdaddy before she went back home—*if* she went back home. Because, if I got my way, I would have that girl mine and pregnant within weeks.

I watched as Parker lifted himself out of the pool. He grabbed a towel and dried off. I had given him a job at the art gallery I'd opened in Chandler Square. It was funny how my career had changed. When Patty, Kayla's mom, had come into my life, I was running a chain of tattoo parlors. You might think they wouldn't do so well in the more affluent parts of New York, but you would be incorrect. All the rich housewives competed with each other for the most beautiful tattoos and my artwork was renowned. My shops had had the best artists in them where you were guaranteed a fantastic inking. Yet within twelve months of Patty being in my life, I had to sell the chain on to keep afloat. Keeping my house had been touch and go until after she had left, and I'd been trying to sell some of the contents of my home. An art collector had picked up a couple of my canvases—things I had painted for fun—and unknown to me, he'd shown them to a dealer. The dealer had gotten in touch with me about securing more of my work. Soon, this hobby had become a passion and had given me a renewed vigor for life. I had opened my own gallery in Port Jeff, a pay-it-forward if you like, some place to buy art from fresh new talent and a permanent display of my own work. I was very fortunate. So I could afford to feed the two twenty-somethings I found living in my house until I worked out how to get Parker to leave without taking Kayla with him. And getting Kayla to want to stay.

I felt hot and uncomfortable. The heat from the day made my t-shirt cling to my body and too many thoughts of Kayla were making me want to jack off. I decided to go for a swim myself now that Parker had gone through to the bathroom in the pool house. I would do a few laps in the pool and try to cool off and calm myself down before dinner when I would see her again.

CHAPTER THREE

Kayla

After unpacking, I had taken a shower and laid down on the top of the bedspread for a while. I couldn't very well stay in here all day, could I? At some point, I was going to have to reappear downstairs. I swung my legs off the bed and lifted myself up, walking toward the window and pulling the drapes open slightly to let in some light. The window was floor-to-ceiling and looked out over the back yard and pool. Daniel stood at the side of the swimming pool. I watched as he laid a towel across the back of a white plastic beach chair and shrugged off his t-shirt, followed by his board shorts which revealed his swim trunks. I couldn't see very well from this distance. I would have given anything for a telescope, so I could have spied on that package in his trunks. After my shower, I had been so hot that I laid on my bed completely naked. I knew that Parker had been in the pool and Daniel had been on the deck, so I felt safe that I wasn't going to be caught in the nude. Plus, to be honest, it was a fantasy of mine for Daniel to walk in on me naked and him not being able to walk away from me if he did. Being close to him stirred something inside me. I scolded myself. I mustn't delude myself that I was here for any other reason than I guessed he still had feelings for my mom and that extended to me. Maybe he was hoping I would go with Parker to find her and bring her home? The thought made me angry. It made me want to pick up the frilly bedspread and rip it apart. How was I going to cope with being this close to him? Keeping such proximity was going to kill me. Daniel dived into the water, a sleek practiced move which made me wonder if all his moves were so smooth and elegant.

I moved away from the window feeling antsy. I picked up a magazine from my travel tote and attempted to focus on the latest celebrity gossip, but my thoughts wandered to Daniel and his body and how the hell I was going to keep my hands away from him.

I threw the magazine down and rested back against the headboard with a sigh. Maybe the only way I was going to be able to deal with him in real life was to have him in a fantasy one? It was worth a shot.

Closing my eyes, I let my hand trail down to the warmth of my cleft. I pressed my finger against my nub and felt a tingle rip through my body. *Yes,* my body almost screamed to me. *Let us come. We need it.*

I trailed a path from my bud down into my wetness, then I brought my finger back up again, flicking my clit. I imagined that it was Daniel's finger that dipped into my core and as I had that thought my pussy blossomed under my fingers. My juices ran thick and coated my digits. Was it taboo to be imagining fucking my stepdad? I reconciled the thought with the fact that this was going to help me relax. I felt the tension in the back of my neck from meeting Parker's belligerent ass earlier, and if I wasn't going to end up with a migraine, I needed to do something about it. It's amusing how a dirty mind belonging to a horny body can reconcile any thoughts. I returned to my fantasy of fucking Daniel.

In my imagination, he was at the end of my bed, laid beside my hip. His hand cupped my mound while he told me how fucking wet I was and how he was going to take me with his huge cock until I could barely walk. I pushed two fingers inside myself and twisted them around while moving them in and out. With my free hand, I pinched my nipples. My breasts were a small handful but oh so responsive. It was like there was a connection between my nipples and my core. I felt like I could come from playing with my tits alone. My fingers continued to tease my clit as I changed my fantasy so that Daniel was between my legs.

I drew my legs up and let my thighs drop to the side.

"Oh, yeah. Right there, right there." I moaned. "Put your tongue on my clit and lick it."

I put two fingers, one on either side of my nub, and squeezed. I placed a finger from my other hand in my mouth and wet it and then flicked it and moved it over my clit as if it were Daniel's tongue.

"Dan," I murmured. "Oh my god, I need you."

I sat up and looked around the room. My fingers weren't enough to get me off. I really needed to fuck something. I grabbed my pillow and sat astride it. Finally, I saw an advantage to frills. The lace on the pillow tickled my clit as I rubbed my cunt back and forth over it. I was facing the wall and so I put a hand out above the headboard to steady myself, the other holding the pillow in place. I moved back and forth across it, feeling the lace as it rubbed across my heat. I left a large spot of my creamy wetness on the edge of the pillow as I rubbed myself. I didn't care. That end would be against the headboard tonight, and tomorrow I'd buy some new linen. I felt the pressure begin to build inside me and fucked the pillow in a frenzy. "Please, please, now, now. I can't wait any longer. I need you inside me. Please, oh God, please. Now. Now. Oh yeah, right there, right there. Ohhhhhhhhh."

I shuddered against the pillow, collapsing face down on the bed with my ass in the air, while the judders subsided. I threw the pillow back to the top of the bed and then turned around quickly, but there was no one there.

I could have sworn I heard my door click.

CHAPTER FOUR

Parker

I wondered whether to stay here or go see a shrink. First up my father dumped me for a whore, then I found the bitch's daughter wasn't who I thought she would be. I'll be honest; I had expected some jumped-up, entitled brat, but no; instead I discovered my new stepsister was prime pussy. When she had sassed me, I thought my dick was gonna punch through my boxers. It was a shame as I watched her walk away that she had that flouncy sundress on. I didn't get to check out her ass.

Then suddenly, I'd had another idea that might

just bring my new stepmommy running back to Port Jeff. It would be a gamble, as by the sound of it, she didn't give too much of a damn about her daughter either. But Dan had told me she raised Kayla until she was eighteen before she ditched her, so maybe Patty did have some feelings for her daughter after all. So I would seduce Kayla. Get my new stepsister into bed and then I would go tell Mommy. If nothing else, it would be great to see the bitch's smug face fall for once; that was if the Botox allowed an expression.

In the meantime, Dan had given me a roof over my head, and I was grateful. I had no problem in working at the gallery in return. I found the place calming, surrounded by all the paintings. It wasn't hard work, thank fuck, as I had never done anything more than hang out with my friends before. As I had gained some independence, I found I really liked it. What I didn't like was having been cut off from my inheritance while I had learned to stand on my own two feet. She was behind that, the bitch.

Still, Dan wasn't charging rent. The guy had a daddy complex, wanting to care for me and by the looks of things, for Kayla too. I needed to make sure he didn't see my attempts to seduce her, or I would be out on my ass. I had to be careful.

After I finished my swim—I was so glad Dan had

a pool as I'd swum at home every day to keep my toned physique—I showered in the pool house and then made my way back to the house. I passed Dan, who carried a towel and was going for a dip himself. It was a hot day. I looked up at Kayla's window and noted the windows were closed. Good job Dan had air conditioning or she would have fainted from the heat. I decided to take her up a glass of iced water. Show her I was a decent guy. Until I wasn't.

As I stood outside her door, I heard her moan. It sounded like she must be asleep, so it looked like my attempt to get friendly would have to wait. Only then I heard her say, 'Oh my god, I need you,' followed by the unmistakable moan of a woman about to come. I placed the tumbler of water on the sideboard and moved closer to her door.

The door was slightly ajar, so I pushed lightly, hoping to God it wouldn't make a noise. As it opened just a centimeter, I could see Kayla was naked, facing the headboard and sat straddling her pillow. Fuck, my cock hardened like I had a candle down my boxers. It was in danger of setting alight all by itself too. She rubbed herself back and forth across that lucky son-of-a-bitch pillow. Her head was thrown back as she gave herself over to her pleasure.

'Please, please, now, now. I can't wait any longer.

I need you inside me. Please, oh God, please. Now. Now. Oh yeah, right there, right there. Ohhhhhhhhh.'

I watched as my stepsister shuddered against that pillow and then collapsed forward. Her backside was pert, and I so wanted to fuck that puckered asshole that winked at me. But I needed to get out of there fast. I needed to not be caught staring at Kayla's limp, satiated body. Instead, I needed to head to my room RIGHT NOW, and jerk off.

I closed the door, then realized too late that I had closed it completely. Quickly, I moved down the landing and into my own room.

I locked my door. There was no way anyone was interrupting me while I jerked off to the image of Kayla masturbating.

Lying on my bed face up, head against the pillows, I pulled my shorts and boxers off and threw them on the other side of the bed. My hand curled around my massive dick and I closed my eyes and imagined it was Kayla's hand. Soon, hopefully, it would be. The next time she masturbated I was going to walk in and catch her. Dirty, filthy Kayla. I held my girth firmly and stroked my hand up and down my shaft. This is what she should have been sitting on. Not that fucking pillow. What a waste, her juices soaking into the cotton when they could have been sliding down my cock. Hell, I thought, I have to get hold of that pillow sometime and smell it. Smell her cum. Fuck, my dick got even harder. Yeah, maybe I would jerk off in her room after I smelled that pillow. Open up the pillowcase and pump my cum into it so that when she went to sleep she smelled my cum. Oh yeah. I pumped faster and faster imagining Kayla had my cock in her mouth. That gorgeous, long red hair falling forward as she bobbed her head up and down. I would fist her hair in my hand and hit the back of her throat with my dick. Make her choke. Maybe I would hold her neck just a little tight. Nothing dangerous, just a hint to see how dirty she would play for me. My thoughts returned back to the pillow and away from Kayla blowing me. In my mind I was in her room with her pillow in my hand where I opened my eyes, grabbed my shorts, and as my balls tightened, I shot my load in a stream of white creamy spunk all over the inside of it. That's what it would be like, baby. Just like that. With a deep sigh, I wiped myself off and closed my eyes.

CHAPTER FIVE

Kayla

I knew I couldn't stay in my room forever and my stomach had started to rumble, so around seven I headed back downstairs. The aroma of food had hit my nostrils as I walked down the stairs and sure enough, as I headed to the kitchen, Daniel was making supper.

"Macaroni and cheese, with salad, and bread. Sound okay?"

"It smells delicious," I told him honestly.

"There's a bottle of red over on the dining table.

It's had its breathing time. Go ahead and pour your-self a glass."

"Thanks."

I took a seat at the wooden dining table. I was pleased the chairs were cushioned as I had put on a pair of shorts and a tank top, and I didn't want any of my uncovered flesh sticking to the seat because of the heat. Reaching over, I lifted the bottle of wine and poured a healthy measure into my glass. Hopefully, it would help to relax me and I could get through a meal with Daniel. Heavy footsteps came from above. I followed the sound as it moved down the stairs until Parker appeared in the kitchen-diner. He immediately went over to the fridge, took out a beer and cracked it open. He was pretty well settled for someone who had only lived here a short time.

"Hey, big sis." He winked, sitting down across from me.

"I'm not your sister. I don't even know you," I threw back.

"Yeah, I was thinking about that," he said, rubbing his chin with a finger. "If you're not going to be able to get your mom away from my dad, maybe we should get to know each other better if we're family."

I took a sip of my wine and pondered what he was saying. It couldn't be easy having been kicked out of the only home you had known for years. Suddenly, he had no money and only Daniel for company.

"Well, I could always use a friend. I don't have many."

"Cool," he said. It made him sound so young. I had forgotten he was only twenty-one. Yes, I was only three years older, but in terms of maturity, it felt like more. Poor Parker was entering a learning curve right now that was for sure.

The table was already set, but Parker jumped up and grabbed the salad. I followed his lead and brought the basket of bread over. Daniel joined us dropping the mac and cheese onto a mat in the center of the table. It smelled divine.

"Ladies first." Daniel nodded at the mac and cheese.

I loaded my plate, adding some salad and bread. When I bit into the mac and cheese the taste was sensational. I moaned as the flavors hit my tongue.

I pointed at my mouth while I was still chewing, "Daniel, this is so good," I said, my mouth still half full.

He looked a little taken aback. Maybe no one ever complimented him on his cooking.

"I'm finding it a little hot," Parker said. "What about you, Dan?"

"I'll get some water," Daniel replied and got up from the table.

We ate the rest of our meal mostly in silence. We all seemed really hungry.

When Daniel had finished eating, he wiped across his mouth with a napkin, setting it to one side.

"So, Kayla. I thought tomorrow if you wanted, we could head out to see my gallery? You haven't been there before, and Parker will be there. I would like to show you the place. Also, there are lots of stores out there. I know you women like to shop. Maybe we could grab lunch while we were there or one of the famous ice creams from Creamy Delights?"

I wondered what Daniel's gallery was like and shopping definitely would pass some time. I wasn't keen on the having lunch with him part, so maybe I could time it so we just did the ice cream?

"Sounds great," I replied. "Anything where I see my little stepbro having to bust a nut sounds fun."

Parker raised his middle finger at me.

I raised my glass at him and took another large sip.

While Parker finished eating, I took the time to check him out. He ate like there was no filling him up, taking not just seconds, but thirds. As I had noted before, he was heavy built. Back out in Los Angeles, I bet he was quite the lothario. He had the gift of the gab and with his being loaded, I bet the girls had flocked to him. He was going to have to work harder for women's attention now that he was relatively broke.

I felt eyes on mine and turned to see Daniel watching me, watching Parker.

"Would you like more wine or water?" he asked me.

"More wine, please. It's going down well."

A smirk appeared at the edge of Parker's mouth, and I realized what I had just said. He was such a juvenile sleazeball!

I kicked him under the table and he yelled 'Ow' really loudly.

"Dad, she kicked me." He winked at Dan.

Dan choked a little on his water.

"Sorry, man. I was just messing with you. Only we're like one fucked-up dysfunctional family, aren't we?"

Daniel took a deep breath. "Well, I rather you

both saw me as a friend than a father figure. I'm not that much older than either of you."

"Eleven years," I said.

"Fourteen years." added Parker.

"Okay, I got it. I'm an old man at the side of you youngsters." Daniel got up and started to clear the table. His mood had turned a little sour. I guess we had really upset him with our jokes about his age.

I shrugged at Dan. "I don't think he finds it as amusing as we do."

"I'll go help load the dishwasher," he replied. "Then we'll take the alcohol out on the deck. That'll loosen him up. The guy's too uptight. It's like he's always worrying about something, but I can't work out what it is. He's financially secure. He has no real dependents, just us two leeches. Perhaps he needs to get laid. Yeah, I'll bet that's it!" Parker leaned back and stretched. His t-shirt lifted upwards revealing a dark path of hair from his belly button trailing down and disappearing under his jeans.

There's no doubt about it. Parker was hot. Now I had to live with two hot guys who were off limits. This place was going to kill me. His talking about Daniel getting laid wasn't helping me either. Thank God, I had masturbated this afternoon or my shorts would be soaked through.

. . .

PARKER HAD LEFT to start work at the gallery for eleven. I showered, dressed, and took breakfast out onto the deck, while Daniel busied himself with loading his truck up with a couple pictures he wanted to take with him. This made me giggle. I guessed that Daniel didn't trust Parker with transporting his precious paintings.

His head shot around the door. "Are you about ready to leave?"

"Sure," I told him. "I just need to grab my purse and I'll be there."

I followed him out front and climbed into the passenger side of the truck. It was high, and Daniel came around and helped me up into the seat by holding my hips. God, his hands were only on me for a second, but I felt the loss when they were gone. I was dressed in jeans and a tank, with an open shirt, and sneakers today, seeing as I wasn't sure how big this place was and whether I was going to be doing a fair amount of walking.

We drove in a companionable silence for a while as we listened to some music on the radio.

"So, what do you think of Parker?" he asked me.

I turned to face Daniel, despite the fact he was looking out of the window so we didn't crash.

"Well, at first I thought he was an arrogant asshole," I replied. "Now I think he's a likeable, arrogant asshole." I laughed.

"You like him, huh?" he asked me. His hands gripped the steering wheel hard, and I wondered if there was something I didn't know about Parker.

"Yeah. Don't you?"

"Sure," he replied.

"Are you okay? You seem a little tense."

Daniel sighed. "I'm fine. It's just strange, the three of us all being together. Patty's still playing her games and messing with my life, and we were over years ago."

"I'm sorry," I told him.

"No," he looked at me fleetingly then back at the road. "Don't ever apologize for your mom, Kayla. None of this is on you. You're as much of a victim as me and Parker."

I shook my head. "I'm no victim. My mom can go suck the dicks of wealthy men all she wants. She has no influence on me."

Daniel started laughing; Big, hearty guffaws that made his cheeks plump up. "Kayla Jackson, watch your mouth." Then he laughed again.

He turned to me as he pulled up at the parking lot. "I wasn't one of them, you know? She never sucked mine. I need to talk to you sometime about me and your mom."

He switched off the engine and jumped out of the cab, leaving me no time to reply. I opened my own door and jumped down, then followed him as he made his way down a sidewalk holding his paintings firmly. The paintings obscured my visual of his face and by the time we entered the gallery the moment had passed as Parker stood there before us with a grin on his face.

Chandler Square was a pretty place, with its run of white fronted stores with matching green signs above their doors. There was a coffee shop, the 'famous' ice cream parlor, and some vintage style shops selling shabby chic. There was also a small restaurant serving home-cooked meals. I gazed out of the doorway at the surrounding buildings until a couple customers left and Daniel had moved the paintings for me to step inside the gallery properly. He had named it simply *Scott's*, his surname. Inside, the walls were naturally covered in paintings, but there were also some sculptures placed on display pedestals. Daniel explained that downstairs were paintings and other art that everyone could buy while upstairs he had a private gallery that had to be booked by appointment. He added that it didn't get booked often, but he had a few regulars who purchased mainly his own artwork for private sale or to sell on in their own galleries.

I followed Daniel upstairs to look at the more expensive pieces and for the first time, I saw his own artwork. Never one to show off, there wasn't a painting to be seen in Daniel's own home and that was a damn shame as they were exquisite. They were explosions of color on canvas. Some just swirls of colors meeting each other; others were portraits mixed with the explosion, like a young woman standing holding an umbrella while the vibrant colors rained down on her. There was a heart exploding outwards in further bursts of yellows, reds, blues and greens.

"Daniel, are these all yours?" I turned to him, my eyes seeking his response, my mouth unable to say another word for a minute.

He nodded.

"Wow," I eventually managed to spit out.

"What are you two doing up there?" Parker shouted, destroying the moment. "I just sold another painting today. Come down, we need to celebrate with some coke."

My brows furrowed as I turned to Daniel, but he just laughed.

"He means the soda. He's not a pothead."

I made my excuses to go to look around the other units while Daniel and Parker talked business. In all honesty, I needed to be away from them for a while. I needed a distraction away from the feelings I was having and the thought that I didn't want to acknowledge screamed in my mind.

They're both hot and I am totally imagining what it would be like to fuck them.

Dear God. What the hell was wrong with me? I'd always had a preference for both older and younger guys, rather than ones around my own age. I guessed Parker wasn't that much younger than me. I allowed myself to think about his body. He wasn't my relation, so why shouldn't I admit he was sexy. It was him filling my mind with this stepsister crap and making me feel guilty.

I carried on browsing in a couple stores and purchased a short, shabby-chic style sundress that came to just above my knees—which would come in handy if this heat continued—and a scented candle for my room, plus some new linens for my bedroom. At the back of a store selling all different kinds of goods, I was surprised to see an 'over eighteen' sign. I followed the arrow on the sign and discovered a display of sex toys and lingerie. I looked around me to make sure I didn't have Daniel or Parker coming into the store to find me, and on confirming I was alone, I began to look at the toys. I decided it would be a good idea to purchase something to play with while I stayed at the house so that I could enjoy my fantasies and stay satisfied. After comparing the feel of a few vibrators in my hand, I finally settled on one called the whisperer. It was named this apparently because it was so quiet which was ideal for where I was staying. It was soft, had a rippled shaft and rounded end, and was nine inches in length. The description on the box said it was powerful and waterproof. I could go take a bath and come out feeling even more relaxed!

I quickly purchased the toy and hid it among the linens I had bought before returning to the gallery.

"Man, look at the size of that." Parker pointed to my shopping bag, and I flushed. "Daniel. Don't let her make the house all girly."

Daniel laughed. "Put that in the truck and then let's go get some lunch."

With my purchases safely put away, I followed Daniel to a quaint looking restaurant where we ordered homemade burgers and fries. They arrived with an accompaniment of onion rings and coleslaw, and I realized how hungry I had gotten.

As I took a bite, mayo ran out from the bun and slid down my jaw. Daniel picked up a napkin, and leaning over, wiped my chin.

"Sorry." I apologized. "I hadn't realized how ready I was to eat."

A look passed between us at our closeness and my words. It was full of something I couldn't or wouldn't name. I sat back in my seat and had a drink of my soda.

"So. I wanted to explain about your mom," Daniel said.

"You really don't have to. It's passed, hasn't it? She's moved on," I told him.

"She has, but I can't. Not until I've explained," he added. His eyes were like pools of shiny black oil. They reminded me of an ocean at night.

I nodded, giving him permission to continue.

He rubbed his jaw. "When I first met your mom, she called one of my shops to ask about a tattoo."

This amused me as my mom hated ink. She thought it made you look like a cheap whore.

"When she requested me in particular, I was

wary. Usually, it was some bored housewife trying to get a hook up with what they assumed was a dirty assed tattooist. She seemed shocked when she met me."

I could imagine. Daniel was clean cut and didn't have his own inkings.

"Anyway, she dropped information to me, like I was a dumbass. No doubt usually men sucked it all up, but I had far too much experience of these desperate housewives and just thought she was another. She told me she was divorced and had a seventeen-year-old daughter who depended on her. Then she put out all this guilt about why was she enquiring about tattoos when she could barely make the rent. She started to cry. I was a little taken aback at that point. Your mom had seemed so confident. Anyway, you know how I am with the homeless and strays. Been like that my whole life. So I told her I had a room she could use while she got on her feet."

"Big mistake," I told him.

He sniffed. "Yeah, well, yes and no. Because your mom asked me to pretend that we were an item. She didn't want you to think she was struggling. I was to act as a stepdaddy while she got on her feet." He laughed. "I even tried to get her work. I thought she was out there trying to fend for herself when actually she was using credit and store cards in my name and maxing me to the hilt. I let her stay because by then I had been introduced to you. I thought you needed a stable home while you graduated, but then you didn't seem to settle and moved in with your friend."

I looked at my burger. I couldn't look at him.

"Everything went to crap and I had to sell the business. Your mom abandoned you and I wasn't ready to let you go. That's why I kept in touch."

"Because you wanted to make sure I got my education?"

"Sure," he said. "And to make sure you were happy."

His voice drifted off at that point and we carried on eating in an uncomfortable silence.

On our way back we walked past the 'famous' ice cream parlor, Creamy Delights, and even though I was bursting full after the burger, Daniel insisted on buying me an ice cream. I settled for a vanilla and coconut cone, and we made our way back to the gallery. Parker was busy with a customer, so Daniel directed us upstairs where he had his office.

The office itself was small with a table and two chairs. There was a sideboard in the corner with a coffee machine and mugs, and a door led to a bath-room to the rear.

"Would you like a coffee?"

I pulled a face. "Not with ice cream, thanks."

I walked next to him while he got himself a pod and placed it in the machine to make a drink.

"Daniel, I'm really proud of you. Your art is amazing, and this place is great. Thanks for what you did for my mom and me. I'm glad you managed to recover, financially I mean, and you didn't lose your beautiful home. I guess it came close, huh?"

He turned to me; his eyes bored into mine. "It did. Very."

I had been ignoring my ice cream and a huge run of white cream dripped down onto my neck and ran in between my breasts. Not missing a beat, Daniel grabbed my shoulders and threw me back against the wall. His tongue dived onto my chest and trailed the whole same route as the ice cream as he licked it from my bare flesh.

He lifted his head up and his hooded eyes fixed on mine. His breathing was rapid.

He let out an uncontrollable moan and dropped his hands from me, standing back. "Fuck. Kayla, I'm so sorry."

"I'm not," I replied, and I closed the distance between us, launching myself at him, my mouth finding his.

Everything happened so quickly after that.

My tank was lifted up and then Daniel pulled down the cup of my bra so one of my tits was free. He sucked it into his mouth and I groaned with the sensation of warmth and the feeling of pleasure that coursed through my body. I felt like I was fitted with underfloor heating—underbody heating! His hands fumbled at the button on my shorts. He managed to undo it and then lowered the zipper. He edged them past the curve of my ass and pulled them to my knees along with my panties so I was stood there—my breast in his mouth and fresh air hitting my lower body. I felt my juices run down my leg. I was so wet for him.

He raised his head and pushed me back against the wall. I felt the coolness of the wall meet my ass cheeks. "I need to be in you. I can't wait. Not this time."

There would be a next time?

I wondered if I was dreaming as I watched Daniel unfasten his own pants and hitch them down along with his boxers. His erection sprang out and I couldn't help but moan at the sight. He had to be a good ten inches. He was definitely larger than the vibrator I had just purchased, and his girth was wider. I could see a bead of pre-cum glistening on his tip. He lifted his knee to spread my thighs apart while he fisted his cock. Testing between my legs with his fingers he brought up a digit coated in my cream.

"So wet." He smiled. "And all bare. I love it."

Then he slammed into me with a hard thrust. The chemistry between us was undeniable. My body broke out in goose bumps. I looked over his shoulder as he continued to thrust and noted the unlocked door. My nipples hardened further, and I got wetter with the thought that at any time Parker could open the door and see us together. I could hear the mumble of his deep bass voice from downstairs and then the flirty laughter of a woman vibrated through the floor. God, some women were pathetic.

I stared at Daniel. His eyes were closed, his breathing jagged and heavy and small beads of sweat had formed on his forehead as he continued to thrust. I leaned in and licked one off. His sweat was salty, and I imagined that it wasn't his sweat, but his cum in my mouth. Daniel opened his eyes, stared at me, and then captured my mouth, teasing my tongue with his own. He tasted of burger and slaw, with a hint of the beer he washed his meal down with. His hand captured my naked breast, cupping it. It fitted so beautifully in his warm hand. His fingers outstretched and then stroked my tit, capturing a nipple and pinching it between his thumb and forefinger. The sensations whirling inside me were incredible. I couldn't get close enough to his body.

"Harder," I told him. "Fuck me so hard I can't walk."

He pulled almost out of me and then thrust back in super hard and rough.

I mewled.

He put a hand across my mouth. "Ssh."

The thought of being restrained, having my mouth unable to ask for assistance made me even hornier. What was I turning into? I had never experienced anything like this before.

Daniel kept a steady rhythm of riding me hard until I felt him go rigid. He reached between us and flicked my clit and I went off like a volcano. I bit down on his thick fingers that were across my mouth. Not too hard, but otherwise Parker and the customers downstairs would have been in no doubt as to what we were doing.

Daniel climaxed, thrusting into me, his seed spilling inside in warm spurts. He rested his head next to mine on the wall and his heart thudded in my chest.

"Fuck," he said, lifting his head up and grasping

my chin in his hands. "Kayla. Tell me I haven't just ruined everything. That I didn't fuck up."

"Oh, you fucked up all right." I smiled at his concerned face. "But only in a good way."

A slow exhale escaped his mouth. He rested his clammy forehead against my own. "I promise next time I'll go slow and give you everything. Put you at the center of all the pleasure. But Christ, Kayla. I waited so long for that. I couldn't go slow."

"You waited so long?"

"Kayla. I tried to explain earlier. I just was going to take it slow." He ran his finger down my cheek and softly brushed the pad of his fingertip on my lips. "I allowed your mom into my home at first because of pity. I let your mom stay in my home because of you."

I gasped.

"Too much." He smacked his own forehead. "I've said too much and made you uncomfortable. I'm sorry."

I grabbed his hand and held it in my own. "No. No, you haven't," I told him. "It's all I've ever wanted. I was so jealous at the thought of you and my mom."

"That never happened. Never, Kayla."

"Okay."

He withdrew from me. My pussy felt the loss of the heat from his cock.

"We should clean up quickly and say our good-byes to Parker."

I nodded. "About Parker. I can't do anything with you while he's in the house. It would be too weird. I know it means we might not get a lot of time together, but I just can't, okay? Can we take things slow? It's a lot to process, that you liked me the way I liked you."

"Sure, baby girl, we can take it really slow. You need to spend some time with Parker anyway and get to know him better. Plus, I have to go away for the evening tonight to pick up a few pieces of artwork. I'll be back tomorrow afternoon."

My jaw dropped.

"Hey, don't look so down. We're going home now aren't we, and Parker's at work. We have the whole place to ourselves, right?" He grabbed my hand and brought it over to his dick. "Feel me." I took his cock in my hand. It was hard as rock. "Does it appear like I'm done with you yet? I told you. I'm gonna make you come so hard and so many damn times."

He left me and headed to the bathroom. I was stood against the wall with my top still pushed up and my breast showing, with my bare pussy on show and cum running down my leg.

I was fucked and satisfied and yet all I could think was that I wanted Parker to come in and find me.

CHAPTER SIX

Daniel

I could barely drive us home. My cock just wanted to be deep inside Kayla as much and for as long as possible. I had one hand on the steering wheel and another one stroking her wet heat every chance I could. She was panting, she was so damn ravenous for my cock back inside her.

I tore up the driveway and we rushed from the truck into the house. I followed Kayla's tight ass that I could now openly stare at as she led me into her bedroom. Closing the door behind me, I pulled her down onto the bed so that she was lying on top of me.

I captured her mouth in my own and gave her mouth a good tongue fucking, teasing her by not touching her elsewhere. Kayla became frustrated with my inaction and sat astride me in her shorts. She started rubbing her mound over the seam of my jeans.

"Oh, Daniel. Fuck, that feels good. Oh."

It was so damn hot that she could moan and scream my name now at the top of her voice. We continued to kiss as she carried on rubbing that hot, sweet pussy over my hard on. I lifted up her top. She had taken off her bra in the truck and shoved it in her bag so that I could keep playing with those cute little tits on the way home. I captured one now in my mouth, sucking on it while playing with the other one. Then I let it slide from my mouth and did the same to the other side. Sucking noises filled the room, along with Kayla's moans from her pussy rubbing. We stripped off all our clothes and I guided Kayla until she was hovering above my mouth.

"I want you to stay there until I've made you come, okay?" I instructed. "Play with those titties while I'm busy."

"Okay." She nodded. My sassy Kayla was gone right now. She was so focused on chasing that pleasure.

She lowered herself onto my mouth and I could

smell her musky scent. My dick twitched with desire. Her pussy lips spread over my face and some of that cream ran from her core and into my mouth. She tasted of sunshine and woman. I ran my tongue down her slit and then up over her clit and I felt her lift up a little as if it tickled. She grabbed hold of her tits, one in each hand and started to play with them. I held her ass cheeks, one in each of my hands and split her open like a juicy peach.

"Fuck, yeah," she moaned as I kept flicking, licking, and sucking as she rotated herself around on my mouth.

I decided to turn up the heat a little and I poked my tongue right up that sweet, wet pussy.

"Oh my god," she screamed. "Oh fuck. Daniel. More of that, please. More."

I stopped and sucked on her clit and then I thrust my tongue in her opening and back out over and over and over. I felt her cunt gather together over my mouth and I pulled her ass cheeks, so she was as close to me as I could get her. She exploded, and I felt each wave of her orgasm upon my tongue. I let her ass cheeks go and she laid at the side of me as if made from a puddle of goo.

I watched her breasts rise up and down with her short, fast breathing.

"Tell me what you want from me next, Kayla. Anything. I want to give you the ultimate pleasure."

"Daniel. I feel so dirty when I'm with you," she replied. Her face was flushed, and those freckles looked cute laid across her pale cheeks. Her long red hair was spread across the pillows. "In a good way that is."

"Thank Christ for that," I said. "For a minute there I thought you were going to say what we were doing was wrong."

She grasped my dick in her hand. "No. It's oh so right. It does feel slightly... forbidden, but I... Well, I like it."

"What do you like?" I started to move within the curl of her hand and fingers. I needed to be inside her soon.

"Can I talk dirty?" she asked. "I've never had the confidence to do it before. We can stop if you don't like what I'm saying."

I didn't like to be reminded that I wasn't her first lover, so if I could be the first she dirty talked and really opened up to... well, that was fine with me.

"Anything, Kayla."

She looked at me with those innocent green eyes that I knew masked the fire of the woman inside. Right now though, with no makeup, she looked younger than she was. Fresh faced. It suited her not having the permanent look of guilt she always carried around me, feeling permanently guilty for the actions of her mother.

"What are you doing in here?" she said to me. Her face had adopted a mock, shocked expression. "You're my stepdaddy. This is so bad. What would Mom say if she caught us?"

Oh holy hell. I stilled for a moment, not sure if I could do this.

Then she put her mouth over the end of my cock and sucked.

I groaned and all bets were off. She could do and say what she liked.

"What are you doing, Kayla?" I played her game. "I know you're eighteen, but we shouldn't do this." It was like we had gone back to when we first met and the times that we wanted each other but couldn't act on it.

"My momma lies. She doesn't love you. I love you. Please. I've never sucked a cock before. Let me try. Teach me." She begged.

I stood at the side of the bed and Kayla knelt on it. "Okay, just this once, all right? Then we must never do it again. You won't tell anyone, right?"

"No, Sir," she replied.

I thrust my dick in her mouth and she widened to take me all in. I went as deep as I could, and she just took it. Fuck, could she suck cock. Her tongue swirled around my glans and around the underside of my dick and she massaged my balls while she did it. Then she started to suck hard and her head bobbed up and down on my dick.

She stopped. "Am I doing okay?"

I thrust my cock back in her mouth. "You're doing fine, baby girl, now hush and keep sucking because your momma will be home soon and I don't want her seeing me spraying my cum all down your throat."

I swear Kayla's eyes flashed when I said this, and she sucked even harder until I couldn't take anymore, and I shot my spunk straight down her throat. She swallowed it all down and then licked around her mouth.

"Before she gets home would you stick your huge cock up my cunt?" she asked.

I didn't even answer. I just pushed her down on the bed and lifted one of her legs over my shoulder as I stuck my dick inside her and started pummeling. The walls of her pussy clenched around me. She was so tight, she fitted like a glove. "Oh fuck, Kayla. Oh, fuck."

She lifted her buttocks and met me with each thrust. "You are such a naughty man. Look at you. Fucking me when you shouldn't. Filling me with your big fat cock. It's huge. It's filling me up and I want all your cum inside me. I need it. Tell me you want me."

"I need to fuck you so damn bad. My cock is stretching your tight pussy lips. Can you feel it? This pussy is only for me. Only for your stepdaddy, do you hear me? You're to wait at night in this room until I can sneak in here and then I'm going to fuck you and you can't make a sound even though you want to scream my name because your mom is down the hall and might hear you."

"What if I want to scream?" she said.

I grabbed her panties from the side of the bed and I shoved them in her mouth. "Now you can't. Now you have your dirty pants in your mouth. The ones you creamed all over before begging me to fuck you. Can you taste yourself?"

She nodded. A little drool ran from the side of her mouth. Her juices drowned my cock, she was so fucking wet. I bucked and thrust within her until I came with a gasp and a moan. I pulled the panties from her mouth as I felt her tense and Kayla screamed.

"Fuuuuck, fuck me. Oh my god, I'm coming. I'm coming."

She fell apart, clenching and spasming around my cock, and I laid at the side of her while I tried to catch my breath. I couldn't believe what she'd gotten me to say to her. But I didn't feel guilty. It's like we went back in time and my fantasies of fucking my eighteen-year-old, part-time lodger—because I never saw her as a stepdaughter—came true. But if she wanted to role play and it was going to make her pussy wet; well, I wasn't going to stop her.

The thought had me hard again in seconds and I spent the rest of the afternoon inside that wet, hot pussy. Finally letting her go an hour before Parker was due home so we could shower and change and pretend we didn't spend half the day fucking each other raw.

CHAPTER SEVEN

Parker

Somehow, something had changed. When Kayla first arrived, I had noticed that she tried to avoid Daniel. I presumed she resented him trying to be a father figure when he wasn't her father. When they'd come to the gallery earlier, she'd looked a little more relaxed as if she could now tolerate being around him, but she still seemed awkward. Seeing the gallery appeared to get her to loosen up a little. You could see she was in awe of some of the artwork and when she had viewed Daniel's own pieces and returned downstairs full of praise, she'd seemed somehow surprised that the man had such a talent. She was scolding him for not having some of his paintings displayed in his home and demanded that he hang some. Daniel looked bemused by her attitude.

Then they had returned from the meal and gone up to Daniel's office while Kayla had an ice cream. I watched her lick that cone and imagined it was my cock. Then I switched my focus to the customer in the store who was ready to part with their cash on a few key pieces. I was busy then, my mind distracted from them being upstairs until they came back down. They said goodbye to me, but it was rushed and false. Daniel was cool, calm and collected. Kayla was awkward and flushed. Something had happened. Maybe they'd had an argument about her mom. They had been in a rush to leave and I guessed that bonding time was over.

Daniel was going away on an overnight trip tonight, so I decided I would ask Kayla if she would like a night out at the movies. We could kick back and have some fun. If things got awkward between her and Daniel she might leave, and I wasn't ready for her to go yet.

Dinner was subdued, and I noticed when one wasn't looking, the other would check them out.

Something had definitely happened. I would check in with Kayla later that everything was all right. She had agreed to the movies, and I'd found out that we both liked superheroes, so we were off to see the latest Marvel flick.

TALKING WITH KAYLA WAS FUN. She relaxed around me, and we had a laugh at the movie when she confessed that usually she and her girlfriends would talk about how hot the superheroes were in their outfits half the time rather than the plot, and they liked to watch the movies on TV and freeze frame them.

"Like Chris Evans in The Avengers." She turned to me as we pulled up in the driveway. "When he did that lift. My god, arm porn time!"

"Hey, I got guns," I replied, flexing my arm. My muscles firmed up and I displayed my biceps and the meaty cords in my arms.

"Oh my god, you really do." Kayla's eyes widened. "I knew you were ripped, man, but jeez."

"Feel 'em." I challenged her. "You can't do that with an actor in a movie. We'll make it a 4D experience. Close your eyes."

"What?"

"Seriously. Go along with it. Close your eyes."

She did so.

"Okay, now think about that movie and Captain America's guns and here, pretend." I lifted her hand and placed it on my arm.

"Jesus, Parker. Your arms are like rock."

I flexed, and she ran her hand over my arms, feeling the contours. "I never felt the arms of a ripped, pumped guy before. It's even better than I expected." She giggled. Then she removed her hand and opened her eyes.

She paused when she looked at me. I guessed my eyes betrayed my mind. Windows to the soul and all that. Windows to the fact that I was enjoying being caressed a little too much. I just hoped she didn't look down and catch my tented erection. Fuck, she just did.

Kayla swallowed. "Well, I guess we should get back inside, rather than sit in the car all night."

We entered the house, disarming the alarm. Kayla headed to the refrigerator and took out two beers. "Want one?"

"Yeah." I ran a hand through my hair. "Jeez, it's hot tonight. I'm gonna take mine out onto the deck."

"Great minds," Kayla replied, following me.

We sat out on the deck for a couple hours,

drinking beer and shooting the breeze. Kayla was relaxed and chatty, unlike how she was around Daniel. I decided to bring it up.

"Daniel and me. It's complicated," she told me. "He's not a relation, yet we want to be in each other's lives. It's deciding how that works, right? A bit like you being here. We're all separate jigsaw pieces trying to somehow fit together. It doesn't quite work, but we're doing our best. Puzzling it out."

"Very deep." I laughed.

"Too much?"

"Yeah, we need to lighten things up," I told her, and with that, I lifted her off the chair and ran with her over my shoulder toward the pool.

"Put me down. What the fuck are you doing? Ah, hell no," she exclaimed as she saw the pool in her line of vision. She was too late. I took a leap from the pool edge and we went under the water and back up.

"I'm fucking wet," she yelled.

"You can't say that to a man," I joked. She wiped her hair back off her face and looked at me in shock, then collapsed into laughter.

"God, you are so bad."

"Soaking wet with the stepbro." I winked. "Sounds like another movie. Let's swim, race ya."

We did lengths of the pool and every now and

then I grabbed her and dunked her under the water. She got angrier and angrier at the fact that she wasn't strong enough to dunk me under in return. I swam away laughing again. We were having a ton of fun and I wished she was like this all the time. I enjoyed hanging out with her. Didn't hurt that her t-shirt clung to her bra and I could perve over her titties when she rose out of the water.

The fact I had gone into a dirty daydream gave Kayla an advantage and so I was completely taken aback when I found my wet joggers pulled down. My boxers came down with them.

Kayla couldn't breathe for laughing. I couldn't tell if it was pool water or tears streaming down her face. "Look, it's a full moon," she quipped, no doubt staring at my bare ass cheeks. I turned around and then Kayla stopped laughing.

"Holy shit!" she exclaimed. "What the hell size dick is that?"

"Twelve inches," I told her, going to pull my boxers back up.

"No." She stopped me. "You gotta let me look. I've never seen a cock that big before. Is it because of the weights?"

"No. Totally natural. I was just blessed." I told her while looking down. She moved over to me. "I know this is a weird request, but can I feel it, like I did your arm?"

"Sure." I dropped my hands and Kayla reached over and grabbed my dick. The woman had my dick in her hand. I immediately got hard and my dick grew to its full potential.

"Sorry for the inquisition, but you manage to have sex with that? It fits in?" she asked.

"Yep. Not had a complaint yet."

She felt me, raising her hand up and down my shaft. I saw her bite her lip.

She gently placed my cock back down; though it kinda waved there at her, it was so damn hard.

"Well, shoot. Thanks for letting me take a closer look. I feel beat now, so I'm gonna go in, take a shower and hit the sack. Thanks for a great night," she told me. "It was fun." She kissed the side of my cheek and then shot to the edge of the water, getting out and walking away.

I took myself into the pool house where I jerked off in the shower before heading back to the main house. I could have slept out there, but as the man of the house tonight I wanted to make sure Kayla was okay.

.   .   .

IT APPEARED that Kayla was more than okay. Once again as I walked past her room, I heard moaning. The door once again was not fully closed. I stood in the doorway and watched her. She was laid spread eagled on the bed pushing a pink dildo into her cunt. I dropped my towel and started pumping my dick which had hardened the minute I'd heard her moaning. She hadn't dressed after being in the shower and her body glistened with droplets of water which had not yet dried on her skin. I was so busy feasting my eyes on her as she played with her own pussy that I stopped concentrating. My hand came off my cock and my fist banged into the door, making it open wider and revealed me standing there, stark naked with my dick stuck up. It was all angry and purple looking.

Kayla gasped and reached for her pillowcase— yeah, the one she rubbed her pussy on—and attempted to cover herself up.

"Oh, man. I'm so sorry, Kayla. I just..." I shook my head. "There are no excuses. I heard you moaning and when I saw you like that. I just... I'm a man, Kayla. My cock went so hard and my balls would be blue if I didn't jerk off. I should have gone to my room though, not stood here like a pervert. I'm sorry. Can you forget I was here? I'll leave."

Then she did something I would have never expected in a million years.

She moved the pillow back, spread her legs apart and removed the dildo from her cunt. Then she said. "Well, it seems a waste for you to go back in your room, and I'm betting that cock would feel much better in my pussy than this vibrator."

Leaving the door ajar with there being only the two of us here, I padded into her room and got on the bed. I took the vibrator from her hand and switched it back on. Then I pushed it into her juicy, wet pussy. All splayed out in front of me, her juices running out. I pushed it in and out. "Well, I think you should do a comparison. Getting off on the dildo, versus getting off on me."

She bit her lip and looked at me while I continued to thrust the vibrator in her wet heat.

"Ohhh," she said, watching my actions. She grabbed her tits and squeezed them.

"You like that?" I asked her.

"Yeah." She almost purred like a cat.

A couple of minutes later she bucked all over that pink plastic pleaser. Her little titties shook as she dripped cum from her core all around it.

"You need a few minutes to recover before we get to trying mine," I told her. "So, in the meantime, you can get mine nice and wet ready to take you. Here, see if you can fit me in your mouth."

I stood near the end of the bed and Kayla moved forward so she was on her knees facing me. Then she opened wide and took my cock in her mouth. The warmth and wetness enveloped the end of my dick and she swirled her tongue around my glans. She grasped the base of me and then opening wider, she took me right to the back of her throat.

"Fuck me, Kayla."

Those eyes looked at me full of mischief. She had no problem handling my massive cock at all. She let me loose from her mouth. "Here, I know how you can go even deeper."

She laid on the edge of the bed on her back and let her head overhang the mattress and then opened her mouth wide again. I pushed into her and it was true. I could fit far more of myself in her. "I'm gonna go nice and slow, but I'm going to fuck your mouth, Kayla."

A slight nod of her head showed I had her approval.

God, I felt good in her mouth. I looked at the woman lying on the bed. Never would I have thought, earlier tonight, that I would be getting her to suck my dick. I was going to fuck her so damn hard she was going to scream the house down. I continued to pump into her mouth, watching as drool slid from the corners of her lips and onto my cock.

I withdrew and told her to get on her knees with her ass facing me.

I shoved my dick in her deep, clutching her hips with my hands to steady her. She squealed and yelled for me to not stop.

"You like being fucked like an animal?"

"Yes."

"Are you a dirty bitch, Kayla? You're soaking me with your cum."

"Yes. I am. I'm a dirty girl. I want your cock to do me hard. Fill me up. Fill me right up with your spunk."

Her beautiful, puckered asshole winked at me from this position. I sucked on my finger and then I stuck it in her ass as I thrust into her pussy.

"Oh my god. Oh my god," Kayla cried out. "Get the dildo. Push that into my ass."

This let me know Kayla was no stranger to ass play. If she could take a dildo up it, she wasn't an ass virgin.

The dildo was long but rippled and wasn't too wide. I put my hand between her legs and gathered up her cum onto my fingers. Then I rubbed the dildo, so it was well lubed up with her juices. Not hard with how soaked she was. In the meantime, she had been left hanging as I stopped thrusting. I looked at her, tits hung down, ass in the air. Withdrawing my cock, I leaned over and bit her ass cheeks and then I stuck my tongue in her asshole.

"Oooohhh."

I wet all around and then positioned the vibrator at her asshole.

I pushed it in and at the same time slowly moved my cock.

"Oh yes, like that. Please, don't stop."

I kept a steady rhythm of slowly moving in and out of her pussy while placing more and more of the vibrator in her ass with each movement. Eventually, she had taken quite a bit of the vibrator and I left it stuck in there but turned it on, while I then fucked her so hard I had to hold her down.

"Oh, oh, oh, yes. Fuck, yes. Fuck, yes. Like that. Just like that." As I felt my balls tighten and felt she was starting to go over, I let go of her hips. I pulled the vibrator out of her ass with one hand and pinched her clit with the other.

"OH. MY. GOD." Kayla screamed. Her body bucked and I once again grabbed her hips as I pumped spray after spray of cum into her pussy. I didn't think I had ever cum that much or that hard.

I collapsed next to her on the bed.

"Shit, Kayla. That was so fucking good."

"I know," she replied, "and I'm not finished with you yet."

She placed her thighs on either side of my head and lowered that cum full and soaked pussy over my mouth. "Eat me. I want to come again," she begged.

I stuck my tongue right up her cleft and then grabbed her ass cheeks and pulled her down firmly onto my mouth where I sucked her nub into me and teased and tasted her. She rotated her hips on me. Then she lifted off. "Can I talk dirty, Parker? I've discovered I like it."

"Sure," I told her. "It turns me on to hear a girl tell me what she wants me to do."

"I'm even dirtier, Parker," she said. "I'm a dirty girl."

She lowered herself back onto my mouth and started to speak. I was not expecting those words from her mouth.

"I'm so bad. I know I shouldn't do this with you, fuck my stepbrother. But I can't help it. Your cock is so huge and your tongue. Oh, your tongue. It's playing me like an instrument. But what if Daddy came in and found us? We would be in so much trouble and look the door's wide open, he could come in at any time. He's only in the room next door. We're so bad. So, so bad, but I love it. I love being your dirty girl, your dirty little secret."

Jesus Christ! My hand was on my cock and I pumped myself for dear life while I brought her over the edge. She collapsed onto me shuddering. I rolled her onto her back and then I leaned over her pumping my cock next to her face.

"That's right, hey? Do you like your stepbrother's cock? You like him fucking you with it, with his fingers, with his tongue. Making you come over and over. Do you want to taste me? Drink up my forbidden man milk. Hey look, we're being watched. My best friend's stood in the doorway watching us. What are you going to do?"

"I'm going to drink you all up and then I'm going to fuck your friend," she told me.

I erupted over her face. She opened her mouth and caught some of my cum, licking her lips. Her face was splattered. She looked like a canvas of cum.

I thrust my dick straight back into her pussy and rode her hard again. "Close your eyes. Pretend I'm the friend now."

"Oh, a new dick. So good. You know what to do with it, baby. Is my stepbrother watching?"

"He is."

"Good. I hope he's fisting his cock while you fuck me."

Sensations took over as we headed toward another climax and I roared out as I once again emptied my spunk into her and she shook as tremors rocked her slim body.

We were soaked in sweat and both needed another shower.

I took her hand and we headed into her bathroom where we fucked one another again. She was insatiable, and I was addicted. Then I kissed her goodnight and returned to my own room, in case Daniel arrived back early from his trip.

THE NEXT MORNING, I headed down to the kitchen, fixed coffee and began making a batch of pancakes, practically the only thing I knew how to make. Being away from my pops had made me realize how lazy I was and how I acted like a young jerk back home, not a man. If I was going to impress a woman like Kayla, I needed to get my shit together. I didn't think spoiled, rich boys were her type.

I heard her footsteps pad down the stairs and she walked into the kitchen raising a hand at me.

"Morning."

She sat at the dining table, looking like she could lay her head on it and go back to sleep. I placed a mug of coffee in front of her.

"Pancakes?"

"Yes, please. Somehow, I'm exhausted. I can't think why. I need energy so keep 'em coming."

"It was all the orgasms that took your energy." I laughed.

She took a hair tie off her wrist and tied her hair back in a bun thing. Then she rubbed her eyes.

"Hurry with the pancakes. I'm so hungry, and then we need to talk."

"Oh. Not sure I like the sound of that."

She said nothing, and I continued to cook, feeling like I had a stone in my gut. Somehow, I appeared to have lost my appetite.

"You don't want a repeat then?"

She looked up at me. "Did I say that? Stop trying to guess what I'm going to say. Pancakes," she demanded.

"You're such a bossy woman."

"I didn't hear you complaining last night."

I brought the plate of pancakes to the table and then the syrup, returning to get my coffee mug.

Kayla dived into the pancakes like she had never been fed before. Syrup ran down her chin. I wanted to lean over and lick it off. Finally taking a break, she leaned back, had a great gulp of coffee, then wiped her mouth with a napkin.

"I need to confess something and then you might not want to sleep with me anymore."

Fuck, what the hell was she going to tell me? She had some disease?

"I'm listening."

"So, earlier yesterday, after I visited the gallery. I, err, I slept with Daniel."

I pushed my chair back in shock.

"What?"

"I know. I know. There has never been anything between us before, I swear. But I had a crush on him the whole damn time I had to visit here. I thought he was with my mom, but he explained yesterday that their relationship had been a sham. He had never been with her in that way. He wanted me. He always wanted me. Things happened."

I thought back to how when they had come back downstairs from the gallery something had been different. It made me feel sick. I pushed my pancakes away from me.

"You slept with Daniel and then a few hours later you slept with me?"

"Yes." She rubbed her eyes. "I'm so confused. I thought all my dreams had come true with Daniel, but I like you too. Now I don't know what to do because I need to figure out which of you I want. That's if either of you still want me after what I've done. I realize I've jeopardized everything.

"I need time to get my head around this, Kayla. You can't just drop this on me and expect me to respond right away."

"I know."

"Listen, come spend the day with me at the gallery. When Daniel returns here, he's going to want to take you to bed again. If you're with me, it buys you a little time to think."

"Thanks. I'll do that. Okay, I'm going to go get dressed. Thanks for the pancakes."

With that, she left the room, leaving me with a plate full of pancakes and no appetite to eat them. I knew one thing. I wasn't giving up without a fight. It looked like me and Daniel needed a man-to-man talk.

. . .

THE DAY PASSED QUICKLY, and before we knew it, we were all home. Daniel had returned and had collected takeout, so we found ourselves around the table eating Chinese. Daniel kept staring at Kayla. Kayla herself clearly couldn't leave the table fast enough and soon made her excuses saying she had a headache. Daniel told her he would check in on her later to see how she was. I bet he would. I needed to talk to him before things got any worse.

I handed him a beer and pointed to outside and the deck. Daniel's brow creased but he followed me outside.

"We need to talk about Kayla," I told him.

His face closed down, guarded. "What about her?"

"I know, man. I know you slept together."

"Fuck" he said, kicking the chair leg. "She told you?"

"Yeah," I replied. "But it's more complicated than that."

"Oh?"

"Last night, Kayla and I fucked."

I should have expected it, but the blow came so fast, ricocheting off my jaw. I clutched my chin in agony then held down his hand as his arm lifted again.

"I'll let you have that one, but now we sit and talk like men."

He took a seat. His face desolate. He looked like I just told him I killed his grandma.

"I should have known she wouldn't want anything serious with me. She's too young," he said, picking up his can and downing his beer in one shot. He crushed the can in his hand and threw it across the patio.

"Son of a bitch."

"I do think she wants you, man," I told him. "But Kayla wants to play. I know this is an awkward conversation, but did she want to talk, like dirty, when you fucked?"

Daniel sighed. "Yes. Very."

"Last night she imagined two guys at once. I think she would be up for that."

"Do you want me to hit you again?" Daniel sneered.

"Hear me out. Kayla thinks she ruined everything by sleeping with us both. We both want her, so why don't we share?"

"Fuck, Parker. This is too much for me to take in right now."

"I know. But I've been thinking about this all day. I don't think we should make her choose. Not right now anyway. We could give her the world between us. I don't know how long I'm gonna stay around here, but for now, as long as you don't kick me out after this, I'm staying.

"How did she imagine two guys?"

"She dirty talked that she was being watched by one guy while with another. Then the mystery guy came in and fucked her. Of course, both were me, but we could make her fantasies a reality."

Daniel pinched the bridge of his nose. "I need time to think on this. I'm going to go swim and I'll probably stay in the pool house tonight. Promise me you won't go near Kayla this evening. If you do, I will throw you the fuck out, after I beat you to a pulp."

"I promise. We all need time to puzzle this out. I'm gonna go out, find a pool game somewhere."

I left my seat, and shortly after, I left the house for a while.

CHAPTER EIGHT

Daniel

I needed to be away from them both for a while. My pool house tonight was my respite. I swam until I could hardly lift myself from the pool. My thoughts were full of images of Kayla fucking Parker. Had I meant so little to her that just a few hours after we had sex, she banged him too? I collapsed with exhaustion on my bed, but sleep wouldn't come. Could I share her? It was a stupid question. If that was the only way to have her in my life, then of course I would. What was she getting from Parker though that was lacking in me? I felt like half a man. I wondered if she was waiting for me in her bed; whether the headache was fake, or whether she really had one from trying to puzzle all this out. Tomorrow, we sorted this. I needed some peace of mind. Kayla needed to tell me what she wanted from me. Tell me why she slept with Parker. I deserved the truth, whether it killed me or not.

I'd had dreams. The gallery was taking off and I was considering opening another one. Eventually, I saw it as a small chain, similar to how my tattoo parlors had run. Kayla was so talented at sales. She was a top realtor at Green's in Brooklyn. So my imagination had her swapping real estate for art. Building the business for a few years and then I wanted her pregnant. So full of my seed that it took and made a baby. My cock got hard and I jerked off to thoughts of filling her with my spunk. It relaxed me enough that I finally dropped off to sleep.

I should have known that Kayla would think it weird for me to stay over at the pool house. She walked in with a mug of coffee the following morning and sat down at the end of my bed.

"He said he told you. He should have let me do that myself."

I sat up against the covers. Thank God at some

point I had cooled down and got inside them so she couldn't see my naked cock.

"It doesn't matter who told me. I'm just glad I know."

"Do you hate me?" She looked at me with tears welling in her eyes.

"I could never hate you, Kayla. I- I love you."

She came up closer to me on the bed. "I love you too, Daniel. I think I always have. But I find Parker hot. I couldn't help myself. I need you, but I want him."

I gathered her into my arms. She curled up, all soft skin and freckles.

"We'll work it out, Kayla. I'm not letting you go now that I have you."

"Thank God," she said, and the tears began to fall. "I thought I ruined everything."

"It's not ruined. It's just different. With any relationship there are no guarantees, you have to see how it goes. This is the same. Except this time, for now, there appears to be three of us."

"I'm a slut."

"No, you're not. It's unconventional. Have we ever been anything else?"

"I suppose not."

"There you go then."

"My friend was in a ménage," she told me. I looked down at her lightly tanned face. "She stopped it after a year or so. Settled down with her husband and now they're having a family. Maybe that's how we'll be?"

"Maybe," I replied. "But this is all new, so let's just see where it leads."

"Okay."

She gazed up at me again and my heart swelled with love. There was no other word for it. If I had to share her for the rest of my life, then I would. I would rather have part of her than nothing at all. I slowly lowered my mouth to hers, brushing my lips softly against her own. "I'm not fucking you this time."

"Oh." Kayla looked disappointed.

"No. I'm making love to you."

I felt a smile break out on her face underneath my own lips. I moved over her and covered her with my body. We kissed for a long time and I trailed my hands up and down her body. Going under her clothing for the bits of flesh I could reach. Taking my time and enjoying the slower pace, the build up.

I guided her arms upwards and removed her t-shirt, revealing her small but firm breasts with their hardened nipples. Then I helped her shrug off her shorts and panties. After that there were no barriers between us. I laid at the side of her, nuzzling her neck and trailed my fingers to between her legs where she was damp. She spread her legs a little further. My fingers rubbed her clit, oh so slowly. I could see when she lost herself to the sensation, gaining a faraway glaze to her eyes.

"Look at me." I took her chin in my hand gently. While we were here alone I wanted to know that she was only aware of me. Only thinking of me. Just this one time, I wanted her for myself. I needed this. Even if we had our threesome, I would sometimes need this time alone with just her. To show her what she could get from only being with me. I dipped my finger into her pussy and she moaned near my ear. I ran my finger down her slit and back up to her nub, rubbing her clit in lazy circles. She continued to moan and began to move her pelvis up against my fingers, starting to rock her hips. I moved over her and rubbed the head of my cock into her juicy wetness and then I slowly inched in. Her pussy accepted every inch of my erection, enveloping me in warmth. I moved lazily inside her, unhurried, and we stayed like that for a long time until our need to climax took over and we both quickened our move- ments. We were still gentle and reached our orgasms almost together. She came apart on my cock and then sent me over, my cum spilling inside her. I wrapped my arms around her again, leaving my cock in her and we dozed.

We got up and took a leisurely shower together.

"Let's skinny dip in the pool." Kayla winked at me.

"You're going to give this old man a heart attack," I told her.

"You are not old," she said. "Let's call you experienced."

She leaped into the pool and I dived in after her. We raced each other doing lengths and then I pushed her against the side of the pool, crushing my lips to hers.

"Can anyone swim or is it a private party?" A gruff voice came from behind me, and I turned around to find Parker standing there, a towel wrapped around his waist.

"Well, Kayla," I asked her. "Do you want Parker to join us?"

CHAPTER NINE

Kayla

It all rested on how this went. After this, I might find myself packing my belongings and heading back to the apartment. I realized that after just these few days I no longer saw the apartment as home. This was my home. I belonged here with Daniel. But my body craved Parker too.

I looked up at him. "Join us."

He dropped his towel and jumped into the pool with a resounding splash. He pushed back through the water and smoothed his hands through his wet hair.

Daniel didn't turn around. Instead, he looked at me and said, "You're going to have to direct me. I don't know what you want."

Parker was also still. He also looked to me for direction. I felt so sexually powerful.

I lifted myself out of the pool and sat on the pool side. I opened my legs and showed both of them my wet cleft. "Daniel, I want you to eat my pussy. Parker, I want you to kneel next to me, watch us and play with your cock."

Daniel held my thighs apart and delved straight in between my thighs. He seemed to be trying to avoid looking at Parker. Although my pussy was wet, I was going to be distracted if I didn't think he was into it.

"Daniel."

He stopped and looked up.

"Watch me a moment."

I reached over and grasped Parker's cock. Daniel's eyes widened and any reticence he had was taken away by shock.

"I thought my dick was big, but you've got to be larger." He stared at Parker's cock in my hand.

"Twelve inches, but don't feel threatened, old man. I'm sure you know what to do with yours if you've been keeping our girl happy."

Our girl.

"Watch me, Daniel," I repeated, and I took Parker's cock in my mouth and sucked.

Daniel moved closer to watch. "Jesus. It's hot watching you suck another guy off." He took his own cock in his hand.

I patted the pool side next to me. Daniel got the message and rose out of the pool, then knelt at my other side. I gripped his dick in my hand and pumped while I feasted on Parker's. After a few minutes of this, I wanted to give them both some separate attention. I lowered myself into the pool and got them to hang their legs over the pool side. I took Parker back in my mouth and deep throated him.

"Ughhhh," he grunted.

Daniel was engrossed watching me suck off Parker. His demeanor had changed from one of sadness, to one of surrender as he fully embraced the fact we were doing this. His own arousal was evident by the large drop of pre-cum at the end of his cock. I made slurping noises as I sucked noisily on Parker. Then I let him slide out of my mouth. "I think I'll keep you hanging," I teased.

"No, don't. I'm ready to come," Parker begged.

"I'll help," Daniel said, and he jumped into the

pool behind me. He wrapped my wet hair around his fingers and he shoved my head forwards. "Suck your stepbrother's cock," he commanded.

My pussy twitched. "Yes, Daddy," I replied.

Once again, I took Parker in my mouth, but this time I didn't have control other than my lips. Instead, Daniel thrust my head up and down on Parker's cock. They got a rhythm going together.

"Go on, dirty girl. Suck me till I cum down your throat."

My head bobbed back and forth, Parker's cock hitting the back of my throat. Then he sped up, pumping hard and fast before exploding into my mouth. I sucked up every last drop.

"Good girl. Shall we let her have a reward?" Daniel asked Parker.

"I think so. I think she should have a little rest before she sucks on yours."

They guided me back to the position I began in. My legs spread apart. Daniel licked my clit and fucked me with his tongue. I cried out, my need to come was so raw. Daniel's eyes looked predatory as they fixed on mine. My reluctant lover had become the conductor of the orchestra.

"So wet for us," he said before diving back in.

I bucked over his face, screaming my delight. I

was so sensitive that when he tried to lick up my juices, I had to hold his head away. "Too much, give me a moment."

"Let's go into the bedroom." Daniel pointed to the pool house.

We all rushed inside, eager to continue our hot fucking.

"I've already fucked her this morning so it's your turn," Daniel told Parker. "She can suck my dick while you pound her pussy."

"Lie on the bed, Kayla, face up," Parker instructed.

I did as asked, but Parker grabbed my calves and pulled me a little further down the bed. I understood why when Daniel threw the pillows on the floor and knelt there facing the bottom of the bed so he was sat above my head. Parker sat astride me and probed my wetness with his fingers.

"So wet for me. Do you want my cock?"

"Yes. I want both your cocks," I answered.

Parker pushed into my pussy and Daniel pushed into my mouth. I sucked on Daniel in exactly the same way I had Parker. Parker fingered my clit at the same time as he thrust his cock in and out of me. There were so many sensations happening in my body all at once. It was hard to concentrate, my attention split between the cock in my mouth and the one in my pussy. Both men started pumping harder. My jaw ached under Daniel's thrusts, but I sucked for all I was worth until he shot his load down my throat. He tasted a little saltier than Parker, I noted. Parker bucked and shuddered as he reached his own climax and with a final grunt he spilled his seed inside me. He withdrew, and I felt it run out of me in a flood.

"Jesus, that was hot," he said. "Watching you sucking Dan's cock while mine was inside you. It was like I could imagine you were sucking and fucking me at the same time."

"So, guys," I said, looking from one to the other. "Is this something you would both be into doing again?"

They both nodded their heads.

I smiled in satisfaction.

OVER THE NEXT FEW DAYS, I was fucked raw. The men were like horny, little schoolboys. Constantly erect and continually fucking me. Last night after dinner I had been laid across the dining table while Parker ate me out and then Daniel fucked me. Today they were both working. I had driven down Main Street to do some shopping as I'd had an idea after yesterday evening. I found the perfect costume and went home, where I spent the afternoon pampering myself, ready for providing the evening's entertainment.

When the guys got home from the gallery, they walked into the kitchen to find me kneeling by the doorway. I was dressed in a French maid's outfit. It consisted of a black thin-strapped chemise. Over the bra part, there were slits exposing my pink budded nipples in all their peaked glory. The outfit had a tiny white apron. My panties were not only crotchless, but they had a strip missing at the back too, showing off my asshole. When I had seen myself in the mirror, I looked utterly wanton. I had become so wet and horny thinking about what was ahead I'd had to fuck my vibrator in front of the mirror while pinching my nipples.

"I'm here to serve," I told them.

"Hell, yeah," Parker replied.

Daniel looked me over and then turned to Parker. "She wants it now. I think we should eat first and make her wait."

"No," I begged.

"Yes. Yes, I think that's a great idea," Parker

answered. "We'll take our seats at the table and you can serve us."

It was going to be like that was it, I thought. Well, a little titillation while they ate wouldn't go amiss.

For an appetizer, I had made them a vegetable soup. I leaned over in turn to serve them, making sure they saw my rosebud nipples falling out of the slits in my outfit. I had expected them to catch a nipple in their mouth to suck it, but each of them smirked at the other. They weren't going to touch me at all.

"Please join us and eat your food. You'll need your energy for later," Daniel commanded.

Following that, I served them ribs in a barbecue sauce with potato wedges. In front of Daniel, Parker trailed a hand up my thigh. I knew they wouldn't be able to wait. He ran his hand right to the edge of my crotchless panties, pulled them back and let them twang, then he picked up his ribs and began to eat. The teasing bastard. By now I was ready to dry hump a chair leg, but there was still dessert to serve yet—a chocolate fudge cake with whipped cream.

When the meal was over, I cleared the dishes and waited for further instructions. Maybe they were just not into this and were tired from their day. I loaded the dishwasher feeling disappointed. Then I jumped as the sound of an aerosol came from behind me and coolness hit my ass. Parker had sprayed the cream directly onto my asshole.

He knelt down behind me and licked the cream off.

"Tastes better on Kayla, Dan. Your turn."

Parker lifted me up and laid me down on the table, parting my legs. Then with the whipped cream aerosol in his hand and a wicked look in his eyes he squirted it the length of my folds. He stepped aside and Daniel moved between my legs. Sitting on a chair he shuffled himself forward so he was sitting between my legs and then he licked and slurped the cream from me. The warmth of his tongue after the coldness of the cream had me thrusting my hips at his mouth. He completely cleaned the cream from me and then he grabbed either side of the panties. "These are pretty, Kayla, but with no crotch and an opening at the ass, I see no further point to them." He peeled them off me and threw them onto the floor. He threw the cream over to Parker. "I think her nipples need it next."

Parker squirted the cream into the boob openings of my outfit and sucked a nipple and the cream straight into his mouth.

I let out a deep moan.

"You like that don't you, dirty girl? Well, I like this cream, but I prefer yours and I'm going to be sucking that later."

"This cream?" Daniel asked as he once again dived between my legs, licking up my slit.

"Oh my god." I sighed.

"I think it's time we saw you with cream in your mouth," Parker said. "Turn onto your side."

Parker squirted the cream around his cock and then he threw it to Daniel who did the same. Then Parker pulled my head towards him. "Take my cream, dirty girl."

I opened my mouth and took Parker's cock in between my lips. My mouth was full of cream and cock and I was scared I was going to choke. I struggled a moment, my eyes watering, but Parker withdrew his cock giving me chance to swallow the cream and empty the inside of my mouth before his cock thrust into me again. Then Daniel pushed his creamed cock into my cunt. It was messy and cold but added to my wetness down there. I was so slippery down below and it felt so damn good. I hadn't realized I was so blissed out that I had closed my eyes and now I opened them seeing the cock in my mouth right in my direct eye-line but also able to see Daniel fucking me. The sensations were off the charts. Both men stood there thrusting in and out of me, their faces schooled in concentration, seeking their own pleasure. Daniel had his hand around the base of his cock and his eyes closed as he rocked in and out of me. Parker was squeezing my tits and pinching my nipples as he fucked my mouth.

I closed my eyes again to submit to all the sensations. The noises they were making became clearer as I closed my eyes. Parker was grunting and liked to talk. He kept calling me a dirty girl and saying that he was fucking me good.

Daniel's breathing was loud, and he kept saying fuck and moaning.

Though my eyes were shut I knew when they must have signaled each other as Parker began to thrust deeper and faster into my mouth and Daniel quickened his pace, adding his forefinger and thumb to my clit and pinching there.

"Oh, oh, oh, oh, oh," I grunted around Parker's cock.

He slipped out into his hand to let me talk. "What's that, dirty girl? What are you saying?"

"I'm saying please fuck me hard. Fill me up, fill my pussy and my mouth with your cum, both of you. I need it so fucking bad. I'm about to come."

My mouth was filled once again, and I didn't know I could be fucked so damn fast. Both men thrust into me like their lives depended on it. Their eyes closed and I once again shut my own and submitted to all the sensations. My pussy built, climbing towards its peak, my cunt and clit started to quiver as they took me to the top of that mountain and crashing over it. I shattered around Daniel's cock as I felt his spunk hit my walls. I bucked upwards with the spasms and at that point my mouth filled with Parker's man milk. I opened my eyes and licked around my mouth.

"What the fuck is going on?"

I turned my head, spunk dripping from my mouth as I laid on my side with two men on either end of me with their spent cocks in their hands, to come face to face with my mother.

I screamed, jumped down from the table and ran up to my bedroom where I locked myself in.

CHAPTER TEN

Daniel

If you would have told me a week ago that I would be faced with this situation, I would have asked what drugs you were taking. Yet there I was, stood naked, in the same room as Patty's daughter and her new stepson. All of us except Patty devoid of clothes. I didn't know how long she'd stood there for, but she had certainly seen our finale.

Her face was shocked, rather than angry, and I waited for the anger to hit. Instead, concern hit her features and she turned to run after Kayla.

"Patty, wait," I yelled. "Not right now. Give her time to get dressed."

Patty turned back round to me and nodded.

"How did you get in here?" I asked. "I'm sure I locked the door."

"I still have a key," she said. "I didn't return one just in case."

I sighed. "Go take a seat in the living room and let us get dressed. Then you can tell me why you're here."

"Your father's in the car, Parker. He wanted to see you. We... we wanted to see both the kids. I- I..." She looked at both of us. "I don't know what to say or what to tell him."

"You tell him nothing unless Parker wants any of his business talked about," I told her. "Now we're going to get changed. Then you can bring in your new husband and carry on like you never saw anything happen here."

Patty crossed her arms over her chest. "Well, that's not possible because I need to know exactly what's going on with my daughter."

"Why? You've never given a damn before."

Patty snarled. "I raised that girl until she was eighteen. I may never have earned the title of 'mother of the year', but I protected her from harm. She had an upbringing devoid of danger and I made sure she was provided for by endearing myself to rich idiots."

"Thanks."

"I didn't mean you, Daniel." She sighed. "You were the catalyst for change. You helped us regardless of gaining any advantage for yourself. You showed me a different way." She smiled. "I actually applied for and got a job selling boats when I left here. My idea had been to get myself set up independently and then let Kayla know there was a home for her with me. One that didn't come with a brand-new stepdaddy. But instead, I met Philip."

"This is great an' all, Mommy, but it's a bit of a weird conversation when we're standing here naked," Parker added. "I'm off to shower and then I'll meet you and my father in the living room."

Patty nodded. It said a lot about her background that other than shock, she had barely raised an eyebrow at the fact we were discovered fucking her daughter. I shook my head and went upstairs to shower in my en-suite. I knocked on Kayla's door but there was no answer and the door was locked. I could hear the faint sounds of the shower running so I walked away and headed to my own room.

When I emerged twenty minutes later and

headed back downstairs, Parker was in the kitchen making fresh coffee.

"They're in the living room. Before I headed for the shower, I told her she could bring my father in, as long as she didn't say a word about what happened here."

"Appreciate it."

"Well, I guessed he wouldn't go away anyhow without speaking to me. He's just that kind of a guy. The way I see it, if I have to take some heat to protect Kayla, then that's what I'll do."

"Yeah, I kind of came to the same conclusion."

Parker gave me a bro fist which I acknowledged with one of my own, though a smirk crept around the edges of my mouth.

"So, do you want me in there with you?" I asked.

"You would do that?" Parker looked at me in shock.

"We share pussy, and I know Patty, so I think it's the least I could do. Anyway, they're in my home, so if they start trouble, I'll kick their asses out."

"I'm kinda hoping they do now." Parker laughed, and I followed him through into the living room.

To say she lived here before, Patty was perched on the edge of the couch nervously, her hand on her husband's. It was hard to miss the giant diamond on her wedding finger and I'm guessing the pendant and earrings she had on weren't costume jewelry either.

I leaned forward as Philip rose and I shook his hand. We made introductions.

"I figured if it was okay with you both, that I would sit in, seeing as it's my house you're in."

Philip looked like he was going to protest.

"I want him here, Pops. He's become a good friend."

Philip nodded and sat back on the couch.

Patty made herself busy pouring everyone a coffee from the tray I had brought in.

Philip cleared his throat. "So, Parker. I came to clear things up. I didn't like how things were left between us. It wasn't my intention to make you feel like you had been disowned. I was just enjoying spending time with my wife."

"A known money-grabber. No disrespect," Parker answered.

"None taken, honey." replied Patty. "I can see why you would think that; but Parker, this time you're incorrect."

His eyes narrowed. "Is that so?"

"Yes." Patty looked up at Parker and then turned her gaze to my own and I could see the honesty in her gaze as she carried on talking. "I fell in love with your father. Right at the time I had sworn off men and decided to stand on my own two feet. Your dad's had quite a challenge on his hands as I resisted him for some time." She turned to Philip and their eyes met and the look that passed between them really was pure love.

"Patty could see you were on a slippery slope, Son. Having hung around money before, she had seen wayward sons who had ended up with drug problems or crashed race cars and ended up in wheelchairs or dead. All because they were seeking thrills because money got them everything. You were on your way to becoming a playboy, Son. I could see it. We agreed that you needed encouragement to stand on your own two feet. I wasn't expecting you to run away from home.

"I didn't run away. I came to track down Kayla to see if I could get her to talk to you." He looked at Patty. "To try to get you to leave my dad alone. I thought you were trying to take him for his wealth."

"Well, I don't blame you for that. I hardly had the best reputation." Patty bit her lip. "But, Parker, everything I did before was to make sure my daughter had a good standard of living."

"I get that, but on talking to her it seems the money was there, but in place of love."

Patty looked hurt. "I was so busy trying to keep the roof over our head and play at being a rich man's wife or lover that I forgot the whole reason why I was doing it." Her eyes went glassy. "There's no doubt about it, I neglected my daughter that way. I see that now and I've come to apologize to her. I fully expect after all these years she'll tell me to go to hell, but at least I'll have made the effort. At least she'll know I love her."

"Anyway, Parker," Philip interrupted. "I came to tell you to come back home. We can talk about your allowance. We don't want to cut you off, just give you a little direction. So, are you coming home, Son?"

"Can I just have a minute outside to discuss something with Dan?"

"Err, yes, of course."

I followed Parker out of the room. We stood just outside the door and I could hear Philip mumbling to Patty.

"Is there something going on between the two of them? Are they lovers?"

"I don't think so, Philip. I think, knowing Daniel, he'll be being a father figure."

"He's got a father."

"An older brother then. Someone steering him right. You can see he's changing already under Daniel's guidance."

"I guess so."

Parker and I smiled at each other.

"He's just looking out for you." I grinned.

"Hey, when we go back in, I should kiss you. That would give him something to really make his head spin."

"Leave the poor guy alone. He'll have a heart attack. Plus, the only person I'm ever kissing from now on is Kayla."

"Yeah, me too." His forehead creased. "Are we freaks, Dan? Wanting to share one woman?"

"Nah, we've got great taste, and luckily for us, we don't have to let the woman choose, leaving one of us disappointed. This way we're all winners. Anyway, what did you want to ask me?"

"I wondered if I could keep my job at the gallery and stay here?"

I patted him on the back. "Absolutely. I'm hoping to expand the gallery. How about a promotion soon to Deputy CEO?"

"Fuck, yeah. Seriously?"

"You seem to have settled into the retail world

well. You've settled here at the house well. Might as well see how far our little empire can go."

"Man, I didn't know when I followed your address to find Kayla, that I was gonna find my own way in life too."

"What can I say? I'm an amazing person. Now let's go back in there and let you sort things through with your father."

We went back into the living room, and I nodded for Patty to follow me out. "Let's leave the guys to it."

"Sure," she said, patting Philip's knee. "I'll be just outside, honey."

She followed me out into the hallway. "Do you want to go up and see if Kayla will let you in? I'm sure she has showered by now. The sooner you sort things out the better as she's feeling ashamed right now when she doesn't need to."

"How long has this been happening? You and my daughter? I know the Parker element is new, but were you seeing her behind my back?"

"No. It all happened this last week. At first, it was just me and her, but she involved Parker. I was hesitant at first, but it seems to be working out for us all. You know I'll take good care of her."

"Daniel, that doubt never entered my mind. It was a shock seeing my daughter stretched out naked across a table and with two men there, not one. But who she was with—I know both of you are essentially good men. Parker's maybe still a bit young and wild, but, hell, I had my own wild adventures when I was young. Kayla's sex life is her business, not mine." She handed me the key she let herself in with. "It's time to return this. In the future, you can be sure I'll be knocking. *Very* loudly."

"I want to marry her if she'll have me, Patty. I want to marry her and give her my babies."

"Well, you'll have no problems from me in that regard, but what about Parker? There are three of you in this relationship and it's all brand new. You might not get what you want, Daniel, just bear that in mind."

I sighed. "I guess as long as Kayla's happy, I'm happy. I'll take her whichever way I can."

"She's a very lucky woman." Patty kissed my cheek. "Just as I was when you took me under your wing. I never did thank you, Daniel, and I know I cost you your livelihood. I spoke to Philip, and we want to settle that debt with you."

"No." I shook my head. "I don't want it. I would have never moved into art if you hadn't done that. I'm a firm believer that things happen for a reason and even though it was tough, and I called you a fair few names behind your back, it's led us to where we are today, Patty. Now go up and see your daughter."

She nodded and started to walk up the stairs. "Blue bedroom," I told her.

She knocked on the door and for a while there was only silence. I heard footsteps in Kayla's room. Then Patty came rushing back downstairs.

"Kayla's not there."

I ran out the front of the house to see that Kayla's car was no longer in the driveway.

She was gone.

CHAPTER ELEVEN

Kayla

The journey back to the apartment seemed to take a lifetime. I had never felt such emotion in my life. The shame. For my mother to see me naked, my mouth dripping with her new stepson's cum. My nipples on display through the slits in my French maid costume and my pussy on full display, having just been filled with cum by the guy she used to live with. I couldn't face her. I felt so dirty and it had left me feeling like I couldn't face Daniel or Parker ever again either. I had showered quickly and then while they were all talking in the living room, I had left. I needed to go back to the apartment. Needed to see my girls. It was a Monday evening and I hoped that Tiff had called around for the usual girls' night, so I would have my tribe around me. Tiff would understand, having had her own threesome until recently. Plus, my roommate, Haley, was the most sensible one of us. I needed her sense and her opinion right now.

What was I going to do?

I parked the car and ran up the stairs to our apartment, quickly unlocking the door and throwing myself through it. Big heaving sobs escaped my mouth as the relief of being home hit. Haley and Tiff appeared in the hallway.

"Oh my god, Kayla, what happened?"

They stood either side of me holding me and took me through the hallway to the living room and helped me take a seat on the couch after Haley had checked that I wasn't hurt. "Not physically, no."

Tiff held up the bottle of wine and a glass. I reached for the bottle and took a huge gulp of wine.

"Everything is such a damn mess," I stated.

I explained what had happened all that week. If Haley's eye sockets had become any wider her eyeballs would have fallen out.

Tiff nodded at me in understanding.

"It's difficult being in a relationship with two different men at once. It's a different set of challenges to face."

"I don't regret any of what's happened between us this week. It's just—Jesus, my mother saw me."

"Oh, so what?" Haley shot back. "She must know you have sex."

"But I was naked."

"She birthed you. She's seen your naked body. Anyway, this is not like you. Where's my sassy, couldn't give a shit roomie? You've gone all soft."

"I have," I said.

"Can't you see, Haley," Tiff replied. "She's in love."

I sat back and took another drink of wine as Tiff's words sank in. I had already said those words to Daniel and then I thought about Parker.

"Fuck me. I am. I'm in love. With both of them. What the hell?"

"So, what are you doing here?" Tiff asked. "You should be back there with them."

I shook my head. "I can't go back right now. I need some recovery time. Time to figure out how I'm going to handle my mom."

"What is it with you two? You've both had two guys each, at the same time. I can't get one." Haley complained. "I'm telling you, I need teaching in the art of seduction."

"You'll meet someone," I told her. "All in good time."

"I'm meeting them, but they are all saying the same thing. That I don't know what I'm doing."

I handed the now empty wine bottle over to Hayley. "Show me."

Haley got a crease between her eyebrows. "Show you what?"

"How you give a blow job. Show me on the bottle."

Bless her, she grabbed it out of my hand without hesitation and stuck it in her mouth. I don't know how the bottle didn't break under all the enthusiasm. There was a lot of that, and spit.

"Oh, hell, Hayley. It's a blow job, not a bunch of fresh flesh at a zombie party."

Her face fell. "See. I told you."

"Let me get my own situation sorted and then, Hayley, I will teach you. We can use a dildo or a banana. Whatever. I will show you how to do a BJ right."

"Thank you."

I looked at Tiff.

"And I'll tell you all about the birds and the bees. See if you're doing that right," Tiff added.

I sat back and sighed. "Haley, I shouldn't laugh, but at least I'm not the only fuck up."

She high-fived me. "Hey, sister. You fuck up, I fuck up, and that's what got us into this beautiful mess."

There was a loud bang on the front door. Haley went to answer it.

She walked back through to the living room, followed by my mother. Looked like someone had told her where I lived.

"Can we talk?" she asked.

"Yeah." I sighed. "Let's go through to my room."

I COULD HEAR the movie playing through the walls, so I knew the girls had given me some privacy and couldn't hear our conversation.

I sat at the top of my bed near the pillows and my mom sat at the edge of the bed.

"Mom..."

She put a hand up. "If you're about to apologize for what I walked in on, don't you dare."

I closed my mouth, now lacking any words.

"Kayla, honey. I've been a crap mom. I put my hands up. I realize that by focusing on providing you with the material things in life that I felt you needed, I took my eye right off what you actually needed most. My love."

"It was like you couldn't wait for me to turn eighteen, so you could leave." I pouted.

She sighed.

"I explained this to Daniel already. I left because I had already woken up and smelled the roses. I got myself a job. Selling boats. Then I met Philip. Kayla, I love him. Really love him. He's not a meal ticket. I could care less if he was the poorest man on earth."

I raised an eyebrow at her before moving my gaze to the giant diamond on her finger.

"Yeah, well, it's just an added bonus. Anyway, we came to talk to you and Parker. I wanted to try to build some bridges with you."

"Instead you saw me naked on a table." I looked down at the duvet cover.

My mom moved further up the bed and tilted my chin up, looking directly into my eyes. "I was shocked at seeing my little girl naked, that's all. I don't care who you are with as long as they treat you right. One, two, a whole harem, my girl. As long as you're happy, I'm happy. Now I know you probably don't give a damn whether I'm happy or not, but I just wanted to tell you before I headed back to LA. I love you, darling, and there's always a bedroom for you in LA. I even had it decorated for you."

I seriously dreaded to think what my room was like with her taste in decorating. No doubt there were more blue frills, but she had made the effort and that's what counted. "Maybe I could come over for a visit sometime?"

"I would love that." My mom teared up. "I really would."

I started to cry. Big fat tears rolled down my face as I realized I might be able to salvage some kind of a relationship with my mother.

"Now, come on. You need to get home to those two men of yours. They'll be waiting for you and worrying how you are."

"I can't. I've been drinking."

"I can drive you back."

"It's okay, Mom. I'm gonna stay here with the girls tonight. It's movie night. I need some time to think about what's happened this last week."

"Okay." She kissed the top of my head. "I can reassure them you're okay, but promise me you'll go back tomorrow to sort everything out. They're good men."

"I promise."

"Right." She stood up. "I'll be on my way." She hovered at the doorway. "Just one thing."

"Yeah?"

She shook her head, "Never mind. I was going to ask what it was like, two men at once; but now I'm settled with Philip, I don't want to know the answer." She winked, and I laughed. "Come see me out."

After she said goodbye to the girls, we said goodbye at the door. My mom went on her way, and I felt more settled.

I texted Daniel and Parker.

Kayla: I'm fine. I'll be back tomorrow.

Parker: Thank fuck. My dick's already hard thinking about it.

Daniel: Can't wait to see you. You belong here.

I smiled and went back to the girls where we enjoyed an evening of gossip and more wine.

· · ·

THE NEXT MORNING, I got a few boxes from a nearby supermarket and returned to the apartment where I started to pack more of my belongings.

"You're not coming back, are you?" Haley hovered in the doorway.

"I'm not that far away and for now while I'm working things out, I'm coming back here at least every Monday for girls' night, but it's true, I might end up moving in with Daniel and Parker permanently. If I do, I'll give you plenty of notice."

"Are you keeping your job at Green's?"

"I honestly don't know. Again, the commute isn't that far, but I need to go back and talk to them both. One thing I've realized is that my life has changed so much in this short space of time, but we've jumped in with both feet. Thinking of the near future, there are questions I need to address with them. So, I'm going back and taking a few more of my belongings because I'll be staying there longer than the couple weeks I first thought."

"I'll miss you. You and Tiff are both moving on and I'm stuck." Haley twisted her lips to one side looking thoughtful. "Do you know what? When you leave, I'm going to place an ad for two male roommates. Then I can learn more about what makes men tick. With that and you and Tiff teaching me about sex and great blow jobs, I might actually start to nail the art of dating."

I stood next to her and ruffled the top of her head as I was a lot taller than she was. "Be patient. It'll happen. Look how fast my life changed. For that matter, the same happened with Tiff. A neighbor moved in and that was her love life sorted. But make sure these two new roommates are hot as fuck. You never know, you might get to bang one of them... or even both of them." I winked.

"Not everyone's that greedy they want two men. Some of us would be more than happy with one."

"Hey, don't knock what you haven't tried." I laughed. "Right, come and help me load up the car will you?"

I WAS HOME BY MID-MORNING, but Daniel had left a note that said he and Parker were working all day and they would see me this evening. I spent the day unpacking, swimming, and then had an after-noon nap as I hoped that I wouldn't get much sleep that evening.

Both men looked so happy to see me home. I cooked dinner. While we ate, Parker and I both spoke about the conversations we'd had with our parents, then we all sat in the living room having agreed we needed to chat about our threesome.

"I know it's very early to be discussing the future of our relationship, but I felt it was important to know where you both hoped it would go," I said. "You know. If this is just a bit of fun or we're seeing if this can lead to something more permanent."

I took a deep breath.

"I'm not getting heavy here; I just thought it would be good for us to talk about what's happened this week."

"Sounds good to me," Parker said. "Now I know I'm living here for the considerable future."

"Well, I'll start," Daniel said. "Time to put our cards on the table and be open and honest. I think I've been in love and lust with Kayla since I met her. This week when we got together, it was everything I had imagined and more. I started thinking of us getting married and having children." He took a drink of the beer he had brought with him. "Then I found out you slept with Parker and you wanted to carry on doing so. I'll be honest, at first, I was devastated and wondered if I was useless in bed. I thought I had failed in some way. I felt threatened because Parker is younger and as it turns out, has a bigger cock than I have." He laughed. "But when we did have the first three-way, I found it exciting. Seeing you enjoying another man's dick and watching you fuck both of us. It's a huge turn on. I liked the fact we can fuck on our own with you or get together for the threesome. It's opened up so many new experiences."

"I agree," Parker replied. "When she told me she had slept with you. I was so pissed. I'd wanted her since I had met her earlier that week and she didn't disappoint with that dirty mind and body of hers. At first, I felt like I wanted to duel with you in the back-yard, but what we ended up doing was far better. I love the three of us together, it's hot."

"Well, I felt like a slut at first, I have to admit," I told them. I could see both were about to protest, but I held up my hand. "Look, I slept with the man who was supposed to have been my stepdad. Then I met a guy who jokingly said he was my stepbrother and I fucked him too. Not only did I like it, but I got off on the fantasy of you being my stepdad and stepbrother. It's naughty and I like that. Just as I enjoyed fucking by the pool and in the office. It's illicit and thrilling. I'm so pleased that we're trying this because I don't want to have to choose one of you over the other. I don't think I could. I think I would have to walk away from you both."

"No one's going anywhere," Daniel almost growled. "But do you think we need some kind of routine or agreement?"

I shook my head. "That makes things boring, and the thrill of this is that we aren't. How about you let me lead the way with all this? I'll make the moves. Some days I might not feel like doing anything at all. Other times I might just want one of you. I'm not saying you can't propose anything, but if one of us takes the lead it might be better."

"And what about sleeping arrangements? Do we spend the night in your room or go back to our own?" Parker asked.

"I'll be honest with you. I love having my own bed," I admitted. "So mainly, I would prefer to sleep on my own."

"Aww, I like to snuggle," Parker said.

"I would like some nights where you stayed with me," Daniel added.

"Well then, how about our three-ways take place either outside of our bedrooms, or we do it in mine and you both leave. Then on nights we're one on one, I sleep all night with you in that room? Though if I get too hot or can't stay asleep, I reserve the right to sneak back out to my own room." I giggled.

"Sounds good to me," Daniel said.

Parker nodded his agreement.

"So, Parker lives here now. I live here. I take it you're moving in too?" Daniel asked.

"I am. I can commute to my job. It'll mean a longer trip to work, but I can put up with that if it means seeing you guys every day."

Daniel moved on his seat. "That's something I was going to talk to you about. I'm going to open further branches of the gallery. Parker is going to run the one in Chandler Square until there may be a need for him to become my deputy. I thought you might like to assist me in getting the others running and help with sales. From real estate to art. They both suit the wealthy. I think it would be the perfect job for you."

"Three of us in the same business, as well as the bedroom?" I bit my lip. "I guess it could work; as long as I get my own role, and I'm not just helping you two guys every day. I need something I can run with. Goals to achieve. I'm very ambitious."

"We'll work it out."

"We need to work out a food rotation too because I don't mind cooking while I'm on my vacation time, but you can both go to hell if you think I'm going serve you dinner every night."

"I can cook," Daniel replied. "I'll take my turn."

"And on my nights, we'll have takeout." Parker laughed.

"I'll give you a few lessons on how to do the basics, seeing as you're learning to become more independent," Daniel told Parker. He was definitely becoming an older brother come mentor to the younger man. I think Daniel would have protested that he didn't need help in order to protect his macho image, were it not for the fact that they were equal in the bedroom. Plus, the fact that even though they satisfied me equally, there was no doubt Parker loved the fact he had the longer cock.

"Can we start with mac and cheese? I love that stuff, man." Parker laughed.

"Okay, now assuming everything works out, what about the future?" Daniel asked. "Because, at some point, I would like to start a family, so if you're not on the same page, we're going to have a problem."

"I always saw myself having kids down the line," I told him. "But how does that work with three of us?"

"Wow, this is a heavy subject for a twenty-one-year-old guy," Parker said. "Like in how many years' time might this happen?"

"I wouldn't want to start a family until I was

around thirty, so that's six years away. Could you handle that, Daniel?"

"Yes. In those six years, we build up the business and all travel the world."

"Well, you and the old man can have the first kid together and then if we're all still living happily ever after, at that stage, me and you could have the next one. See how it goes. We could still all live together, right? I like kids. Perhaps we could be Dad and Pops?" Parked looked at Daniel with a cocked eyebrow.

"Sounds okay to me."

"Well, we've been together a week and we're plotting out potentially the next six or so years." I sighed. "This is all getting a bit heavy for me. I like knowing where our minds are at right now, but I think it's time to get back to concentrating on the immediate future of me sucking and fucking your cocks. And can I let you both know that I've been put off wearing the French maid outfit for life."

Everyone laughed.

"Yes, I think we'll burn that sometime, along with the memory of your mother coming in and finding us."

"I don't know," Parker added. "I found it quite hot."

Daniel and I rolled our eyes at him.

"So, for one night only," I addressed them. "Who wants to come to my room for a sleepover?"

PARKER WALKED INTO MY ROOM, picked up my pillow and inhaled the top of it deeply.

"Aww, look," Daniel said, "he can't get enough of the smell of Kayla's hair."

Parker looked at me, a wicked glint in his eye. "I caught a glimpse of Kayla when she first stayed here. She wasn't laying her head on the pillow were you, Kayla?"

My face flamed. "Oh my god, you mean you saw..."

"What?" Daniel asked.

"Kayla got herself off on the pillowcase. Shame, because I can only smell laundry detergent, so it would appear the dirty girl got cleaned up."

"You fucked the pillowcase?" Daniel asked.

"Yeah, needed to find some way to like the frilly bedding and it felt nice against my clit." I laughed.

"Well, that's great, but tomorrow we go get paint and you buy some new linen. This blue is a migraine and needs to go."

"I bought some from Chandler Square," I told

him. "I just haven't got around to putting it on yet. I keep being distracted."

"Hey, can I paint my room?" Parker asked.

"No, I think the pink suits you." Daniel laughed, a deep hearty laugh.

"Oh God, I totally forgot that the other guest room was pink. Oh, poor Parker. You could have let him have my blue room."

"It's still girly, even though it's blue. Hell, there are a shit ton of these frills." Daniel looked at the décor as if seeing it for the very first time.

"Well, by all accounts, looking isn't what she does with them," Parker quipped.

"Very amusing," I said and then I pulled my top off over my head and the joking stopped.

WE ALL GOT naked and under my duvet. The guys were on either side of me. I was curled up within their arms and warmth. Their erections pressed against my legs. Hands swept over my body, trailing, teasing, pinching. They both dropped a hand down to my pussy; one concentrating on my clit while the other plunged their fingers inside me, stretching my walls. I sighed and took a cock in each hand, enjoying the feel of their silky-smooth lengths as I pumped them slowly. Daniel kissed my mouth while Parker leaned over and took a breast in his. We were all so close in my queen bed and the duvet was making us hotter still. But I liked the fact I couldn't see what was happening further down the sheets. I could only guess as to whose fingers were doing what. I closed my eyes as I concentrated on the fingers plunging deeper into my pussy and raised my hips so that they could get deeper still. Then their cocks left my grasp, the duvet cover hit the floor, and my pussy was empty. All that remained were the juices running down my leg. Parker sucked on the breast nearest to him and fondled the other while Daniel raised himself above me and rubbed his cock against my entrance. He slipped inside me, filling me, and creating a greater need for me to reach my climax. I hungered for his thrusts to increase and raised my hips. Daniel stared directly into my eyes as he fucked me. "God, yeah, baby. This is where we belong. I needed this. Missed you last night."

"Please, I can't wait any longer. Please, fuck me, Daniel. Make me come."

His thrusts increased in pace and sweat started to break out on his forehead. I brought my hand up from my free side and held onto his ass cheek, feeling it clench as he pumped. His pace suddenly became fervent as he rocked into me quickly before tensing and spilling his seed within me. As his last thrust hit, he took me over the edge, my pussy spasming around him and I cried out.

"Oh God."

Daniel withdrew and before I could recover from my last orgasm, he had moved to my side and Parker had taken his place. He knelt on the bed, placing one of my legs around his neck. His cock plunged straight into me, stretching my walls. He thrust to the hilt, making me cry out as those extra couple of inches pushed inside, this position meaning he could hit me oh so deep. He placed his thumb on my clit and strummed me at the same time. Daniel took his hand off his cock and pushed his fingers into my mouth making me taste his cum. Then he took his now wet fingers and pinched my nipples.

Before long, I was bucking up off the bed straining to reach my climax.

"Come on, dirty girl, fuck me good. Oh yeah, baby. Oh yeah. Like that." The familiar shudders shook around Parker's dick as he pumped his spunk inside me.

After a few minutes coming down, Parker rested back at my other side. Daniel picked the duvet from the floor and put it over us, turning the top down to give us some air while we cooled down.

"Welcome home," he said and leaning over, he kissed me, hard and deep.

"Yeah, welcome home," Parker added, and he licked and bit up the side of my neck, making me shiver.

We all fell asleep, limbs entangled.

CHAPTER TWELVE

Kayla

I woke very hot and sweaty and wanted to get out of bed, so I shook both Daniel and Parker awake.

"Guys, I want to get out."

"Hmm." Parker stirred and groaned. "Sure you don't mean you want us to get up?"

"No. I have paint to buy and I need a shower so bad. Come on," I moaned. Daniel was still dead to the world, but Parker swung his legs over and got to his feet. "Sure, now you've had me, you discard me. I get it. I'm used goods right now."

I threw my pillow at his head. He caught it and

sniffed the top of it again. "I'm keeping this," he said and began to walk away. "Buy some new pillows while you're out."

I got in the shower and by the time I came back out Daniel had also left the room. I dressed quickly in a loose-fitting sundress, determined to have breakfast and hit the stores.

Daniel had made pancakes, and there was fresh orange, plus steaming hot coffee waiting when I arrived downstairs. Parker had already left for the gallery.

"So what are your plans today?" I asked Daniel.

"I'm going to buy some art supplies and then I'm painting," he informed me. "Only I'm doing canvases, not walls."

"Will you show me?" I asked him. "I never asked to see where you actually create these masterpieces before, did I?"

"Come on. Follow me," he said, picking up his mug of coffee. I did the same and followed him out of the house. Just around the side of the property, set back, was a separate small building which, when he had lived with my mom, had housed spare tattoo equipment. Sometimes his more important customers had preferred to come to the house for their work, rather than have to sit among others. I had presumed, wrongly, that it was still full of old equipment, but as he pushed open the door, I saw canvases in various stages of completion, and art equipment. He'd had a small kitchen fitted to one end so that he could make refreshments and there was now a small room cornered off at the rear which I presumed housed a bathroom. No need to leave when he was lost in his art.

"Oh, wow," I said, gazing around, taking it all in. "This is amazing. Your work is amazing."

I stared at his works in progress: some abstract, some portrait. All with his trademark bright colors. "Which do you prefer to paint? The portraits or the abstracts?"

"I just paint whatever comes into my head and then whichever shouts loudest. Right now, neither of these are calling to me. I'm looking for fresh inspiration."

"Then what are you going to do today?"

"I'll mess around with some old canvases for a while, let my mind untangle, and then hopefully inspiration will hit."

"And if it doesn't?"

"Then I'll come help you paint your room."

"Okay. Well, I kinda hope inspiration doesn't hit. Then you could paint my room while I hit the pool."

"I don't think so, girlie. Painting your room isn't going to pay the bills. Do you think one day you might pose for me? I never did a nude before."

"And you won't be doing one now. There is no way my naked body is going to be hung on a wall for all to see. Not my portrait either. You'll have to paint me in some weird abstract way." I pretended to be an art critic, "Kayla is represented here as a series of stripes and dots."

We finished our coffees and then kissing Daniel's cheek I said goodbye and went shopping to get everything I needed for my room.

THE NEXT COUPLE of days were spent with me almost imprisoned in my own room. I had cleared it, prepped it, and then started painting. The previous night I had shared Daniel's bed and tonight I was sharing Parker's, but I couldn't wait to get the room completed. I'd decorated in a light vanilla and my en-suite, which would need decorating next, was crammed with the purchases I had made of new lamps, linen, and floor rugs. I was determined to have a sophisticated room all of my own. I was lucky, the room was larger than both my rooms at the apartment put together, so I wasn't downsizing. Daniel had said I could organize the study downstairs next, ridding it of his dark furniture and making it somewhere that all three of us could use for the business. In the meantime, Parker had bought paint ready to start his own room at the weekend, saying he could take the pink no longer.

By the end of the following day the room was done. That night I slept in my new room, all alone, enjoying the feel of my new mattress and duvet and the soft linens I had bought. I had the best night's sleep and woke refreshed and ready to seize the day.

"So it's the weekend. Do we have plans?" I asked the men of the house.

"Well, yes we do," Daniel replied. "Because something you said to me the other day inspired me, so I want you both to come to my studio to help me with a painting."

"What are you wanting me to do? Hold the canvas up?" Parker jested. "Because I don't have an artistic bone in my body."

"No. I bought some special paints yesterday." Daniel explained. "Ones that are non-toxic to the body but will stay on a canvas."

I turned to stare at him.

"Kayla gave me the idea when I asked to paint her. She said only in abstract. It gave me an idea, and don't laugh but I had a try myself and it made this." He held up his cell and we looked at an interesting abstract picture.

"What did you do, roll around on the canvas?" I joked.

"Yes," he replied. "While thinking of you."

My mouth fell open.

"All the times my body moved as I jerked off are captured in the swirls on the canvas. I want to try one of us all. I've placed two large canvases out side by side in the room. I want us to paint each other and then fuck while lying on the canvas. The worst that happens is paint in an awkward place and the potential waste of two canvases, but I have high hopes. Are you in?" he asked us both.

"Why not," Parker replied. "I don't have any other plans and rolling around naked with Kayla sounds good to me."

"Why not." I laughed. "It's certainly different."

"Okay, you finish your breakfasts and give me thirty minutes to get things set up," he said, walking out of the room.

WE GATHERED in Daniel's studio. He had fixed a tarp to the floor and the canvases on the top of that.

To one side were some of those plastic slip-on shoes for your feet that you got at public swimming pools. He pointed to them and explained. "For when we're finished, so you can get to your showers without leaving a paint trail."

There were open pots of paint in the usual bright colors and several thick paintbrushes. I picked one up. It was very soft, and I stroked it down my hand. I walked over to Daniel and pulled down his shorts and brushed it over his cock. "How does that feel?" The answer came directly from his cock which burgeoned under the bristles.

I walked over to Parker who had already removed his clothes and placed them on the kitchen counter. I brushed the paintbrush over his dick. "That's nice," he said. "But I prefer your mouth on it."

I dropped to my knees and took him in my mouth. He pumped gently against me as I sucked him deep into my throat.

"Over here, you two," Daniel demanded.

We stopped what we were doing and walked over to him. He took us onto the canvas and asked Parker to lift up his feet in turn, painting his soles a bright yellow. Then he painted my knees in orange. I dropped back to the floor. When Parker had come in my mouth, I got up and looked at the canvas. There were smudged marks from my knees and smudged footprints from Parker where we had moved a little as I had sucked him dry. Daniel brought the paints nearer and we painted different colors onto different body parts, leaving our hands and most intimate parts free of paint. Daniel directed Parker to lie on his side on the canvas. He then helped me lie next to him so that my butt was positioned next to Parker's ass. Then Daniel placed lube on my butthole, letting Parker take over rubbing it in. Finally, Daniel laid at my other side so his dick was to the front of me.

"Now we do what comes naturally," he said.

My juices were pouring. I was soaked between my legs at the thought of the double penetration about to occur. Parker placed a hand on the front of me, feeling my pussy lips and then dipping a finger inside me. "God, you're wet."

He took his cock in his hand and slowly, an inch at a time, pushed inside me, as I relaxed to accept him in my ass. Then Daniel slowly entered my pussy, filling me up. I had never felt so damn full. It was amazing. They moved together, both thrusting inside me in a steady rhythm. I wondered if they could tell that the other's dick was there. If it gave them any extra friction. But my thoughts were soon lost as I gave myself over to the sensations. "That's it," Daniel whispered. "Submit to us. Give us everything."

That was all I needed for my mouth to begin shouting out what was becoming unleashed from my filthy mind.

"Oh my god, you both have the biggest cocks. I can't believe they're both inside me, filling me up."

"Do you like being fucked in both holes, Kayla?" Daniel asked.

"Yes." I gasped. "Is it bad that I like that my stepbrother is fucking my ass while my stepdaddy fucks my cunt?"

"No, you're not bad; you're very, very good," Daniel replied, his voice husky. His mouth dropped onto my neck and he licked and nibbled there making me gasp. "Keep doing that," Parker ordered him. "It's making her pussy tremble against my cock."

"Dirty girl," Parker whispered in my ear. I loved his nickname for me. I was his dirty girl.

We slid against each other's bodies with the paint on our skin, until the guys were ready to come. "Shoot onto the canvas," I asked. "Please." Their thrusts built, and I was being rubbed up and down the canvas as they got closer to their climaxes.

"Fuck," Parker's hips jerked against my ass. "I'm about to come, sweet little stepsister. Right in front of daddy." He withdrew and shot his load out onto my back. "There, after, you can rub it into the canvas. A mixture of paint and spunk," he said, lying on his back.

"Turn around," Daniel ordered, slipping out of me and holding his cock in his hand. "Lie on your front." My painted breasts, smeared where they had rubbed against Daniel, plus the rest of the front of my body, laid touching the canvas. Daniel knelt behind me and slid right back into me, continuing where he had left off.

He placed a hand on my hipbone and pummeled into me. My body kept sliding back on the canvas with all the paint on me. At the brink of my orgasm, Daniel cruelly withdrew and pumped his cock until I felt the familiar splatter of cum hitting my skin.

"Now turn over, spread your legs apart and make yourself come," he said.

I did as instructed. I was so damn horny I was almost delirious. I opened my eyes, watching the guys watching me as I put the fingers of one hand in my pussy and frigged my swollen bud with the others. All the while the paint and cum on my back were decorating the canvas. "Yes, we're watching you, dirty girl," Parker said, licking his top lip.

"I can't believe you've caught me," I told them. "I'm so embarrassed, my stepfamily watching me, but I'm too close to stop."

"You're a disgrace," Daniel told me. Instead of this turning me off, it made me strum myself harder, my cream running down all over my fingers. "Don't tell my mom," I asked them. "Maybe if you both jerk yourselves off, it can be our little secret."

The guys begin fisting their dicks again, but I couldn't wait for them. I came hard all over my hands, bucking violently. The men descended on me, Daniel fucking my mouth and Parker now taking a turn in my pussy. We writhed all over the canvas until we were entirely spent.

After a few minutes, we lifted ourselves off and looked at the work before us.

"Hey," I said looking at the starburst of colors across the canvas, mixed in places and complete with swirls where my ass moved around. "They look really good. I thought they would just be a complete mess."

Daniel stood studying them, his chin resting on his hand. "I think mounted they'll look sensational."

"Kayla does," Parker quipped.

"I'm going to call this one sensational," Daniel pointed to the canvas on the left. "And we're going to keep that at home. I'll hang it in the living room."

I nodded. "Perfect. And the other?"

"This one is going to the gallery with an explanation that will make people wonder. I'm going to call it submit."

I didn't ask what he meant by an 'explanation'. I trusted him to do what was right for us all.

We slipped on the plastic shoes and made our way through the main house to the massive shower in the family bathroom. Daniel figured it was better to mess up one bathroom than them all. We helped loofah the paint from each other's bodies and sucked and fucked each other until we were all struggling to keep our eyes open.

"Siesta time," Daniel said, and we all retired to our own rooms to rest.

CHAPTER THIRTEEN

Two years later...
Kayla

I stepped out of the limousine, taking Daniel's hand, and we walked the carpet laid out toward the venue hosting the night's ceremony. Parker walked behind us, not wanting to steal the limelight from Daniel. We were at the prestigious Artariad awards. Daniel had been nominated for a breakthrough artist award. The nomination on its own meant a rise in popularity, taking the galleries to ever higher levels. We now had three of them and were hoping to complete on a fourth venue soon.

We were greeted by so many people, some friends in the trade that I recognized—others sycophantic lovies who hung around the popular people only to disappear when a new name arose. I stood with Parker and we watched as several women fawned over Daniel.

"Bless him, he looks scared to death," Parker said, a smirk appearing on his face.

"I don't think it helps that he's so nervous. I know how much he wants to win the award."

"You don't have to tell me. I live with him too, remember?"

"Oh shut up, and get me another glass of champagne," I scolded.

The last couple of years had been amazing. We had fallen into a healthy relationship and though at times we all argued, the majority of the time we had lots of fun. The sexual side of our relationship was still scorching hot, but I did get some days where I managed to head to bed with my Kindle rather than two horny men!

Parker was overseeing all the galleries now, whereas I had settled into managing the store at Chandler Square. It was where it had all begun. The unit next to it had come up for sale and Daniel had purchased it. After a renovation, we had a much larger gallery and it had a huge turnover. Daniel kept his model of affordable art mixed with more expensive pieces, so each gallery had the upstairs viewing area that was by appointment only.

It was the canvas 'Submit' that had led Daniel on a path headed toward the nomination for the award tonight. When an art dealer had asked about it, Daniel had been candid in explaining that it was the result of lovemaking on canvas. The dealer had purchased it and hung it in a top New York gallery. The publicity had soared when Daniel had been asked about it on opening night at the gallery. The question had been posed as to was it Daniel himself and a girlfriend or boyfriend who had done the love-making, to which Daniel had replied it was with his girlfriend and her other boyfriend. Nothing truly fazes the art world, but that five minutes of fame put Daniel's name on the map and the three of us had long since decided we weren't hiding our relation-ship from people. We were happy together and we didn't care what anyone else thought. Well, that wasn't strictly true. Parker had worried about what his father would think, but my mom must have talked to him about it because he just patted Parker on the back when we told him and asked if he was happy. My mom had winked and given me a thumbs up.

My relationship with my mom was much better. We didn't see each other very often, but we spoke on the phone once a week and were focusing on the future, and not the past.

I still saw the girls on a Monday night. Tiffany was now a mother of a five-month-old baby girl and so Monday nights were her downtime. It was perfect that she only lived next door if needed. Haley, well she had got her two new roommates when I'd left, and they knew to make themselves scarce on a Monday night. I would tell you about them, but well, that's Haley's story to tell, not mine.

We took our seats in the venue and enjoyed a fabulous five course dinner. By the time the award ceremony started, I had to confess I was quite tipsy. We waited through several awards and while it was exciting for the winners, I really just wanted them to get to Daniel's award and put us out of our misery.

Then it was the opening of the envelope.

"The Artariad Breakthrough Artist of the year is... Daniel Scott."

Parker and I leaped to our feet. I hugged and kissed Daniel before he extracted himself from my clinging and made his way to the stage.

"Oh my god, he won." I squealed at Parker.

He high-fived me. I wouldn't admit it, but due to his strong physique, it stung a little. I was going to get my own back later with the paddle.

We watched as Daniel accepted his very fancy award and faced the audience.

"Thank you very much to the judges who considered me as a potential nominee for an Artariad Award. It's beyond my wildest dreams that I am on this stage tonight accepting the award for Breakthrough Artist. Now, as you know, the piece that cemented my name as an artist was one called Submit. I would like my partner, Kayla, and her other partner, Parker, to stand, because they have been intrinsic to my appearing here tonight."

Fuck, everyone was staring. Oh well, I'd had a shit ton of wine and my dress was designer. I rose onto my four-inch heels and raised a glass at Daniel. Parker followed suit, standing and raising his own glass and the people around us applauded.

"Submit is a one-off," Daniel lied to the audience. We had made an agreement that knowledge of the other picture would never go beyond the three of us and after Submit's fame we took it down from the living room wall and had hung it in my bedroom instead. "It's a public declaration of our love for

Kayla, and our respect for each other," he continued. "But our adventures will continue behind closed doors from now on. So, thank you to Kayla, to Parker, and to anyone who has appreciated or purchased my work. It is truly an honor to be accepting this award tonight."

The audience got to their feet as they had with the majority of the night's winners and I stood, my arm through Parker's as we watched Daniel take in his new celebrity status.

"That award's lovely and all," Parker said, "but the true star of the show is you, baby."

"Why thank you, Sir."

We sat back in our seats and I massaged his cock over his trousers, my hand concealed by the table.

Daniel returned to the table. "Can we get out of here soon? Now I have the award, I'm scared I'm going to be bored to death by the freeloaders for the rest of the evening."

We rose and left, right in the middle of the ceremony. No one batted an eyelid. It was the art world after all and full of divas.

"I think tonight we should fuck in my room right in front of the other painting," I announced in the limousine that was taking us back home.

"That would be... sensational," Parker quipped.

Daniel and I rolled our eyes.

"Actually," I told them. "I never made out in a limousine before, how about you two?"

There was no more talking on the journey home.

THE END

Double Delight continues with SHARE – Haley's story.

SHARE

DOUBLE DELIGHT BOOK THREE

Haley

It was official. I sucked. I sucked at sucking. And no doubt at sex itself. But definitely at sucking if my friend's faces were to be believed as I attempted to give a wine bottle a blow job.

"Oh, hell, Hayley. It's a blow job, not a bunch of fresh flesh at a zombie party," noted my roommate Kayla.

My face fell. "See. I told you." Being crap at coitus was no joke.

"Let me get my own situation sorted, and then,

Haley, I will teach you. We can use a dildo or a banana. Whichever. I will show you how to do a BJ right."

"Thank you."

"And I will tell you all about the birds and the bees. See if you are doing that right," Tiff, my ex-roommate and now next-door-neighbor added.

At that point, a knock came at the door. Kayla's mom had come to see her about a tense situation she had just left. Kayla had come over tonight from Daniel, her ex-stepfather's house because she had started a relationship with him and a guy called Parker, her mom's new stepson. Here I was with no man in my life and Kayla had two!

Tiffany returned to the living room. Monday night was girls' night. Even though she now lived next door with her husband, Brandon, Monday's remained a man-free zone, rather like my pussy. "I hope they are going to be all right," Tiff stated, nodding toward the hallway. Kayla and her mom didn't have a great history.

I shrugged my shoulders. Kayla's mom had just walked into Daniel's home to find her, Daniel, and Parker in the throes of passion. "Well, we are here if not."

.   .   .

KAYLA WORKED things out with her mom, and then also with Daniel and Parker, and the three of them were cohabiting in Port Jeff. Kayla had given notice on her share of the apartment and so this evening, her and Tiff were coming over to help me interview potential new roommates. I had jokingly said I wanted two hot males, but to be honest, as long as the newbies didn't look like serial killers or other such weirdos, I would be happy. Good references were key to getting a key. My apartment had three bedrooms. Mine, at the front, had an en-suite. It over-looked the parking lot for the apartments, but beyond that and the street, there were nice views. We had all worked for Green's, a Realtors based in Brooklyn. Kayla had now left to join Daniel's art business. He was an artist, owned a gallery and was looking to expand. Tiff still worked at Green's but was plan-ning on trying for a baby with her husband, so I didn't know what her long-term plans were. I felt like the only one of us with no life. Maybe I should ask all the apartment applicants if they were boyfriend-less and downbeat? Make sure we had common ground. I tried to shake the melancholy hanging over me. I was pleased my friends were both in love, and as they kept on telling me, it would happen for me too, one day. In the meantime, I needed to get better at sex. I figured if I watched some porn that could help. Though Kayla and Tiff had promised to help, they were just too busy getting on with their own lives. Anyhow, they didn't have dicks. I kinda needed the real thing to practice on. I wondered about paying for a male escort, that was how bad things were getting.

Out of the three of us girls, I was by far the most innocent. Through college, I had dated Liam and he had been the guy to take my cherry. I had thought we were good together, but once we graduated, he graduated onto another girl. We had hardly ever had oral. He said he didn't like it, either the giving or receiving, so it wasn't until I started dating other guys that it all went wrong. I had not got past first base with many dates. I always got shy and clammed up. Having no idea what to converse about other than my friends and work, most dates didn't progress to a second. A couple times things had gone to the bedroom, it had been a disaster. My pussy was so dry men couldn't get near it. My latest date, another realtor from Green's, Malcolm, blamed me for the fact he had not been able to get it up. Truth was, my only real joy came from my other best friend, B.O.B., that's right, my battery operated boyfriend who never let me down. He was a bendable rabbit vibrator who I could position to hit my clit and my pussy at the same time.

I noticed the time and realized I needed a final flurry of domestic activity. The two bedrooms down the hall were where the two new roommates would be and there was a shared bathroom for them to use. Both rooms had been given a fresh lick of paint last week and thoroughly cleaned and aired. Each had a queen bed, fitted closet space, and a dresser. A TV was fixed to a wall in each, so they'd be able to escape to their rooms if they wanted each night. Butterflies hit my gut followed by a feeling of dread. What if they seemed nice, so I gave them a key and then we didn't get on at all? I shook my head and went through to my en-suite to shower before the girls arrived. We were having pizza after the interviews, so I grabbed a bag of potato chips to eat before I hit the shower. It was a shame I couldn't afford the apartment on my own. Peace and quiet could be nice at times and at least there would be no more witnesses to my dating disasters. By tonight I might have one or two new roommates. I crossed my fingers, closed my eyes and said pretty please.

·   ·   ·

"I AM SO FREAKING HUNGRY. How long is this gonna take?" Kayla moaned. The redhead patted her svelte stomach and it emitted a gurgle.

"Yeah? Well, I might have had more sympathy if your hair didn't look all fucked up. You had sex before you came here, didn't you?"

"Might have." Kayla winked.

There was a noise from the vicinity of the unlocked front door, followed by a flurry of footsteps. "I'm not late. There's one minute to 6pm," Tiff announced like I hadn't been checking my wristwatch every thirty seconds since 5pm.

"Oh my god, not you too!"

"Not me too, what?"

"You have sex hair. I need to get laid. I need to learn sex and get laid."

Just then the doorbell rang.

"Take a seat, you two, for Christ's sake and straighten each other's hair. There is serious decision making to be done," I chastised them.

The interviews were a complete waste of time with just two people to go. We had interviewed a pregnant woman, who didn't announce she was pregnant even though her stomach kept moving. She kept repositioning her wrap. If she wasn't pregnant, she had weird medical problems, so she was out. The second woman we interviewed was clearly a call girl, asking if men were allowed back before I'd had a chance to ask her to confirm her name. The others seemed fine but had not shown that we had any common ground and after the fantastic apartment share I'd had with Tiff and Kayla, I was reluctant to settle for business people.

"Well, this looks like a complete bust," I said to Tiff and Kayla.

"Don't give up yet. There are two men to come. They might be the sex on legs you've been looking for," Tiff said.

"Of course they will, Tiff. Dreams like that come true all the time, especially with me. They will be two sex gods who want me as a filling in their sandwich. Now if we could all wake up, I am going to open a bottle of wine. Screw this."

Tiff went to answer the door to the next-to-last applicant while I stood in the kitchen in the corner of our apartment pouring a very large glass of red wine. I couldn't afford to keep the apartment going on my own, so if these next two weren't of any use, then it looked like business bores were moving in with me. I took a secret large swig of wine with my back to the room and then turned around where I choked and spat red wine straight down my white blouse. For fuck's sake!

In front of me and stood at the side of Tiff, were two of the most gorgeous men I had ever laid eyes on. Seriously, if Victoria's Secret ever had a brother business called Victor's Secret with men modeling boxer shorts, these two needed to be included. In fact, in my head, that was all I could see.

"Erm, Haley. You have an, erm, strawberry cordial situation going on," Kayla said. "Take a seat, you guys, while we get sorted. Haley had the hiccoughs." She gave me a steely gaze, and I knew better than to say anything. I jolted out of my daydreams, back to the reality of my surroundings and blushed to the roots of my hair. I had red wine dripping down my chin and it was all down my blouse.

"Hi." I decided to add to the charade by doing a hiccough, then I headed for the sink.

"What on earth are you doing? Best behavior. You need these two in your life," hissed Kayla.

I sponged my blouse down, dried it the best I could and sat back down.

"Sorry about that, erm—"

"Chase. Chase Collins."

I stood and held out a hand for him to shake. "Pleased to meet you." I took in Chase's vivid blue eyes and his smile. He had short, blond hair. I'd put him at about six feet tall. At the side of my small frame, he was a giant.

Tiffany turned to me. "And this is your last applicant too, Todd Ross. They are friends and so thought they would attend together."

My mouth dropped open. "Oh, friends, that is so cool. How long y'all been friends for?"

"A couple of years now," Todd said. "We met at work." Again, I spent a moment taking in the appearance of my potential new roommate. Todd was dark haired; olive-skinned; and had deep, dark-brown eyes. He looked like that actor from Lucifer.

Realizing I had been staring, I looked at my list of questions. "And what do you do for an occupation?"

Chase looked across at Todd, who nodded. "We run an adult entertainment company."

"Like paintball?" I asked.

Kayla snorted which I didn't think was amusing or professional.

"No, we film adult movies."

"Porn?" My mouth dropped open again.

"Yes. If you want to call it that," Chase said. "We run a small, reputable company which is like a little family."

"Wow, I bet that is so interesting," Tiff said. "I bet you have a few stories to share."

"We certainly do," Todd replied. His eyes twinkled as he smiled. I couldn't let these two move in. I would be hopeless. I would probably keep forgetting to move. In fact, I would win the record for the longest mannequin challenge while I ogled these two all day.

I managed to conduct myself for the rest of the interview in what I hoped was a professional manner. Then I showed them around and thanked them for coming.

"I have a few applicants to consider, but I will let you know later this evening," I told them. It was very hard to not jump up and down and ask them when they could both move in.

"Not a problem," Chase said. "We will leave you to the rest of your... strawberry cordial..."

I followed his gaze to the kitchen countertop where the opened bottle of wine was on clear display.

I looked back at Chase, and he smirked. He was a cheeky one, this guy. I liked him already.

"Strawberry cordial is the best," I replied. Then I showed them out of the door.

"OH MY FUCKING GOD, they were scrumilicious," I shrieked. "I can't live with them."

"Why not?" Tiff's face had hardened into a frown.

"I mean how am I going to live with them? I'll be permanently in my room with my vibe!"

"They met at work. I wonder if they met behind the camera or in front of it?" Kayla asked.

"You mean they might do the porn?" For the bazillionth time that day my jaw hung open. I was going to need a physician for lockjaw if I carried on.

"Could have started that way. You will have to ask them once they live here," she added. "You need to phone them, like now, before they look anywhere else. They are sexy as fuck and they can help teach you sex by showing you their movies. They might even let you visit the set and get some hands-on expe-rience." Kayla chuckled wickedly.

Taking my cell from my purse, I called the

number Chase had given me and asked if he and Todd fancied being my roommates.

Walking back into the kitchen, I drank some more red wine. "I did it. Jeez, I fucking did it," I told the girls. "I got two hot as fuck male roommates. Now get the pizza ordered. We need to celebrate."

CHAPTER TWO

Haley

I was amazed at how fast we all settled into the new arrangement. The guys worked long hours and often called to see if I wanted takeout. They were going to make me fat. I already had an ass larger than Kim Kardashian's. If they didn't stop feeding me, I was gonna be as wide as I was tall, being as I was only a little over five feet. Chase was a talker. I reckoned I knew his whole life story by now and that of Todd too, as Chase had no filter and just said everything he thought. He was so cheeky with it though. His blue eyes sparkled when he said something risqué. Todd wasn't quiet either, though he struggled to get a word in edge-ways with Chase. Often, he rolled his eyes at me and shook his head. It was nice then on times like tonight when Todd was home and Chase still working and I got to talk with him a little more.

"So, tell me more about how you started GoDown Movies," I asked him while trying to capture noodles with chopsticks. Chase had given a very speedy version of events, seeing as he ran at the mouth, but I wanted to know the full version.

"Simple really. I was working as an attorney and had to assist a company with the legal side of getting their business started. I saw how the big players in the porn world didn't take kindly to anyone muscling in on that territory. Came across a few guys I would rather keep on my good side. I learned it could be pretty lucrative as long as you didn't overstep. So, I set my own small business up, that didn't threaten any of the big players. Soon I didn't need to be an attorney anymore, which was twisting my balls. I had met Chase via the other company; he was a camera-man. We had had drinks a few times and hit it off, both of us wanting to make money, and he left the other fledgling business and joined in my enterprise. We never looked back. By keeping it small, we are left to get on with it."

"God, it sounds dangerous, like the mob or something."

"It's like any business, you have competition. With the adult entertainment industry, some of the bigger players send in the heavies if you are taking money or models away from them. We've learned how to work alongside them; we're no threat and they leave us alone. We reckon we will only need to work for about another five years and we should be financially set. Then we are done. It will be time to look around for the perfect woman and do the whole having kids bit."

"Wow, sounds like you have it all worked out," I said, wishing my own life had any hint of a happy future in it.

"It's all still dreams at the moment, Haley. Gotta have dreams."

"I have nightmares instead," I told him.

"How so? You're a beautiful woman. How come there is no Mr. Haley?" Todd's eyes fixed on me with that dark, brooding stare and I kinda lost my train of thought for a second.

"I don't have any luck with men. Tiff and Kayla are trying to help me. I can't really say why, because it's embarrassing."

"I wouldn't say anything, Haley. I know we have

only been roomies for a couple of months, but you can talk to me."

I sighed. "I suck at sex."

Todd almost choked on a noodle.

"Why on earth would you think that?"

"I've been told several times. Even Kayla and Tiffany seem to have given up on me as I can't get the hang of practicing blow jobs on bananas. I hate bananas."

I realized Todd was almost puce in the face and I couldn't work out if that was because of my declaration or because of his almost choking. I got up and got him a glass of water which was gratefully received.

"Sorry," I told him. "I tend to overshare."

"No, I asked. I just wasn't expecting you to say that."

"Well, Tiff wondered whether you might let me watch filming some time, so I can get an idea; but I'll be honest, I've watched pornos and I don't know how the women bob up and down like that."

"You can't learn from porn, it's unrealistic. We have all sorts of tricks of the trade and most people don't conduct their sex lives like that."

"You say that, but Kayla lives in a polyamorous

relationship, and Tiffany had threesomes with her husband and a man who owns a sex club."

"Did someone say sex club?" Chase walked through the door. "Where, and when are we going?"

"You need a beer, buddy?" Todd asked. "Even you are going to be rendered speechless by what Haley has to tell you."

Chase threw his jacket on the floor in the center of the room, walked over to the fridge where he grabbed a beer, and with the bottle opened, he sprawled across the couch with his feet up.

"Tell me everything." he said. I swear the guy should work for the National Enquirer.

"I have only heard a shortened version of the 'my roommates like threesomes'," Todd added. "Seriously, I figure we could make a movie about Haley, the innocent roommate."

"Screw you," I said and flounced into the kitchen area where I grabbed a bottle of wine.

"You drove her to strawberry cordial, dude," Chase yelled.

I gave him the finger.

"Come on, tell Chase everything." He patted the couch in front of him, indicating a space near his chest. I walked over and thought 'what the hell' and sat down, resting my back against his midriff. His body heat soaked into my skin. I had an urge to snuggle.

"Which bit do you want to know? The I'm hopeless at sex bit, or the gossip about my ex-roommates' romantic lives?"

"Both but start with the roommates. So, they didn't just leave because they fell in love?"

"Well, they did, but they both had awesome, amazing sexcapades."

"Aww, honey. You sound jealous." Chase sat up and pulled me under his arm. I thought I would die of lust as his toned arm wrapped around me and he pulled my head under his chin, stroking my hair. "You will get laid, sweetheart. It will happen. No need to be embarrassed about still being a virgin."

I knocked his arm off me. "I am not a virgin. I am just awful at sex."

Chase looked at me and smirked.

"Stop tormenting her, Chase, or she will withhold the gossip," Todd threatened.

"Sorry, Haley." Chase tried his hardest to make a contrite face but the smirk at the corner of his mouth remained.

"Do you want to know about Kayla and Tiffany?" I asked.

"Totally, yes," Chase answered.

"Then give your mouth a break and your ears a turn."

Todd laughed, a great hearty rumble erupting from his throat. "You've been told." He went to get himself a beer and made himself comfortable in the chair near the couch.

"Okay, so Tiff first. None of the girls hide anything, so I'm not telling you anything I shouldn't. She works for Green's like me and one day she got an email from a mystery guy called H. It said all this stuff he wanted to do to her, you know, dirty stuff. She thought it was from a creep and then she went to show a condo and the businessman was H. His name's Henry Carter and he owns a sex club called Club S.

"Club S? Yeah, we've been there. I might open a Club O, that's the one everyone would wanna visit."

Todd rolled his eyes.

"Anyhow, Brandon moved in next door and he and Tiffany fell in love, but they ended up having threesomes for a while with H. Meanwhile, I couldn't land one guy."

Chase and Todd exchanged glances.

"I know. You want me to carry on. Okay, so then there is Kayla who'd had a crush on her stepfather for-ev-er, except he wasn't really sorta her stepfather because it turned out he and her mother were never together, if you get me, and then she goes to visit him, and Parker is there, her mom's new stepson and she starts a relationship with both of them. Here I am again with no one, I repeat no one, and they have both had two guys."

I then realized I was shouting this fact out to two hot guys and clamped my mouth shut, because what if they thought I was hinting. I kinda hoped they thought I was hinting.

"Anyhow, Tiffany moved in with Brandon and they got married; Kayla moved in with Daniel and Parker a few months back; and now I have you guys to be my new roommates who have to listen to my tales of woe in the dating department."

"I don't remember that being on the lease," Todd added, with a wink.

"Small print. So tiny ya can't see it," I replied.

"So, onto you and your 'tales of woe'," Chase said.

"Okay." I shuffled myself closer to Chase. "I have only had one full on lover and he said I was a pretty bad lover. I thought he was just being bitter when we broke up, but since then when I have gone past first base with other guys, I have either had radio silence afterward, or they tell me I can't perform blow jobs properly. The guy I dated last, another realtor from Greens said I was the reason he couldn't get it up."

"That's bullshit. My dick often goes stiff in your presence, Haley," Chase added.

"Chase. For God's sake," Todd said.

He shrugged. "It's true. Yours does too; tell her."

I held my hand up. "That's okay, Todd." I leaned over and hugged Chase. "But thank you, Chase, for trying to help."

"See, now you made it happen again."

I looked at him horrified and moved a little further away.

"Joking! Oh, girl, you are so cute. Seriously, these guys who you've been dating. They are losers. They are making shit up to cover their own failings."

I shook my head. "Maybe, but there is truth in it. Kayla had me demonstrate a blow job on a bottle. I was hopeless. You should have seen their faces. Complete disbelief. She told Tiffany that she had to teach me with either bananas or dildos. I chose bananas and I bought my own because you never know what is happening around their apartment." I pulled a face.

"So, what happened?" Chase asked.

"I still suck at blow jobs, and I now hate bananas."

"Oh, girl, you need to get some proper practice. You can't learn how to suck a guy on a banana. Our man parts aren't fruit, although my ass is kinda peachy," Chase added.

"She wanted to come watch a movie being made," Todd said. "To learn."

"We will take you to watch one sometime, but that is not how you learn. Now, here, take my beer bottle. Show me. It can't have been that bad."

I took the bottle from him and wrapped my mouth around it like Tiff had said to do, then tried to hollow out my cheeks and suck.

"Oh my god, it's like a puffer fish," Chase exclaimed.

"I told you. I suck at sucking," I yelled. Then I stormed out of the room, slamming the door behind me.

I SAT BACK on my own bed, tears welling in the corner of my eyes. I had done my damnedest to be a good girl my whole life. Never did drugs, passed my exams by studying hard. I deserved to be able to have a damn good fucking. It wasn't fair. My rabbit made me feel things my first boyfriend, Liam, never had, so I knew there was more out there to experience. I just needed to do it. Maybe I would have to ask Henry for a membership to Club S. I could wear a mask and ask men if I could suck their cocks. At least if I was useless at it, they wouldn't see my face, and hey, practice made perfect, right? I decided that after work that next day I would ask Tiffany if she was still in touch with Henry and to get me a membership card.

THE NEXT MORNING, I apologized to the guys. I hoped I hadn't put them off as tenants by being such a girl. I grabbed a coffee in my takeout cup, stuck a slice of toast in between my teeth, and headed out for Green's. I was hoping to get a good bonus this month as there was a pair of five-inch Ferragamo's with my name on them. When you're short like me, heels are everything, and these were everything and more. They were a high heel pump with a black ankle strap and a see-through mesh body with a matching trim.

I headed through the door of the office. Green's was a glass-fronted building located on 7th Avenue. I said good morning to the reception staff and strolled through to my part of the large open-plan office. Deciding I needed more stimulation before I attacked the day, I went into the staff room and pressed the necessary buttons to ensure a perfect latte emerged from the expensive coffee machine in situ.

"Morning, Haley." I turned around to see Malcolm had just come in. Malcolm of the disastrous 'I can't get it up and it's all your fault', date.

"Malcolm," I said tersely. I really didn't want to speak to him.

"Haley." He walked in front of me, so I had no choice but to look at him. He was around five feet ten, slim built, with ash-blond hair and green eyes. His eyes were nice, they looked kindly, which kinda sucked. That's why I had said yes to a date. Shame he was an asshole.

"Sorry, do you want to get to the coffee machine?" I grabbed my drink and backed away.

"No." He placed a hand on my arm. "I wanted to apologize. For when we went out. I was an idiot and not a gentleman. I was embarrassed, you know. I- I've never had that happen to me before. So I blamed you. It was bad form and I'm sorry. I'm also sorry it has taken me so long to come and apologize to you."

"It hurt me, Malcolm. I felt embarrassed too. Like I was less of a woman, you know."

"That's how I felt, Haley, less of a man. I really am so, so sorry. Please, could I take you out again?"

I opened my mouth to protest, but he interrupted.

"Just dinner. To a really nice restaurant. We can talk, get to know each other. Please. Let me take you out and spoil you. You deserve it. I want you to see that is not who I really am."

I sighed and closed my eyes for a moment. I did enjoy eating and here was a free dinner. I opened my eyes. "Okay. Dinner only. I will not be coming back to yours."

"Well, maybe another time we might try again, but for now, dinner. Fantastic. I will pick you up at eight?"

I nodded and then took my coffee back out to the office. We had a large apartment development coming up to sell soon and I needed to spend some time working on my sales pitch if I was to land it for my portfolio. I looked down at my feet and admired my Jimmy Choos. *I won't abandon you*, I promised them. You just have to learn to share.

"YOU'RE DOING WHAT? Going out with that asshole again? Over my dead body, Haley Martin."

I had never seen Chase angry before, but he

looked like he was going to punch a wall. "Todd," he shouted down the hall. "Get out here now."

Todd emerged from his room out into the hallway, rubbing his eyes. "I was having a nap. What's going on?"

"Haley here, has decided to go on another date with floppy dick."

"His name is Malcolm."

"I can't think of anything that goes with an M, all right? So I have named his penis instead."

"You named another man's penis?"

"Yes, and it is not the first time. Is it Todd?"

Todd shook his head, "It really isn't."

"Cancel, and we will take you out instead," Todd said, looking at Chase for his approval.

"Yes, let us take you out. We're much more fun," Chase agreed.

"Thanks, guys, but it is just dinner. He is taking me out because he wants to say sorry for what happened, that's all. It's just to clear the air. I'm going because it has made work awkward, so I need to do this, okay?"

"I am not happy," Chase replied. "Do not give him anything. Not any tongue, or a hand job. Nothing."

"Yes, all right. I won't anyway in case I give him another reason to tell me I'm hopeless in bed."

"Go on your date, lady. Sorry, on your dinner. We are not even calling this a date, and then straight home. We'll be having a chat tomorrow about this whole," he flamboyantly wafted his hand all the way down the front of me but did an extra couple of circles near my pussy, "situation."

I sighed. "Fine, but right now I am going to get ready for my dinner." I left them in the hall and returned to my room. They were more trouble and more dramatic than the girls.

Haley

Malcolm had chosen a steakhouse on 84th Street. When he was due to come pick me up, I had waited outside, rather than let Chase be in shouting distance of him. Malcolm's eyes had trailed down my body and I was about to call him on it, when he informed me I was probably overdressed for where we were going.

When he had said he was taking me for an apology dinner to a nice restaurant, I had wrongly anticipated a nice little Italian like we had gone to on our first date, so the steakhouse had taken me by surprise. Don't get me wrong, I loved eating in any place, but I wished he would have given me a heads up on the location of dinner. I had on a little black dress and heels and wished I could tap my shoes Dorothy style and be in a pair of jeans and a checked button down, with sneakers on my feet.

We ordered two porterhouses on the green, and Malcolm ordered a beer while I asked for water. I wanted to keep a clear head and make sure I didn't fall for any of his sales bullshit. He was a good realtor and that sales charm extended outside of work.

Within five minutes of being there, I once again wished for sneakers, so I could run the hell home. We had shared about three sentences of conversation and the subject of the weather was completely exhausted.

I took a sip of my water and looked around the restaurant. There were couples and families, all engaged in conversation. They wore happy smiles on their faces while they tucked into their food. I wanted that. I wanted to be in a restaurant with my significant others, having a great time. Not stuck here with Malcolm. God, please let my steak get here soon, so I could make my excuses and leave.

"So, about the last time we got together—"

"It's okay, really."

"No, look. I wanted to say. It had been a while for me."

"Oh, okay."

"So, that is probably part of why we had trouble that night, as well as, you know."

I felt my neck tense up. "As well as what?"

"Never mind."

At that point, the waitress delivered our steaks and mine looked so mouth-wateringly delicious that I didn't question Malcolm any further because I didn't want to stab him to death with my steak knife and be prevented from eating my food.

"What do you think about the development of King Park on the Upper East Side?" Malcolm asked. That was the new development I had been trying to get for my portfolio and no doubt a hungry salesman like Malcolm wanted it too.

"It looks great. I'm sure we'll sell most of the apartments off plan, given the location."

Malcolm rambled on about how amazing for families it would be. Personally, I didn't agree. I thought it would make a great place for wealthy businessmen to install their mistresses in a home from home when they were in New York on business, but I wasn't going to share my views. I finished my steak, wiped my mouth with a napkin and sat back.

"Would you like a dessert?" he asked.

"No, thank you, Malcolm. I'm feeling beat. If it's okay with you, I'd like to go home now."

"Before you go…"

"Yeah?" I sighed.

"I have a proposition for you."

I started to get up from the table before he tried to get in my pants again.

"It's about Green's."

When I realized it was about business, I relaxed and turned to him.

"What's that?"

"I thought we could partner up on King Park. We could be a killer team, Haley. We're both great at sales and we're both hot. You can flirt with the husbands, and me the wives, right?"

I was simply speechless. Was this man for real?

"Then I thought we could extend our partnership back home." He winked. He actually fucking winked at me. "I figure I'll have no problems from here on out, and I don't mind giving you a few pointers on technique."

Thank goodness I had not finished my carafe of water because it was in easy reach and gave me much more satisfaction dripping down Malcolm's face than it would have my throat. I most definitely preferred red wine.

"You arrogant ass," I screamed.

Malcolm's eyes swept around the restaurant, noting the faces of the people who had stopped eating and were now our captive audience.

"I will land King Park by myself and as for your limp hot-dog, (I was mindful there were children listening), find another roll for it because it is certainly not getting eaten by me." I threw money on the table to cover my portion of the bill because there was no way I was owing the guy anything, then I turned on my heel and stomped out, waving down a cab and heading back to my own apartment far earlier than I had envisioned. I had really wanted a sundae too.

It wasn't even 10pm and yet the lights were out at the front of the apartment. Looked like Chase and Todd might have gone out too. I was glad. It meant I could sulk on the couch for a couple hours and watch a movie, preferably something where a godawful guy got beaten to death. I opened the door of the apartment and saw a light was on in Chase's room. Did he ever turn them off and think about the environment? I hung my jacket, dropped my purse in the hallway and walked down to his room to turn it off. Then I heard moaning. I stopped in my tracks. Shit. Did Chase have a woman in his room?

Then I heard Chase's voice, as clear as day, yell out, "Fuck, Todd, I'm coming."

What the hell?

I tiptoed down the hall. My mind yelled at me to go back to my room, but my body propelled me forward. I stared through the crack between the door and the door jamb and my heart thudded at the scene in front of me. Todd was laid across Chase's chest, his cock in his hand. His dick was huge, with thick veins, and was an angry purple as if it was desperate to explode. Chase's dick laid at the side of his leg, cum smeared on it after he had clearly just shot his load. I knew I should back away, this was private, but I was in shock. How had I not realized they were a couple? Had they deliberately tried to conceal it from me, or was I just that goddamn naive and stupid I hadn't noticed what was in front of my face? I was certainly noticing what was in front of my face now. Two cocks. I examined Chase's. Though it was currently not erect, it appeared a decent size and was quite wide. Two huge dicks. They were lucky guys. I stayed by the doorway as Todd reached over to grab a bottle of lube. He tipped some out into his hand and then coated his dick. Then he lowered himself further down and lining his cock with Chase's ass, he thrust forward into Chase's puckered hole. Chase gasped, his face contorting in ecstasy as he placed his hand back on his own cock, which stirred into life. I watched the men in front of me fuck: Todd thrusting away until sweat beaded his forehead, Chase's head hitting the headboard with each thrust. They were caught in a frenzied fuck until with a shout Todd reached his release, filling Chase's ass with his cum. Then he shuffled right off the end of the bed and took Chase's cock in his mouth where he sucked it until Chase came again, swallowing his load and licking his lips. I quietly backed away, not wanting to intrude on any intimacy. What I had done, spying on them like that was bad enough. I tiptoed back to my own room, where I stripped off my clothes, wiped the makeup from my face and hit the shower. In the privacy of my own bathroom, away from the other bedrooms, and with the shower masking any sounds, I let the tears fall, while I reached some kind of high level of hysteria. Not only was I so bad in bed people felt they had to offer me lessons, but I was the only woman in the world who could get herself two hot roommates and discover they were gay. I sat on the floor of the shower while water cascaded down me and sobbed until I had nothing left to give.

When I eventually left the shower and toweled myself off, I put on my sleep shorts and cami, climbed under my comforter, and came to an agreement with myself. I would definitely see Tiffany tomorrow and contact Henry Carter. I was going to become the best fucking fuck there was. A blow job queen, and nothing was going to stop me. Haley Martin was not going to take this lying down I thought, then I realized that yes, I probably was. That thought made me smile and with that, I fell asleep.

USUALLY, on a Saturday I still got up early so I could make the most of the day, but this morning I stayed in bed and waited until I heard Chase and Todd leave. They had started going to Brandon's gym as he had promised to help them develop a fitness regime, and Saturday mornings were a day they could stick to. It also meant I knew that Tiffany was probably at home. She may have become a gym bunny with a fitness instructor husband, but I knew she was a lazybones and was no doubt currently making the most of being able to starfish in bed.

I got out of bed, wrapped myself in my robe, added bed socks to my ensemble because my feet were like ice, and then I padded down the hall and into our living space where I headed for the kitchen and set up the coffee machine for some fresh heaven in a mug. I grabbed my phone from the side and saw I had a message.

MALCOLM: **You embarrassed yourself last night. You owe me an apology.**

WAS HE SERIOUS? I felt my temper build again. I hit Tiff's number and listened to it ring.

"Mmmmph."

"Tiff. Code red."

There was a muffled response which sounded akin to 'hold on' and then I heard bedlinen rustle.

"What is it, girl. Who do I need to kill?"

"Can I come round? I'm still in my sleep shorts. I'll bring coffee."

"I'll leave the door unlocked. Lock it behind you. You will find me under the comforter."

I made two coffees and put them in reusable

cups from a local coffee shop chain and went around next door. Pushing open the door, I was always surprised at how similar their apartment was to ours. The only difference being theirs was a two bed apartment.

I pushed open Tiff's bedroom door. I could just see a bird's nest of blonde hair poking out of the top of the comforter.

I put her coffee on her nightstand and got on the top of the covers and huddled next to her.

Tiff emerged slowly, an inch at a time until her head was visible. Then she sat up and grabbed her coffee from the nightstand.

"So, code red, huh?"

"Yes. Like the quote I saw on Pinterest last week, it would appear rock bottom has a basement."

She placed an arm around me. "What's happened, honey?"

"I went on another date with Malcolm."

"You did what?" she screeched.

"I know, I know. He said he wanted to take me to dinner to apologize for his behavior last time. Really, he just wanted to feel me out for my secrets on King Park. He wants to muscle in on the development he knows I will get. I have worked my ass off, there's no way he is getting his hands on it. Especially not now, the limp-dick."

"Oh dear. So another unsuccessful date?"

"Well, one of us ended up wet, but it wasn't me, and it was courtesy of a carafe of water."

Tiff burst out laughing.

"Good for you. I'm not seeing why this is a code red though. You already knew the guy was a dick."

"I came home and discovered Chase and Todd fucking."

"Oh."

"Yes, indeed, oh."

"So, that must have been embarrassing for you all?"

"They don't know I saw. I spied on them through the crack in the door, like a voyeur. Seriously, I couldn't avert my gaze."

"So is it hot seeing two guys together?"

"Tiff! Are you not listening to me? My roomies are gay. Gay! The roommates I chose with a potential apartment orgy in mind are gay. Not only do I get no sexy times, but I have to hear them at it!"

"It's not that bad."

"Not that bad? Sure, perhaps they could move Malcolm in and then all three could go at it while he tells me their cocks get him hard."

Another round of laughter burst from Tiff.

"God, you are not taking this seriously. I'm hurting Tiff. I came by for sympathy. You don't even sound surprised. Was it obvious to you they were together? Is it just me with no gaydar? Anyway, I need you to get in touch with H for me."

Tiff sat up straight in bed. Holding a hand up at me to get me to be quiet, she took a large gulp of her coffee before placing it back on the bedside table. "H? Henry? Why do you want me to contact him?"

"I want a membership to Club S. Do they have nights where they wear masks? I need to go in without anyone knowing who I am, so I can practice sex and sucking cock."

"Seriously, there is no need, Hales."

"No need! You are hearing about my sad, desperate love life, aren't you?"

"Yes, and that's why I gave your apartment details to Chase and Todd."

My hand flew to my chest and I gasped.

"What? You gave them my details? You knew I wanted hot guys and stuck me with two gay men?"

"They are not gay, they are bisexual. They like pussy too."

"Fuck this coffee's strong. I swear you just said you set me up with bisexual roommates," I yelled.

"Calm down. Yes, I did. I knew you wanted some hot roommates and I'd seen your applicants. There weren't any. So I called Henry and asked him if he knew anyone who was looking for a place. He put out feelers and came back with Chase and Todd. They are looking for a permanent partner. A female. They are together, have been for a while, but as I said, they like pussy too and they are thinking of the future and potentially having a family.

My mouth did its usual jaw drop. Seriously, I was going to need plastic surgery for saggy skin around my jaw if this kept up.

"What the, erm..."

"I'm sorry, Hales. I know this must be a shock, but I was thinking of what you said. There is no pressure. Chase and Todd were looking for an apartment, but they didn't move in expecting you to be part of the arrangement. They planned on looking around and then moving when they found someone. I was just wanting for you to have the option. That is if maybe you liked them and they you... well, it could work out. Or at least give you some practice."

"I seriously, like don't know what to think. I forgot I'd been asking advice from Mrs. Tiff Three-way-I-went-out-on-stage-and-had-sex-with-an-audi-ence-watching Bailey. So, get a hot roomie Haley.

Why stop there? Get two roomies, hell, make them bisexual and wanting a female as a trio. Is there some three-way club you and Kayla joined and now you're co-opting me or something?"

Tiff smiled. The girl could have been offended but she was so happy she didn't give a crap about my outburst.

"Hey, I know how much fun it can be. I got it out of my system, but look at Kayla. She's in it for life. Normal dating isn't working out so well for you, so why not try this?"

"So, what do I do? Just go home and say, 'hey guys, I saw you fucking and well I would like to join in, can I have a sample. Is there an audition?'."

"Well, not quite like that, but I would tell them you saw them and just open a dialogue. Ask them about themselves. They are really open according to Henry. I figured they would have told you soon about themselves anyway once you were all settled."

I sat back and thought about what I had just learned. Tiff yawned so wide she nearly broke her jaw. I crawled under the comforter. "Okay, I'm staying for a nap. My mind has exploded. Put the alarm on for in a couple hours."

"Oh, thank Christ, I'm beat," Tiff said and with that, we both fell asleep.

. . .

"OH, Tiffany, all my dreams have come true. Are we having a threesome with Haley?"

Tiff had failed to set an alarm and it was now early afternoon and Brandon had returned from his classes. He stood in the doorway and took his tee off revealing a muscled torso and corded arms. She was a lucky girl, but even if he had been serious, there was no way I was doing anything with a) my friend's husband, and b) girls. No thank you.

Tiffany leaped out of bed and threw her arms around her husband. "Missed you, baby."

"Missed you too. I'm just going to hit the shower."

I took one look at my friend's face and launched myself out of bed. "I am off back to mine. Thanks for the chat, Tiff. Good to see you, Brandon. Now it looks like your wife wants to join you in the shower, so I am leaving before you guys do something in front of me that makes me want to vomit."

"And there I was thinking you liked to watch after last night," Tiff quipped.

"What about last night?" Brandon asked.

"Shut it, Tiff, and Brandon, never you mind,

although Tiff's mouth is so big, no doubt you'll know before I've even left."

"Hey, I have no complaints about her big mouth. She needs it for my big—"

I placed my hands over my ears, "Lalalalala." I reversed out of the room and left. I'd get my coffee cups back later. For now, I made my escape.

CHAPTER FOUR

<u>Haley</u>

My mind was reeling.

Bisexual roommates.

Hot roommates.

Threesomes.

The fact Tiff had engineered this on purpose.

Would Chase and Todd see me as a potential lover? I would seriously doubt it given I had told them how hopeless in bed I was. It was like winning the booby prize on a chat show and even then, I only had a small handful—what should have gone to my breasts had wandered off and accidentally added to my ass.

I hated my inexperience. At twenty-four I should know what I was doing.

I crawled back into my own bed. There was no sign of the guys and stuck for anything else to do that wasn't a chore, I powered up my laptop, positioned it on its laptop cushion and went to a porn site that Kayla never stopped raving about. I typed in two men and one woman and a host of videos displayed. I kept seeing the words MMF and MFM so I went onto Google to find out what the definitions stood for. I quickly discovered that MFM was like what Kayla and Tiffany had experienced, a threesome where the guys didn't get involved with each other; but MMF was everyone involved with each other, so as well as fucking the female they'd have sex with each other too, do blow jobs, etc. The videos were rated and so I chose one with a high percentage which hopefully meant it was good and sat back and watched.

In this video, a couple: one man, and one woman had advertised for a male partner to join them. It wasn't long before everyone's clothes were off. In the beginning, the woman laid back on the bed while one man licked her pussy and another thrust his cock down her throat. I felt my legs pulse and my pussy instantly got wet. The man withdrew his cock and started sucking on her breasts. Hands, mouths, and cocks were everywhere. I started to see why Kayla and Tiff had been so into their threesomes. This was HOT. Then, as one man started to fuck the woman, he leaned over and took the other guy's cock in his mouth. My heart beat faster. It was so erotic! I was surprised at myself. Why was the thought of a man with another man turning me on? I couldn't explain it, but I wasn't about to stop watching! They switched around again and this time the woman was being fucked in the pussy by a guy who was himself getting fucked in the ass. I moved my hand down my pajama shorts and started flicking my nub as I watched. I wanted to watch another scene with a woman getting her pussy eaten so I clicked on another clip. Once it got to a scene where a man was between her legs while another man fucked him from behind, I frantically rubbed at my clit while two fingers from my other hand pistoned inside my pussy. I tried not to be distracted by the fact that the laptop was jiggling up and down on my lap while I did it. I was pleased there was no one home, so that when I came, I screamed out loud as the tension I'd been holding dissipated from my body and left me in some kind of come-coma.

"Sounds like someone is having a good time." Chase's voice came from the hallway.

"Yeah, she must have brought the guy home. He is obviously very good at apologizing," Todd added.

My face flamed red. Oh my fucking God, they'd heard me and there was no one else in here. I was going to have to lie and somehow fake I'd just snuck him out of the apartment.

I quickly showered and then I left my room walking over to the apartment door, opening it and yelling, "Yeah, see you again sometime." Then I closed the door with a slam, so my roommates could hear it. I walked through to the living area and stretched like I'd had a great evening. I hated lying but there was no way I wanted them to know I had been solo when I'd climaxed like a singer practicing scales.

"Some mighty skills your guy has there, Haley. The power to make you screech like a freight train and then invisibility. Is it a cloak like in Harry Potter?"

Chase was staring out of the front window.

I tilted my chin up at him. "He jogs. He got out of here in no time."

"That may have worked if Chase hadn't been looking out of the window for the last ten minutes as he thinks the mailwoman is fit," Todd added. "Don't be ashamed about enjoying your body, Haley. We all do it. Perhaps your confidence would grow if you owned your body a little more. We are all adults. Chase and I don't care."

"Yeah, about that," I answered, seeing an opportunity to divert attention away from myself, "Last night when I got back home, I heard you two."

"Ah," Todd said. "Looks like we could use a chat. Shall we order pizza? I'm ravenous."

"You don't have anything to explain. I just wanted to let you know that I knew and that I am totally cool with all that, anything at all, any scenario you have going down."

Chase looked bemused, a smirk quirked his lip. "Like what? We didn't have animals in there or torture equipment."

I blushed again. "I don't know. Anything men do together, or if they have a woman in there as well. I am cool with it all. Go for it."

Todd walked over and folded me in his arms. I only reached his chest and so my face was smushed into his rock-hard pecs. I didn't want to move. "Oh, Haley. I might not have known you very long, but, babe, I adore you. You are so entirely sweet and endearing and innocent."

"I find it a problem myself," I mumbled into his chest.

"I'm going to order pizza and then we'll crack open some beer. For fuck's sake don't tell Brandon, after we just worked out with him. He was advising us to eat poached salmon and a side salad for lunch."

I giggled. "Your secret is safe with me as long as we get pepperoni."

"Blackmail, hey?" Chase added. "Well, this time I'll allow it seeing as you now know Todd and myself both like to eat meat."

"Oh my god, you didn't just say that." Todd covered my ears. "Don't listen to him, he's disgusting."

"Yeah, that's not what you were saying last night," Chase quipped. "Now while I order the pizza, Todd you get the beers, and Haley, please set the table."

I was pleased to note that rather than my operatic orgasm making me uncomfortable around the two men, now that they knew I knew they were a couple, everything was actually more relaxed. It was like a barrier had been broken through and we could talk about anything. I loved it because it was similar to the relationship I had with the girls, but now I was getting a male perspective on things, something I sorely needed.

When I told them about Malcolm they went insane.

"I am coming to your work. I am going to kick him in the balls," Chase said.

"If you need me to have a word, Haley, just say it and I'll be there. Only I'll use words rather than physical violence." Todd rolled his eyes in Chase's direction.

"No. I will get my revenge. I am going to get that development and rub his face in it when I make a huge commission."

"You need a goal, other than to beat Malcolm," Todd said. "Something to aim for. What do you want to get with the money?"

I explained about the shoes.

"Fuck the fuck-me heels. You can have those, but you're going to earn megabucks. What's something huge you want to aim for?" Chase asked.

I sat back for a moment resting against the back of the couch. "I would really love to go on a vacation where you are at the edge of the ocean and you eat on the beach. What people have for honeymoons, except I'm not married. But I have no one to go with and I'm not doing that on my own. I just don't see why honeymooners should own that kind of vacay. I want to be spoiled and massaged."

"We will come with you, babe. We need a break," Chase declared, looking at Todd.

"Yeah, well, great that we have these full and frank discussions where everyone gets their say." Todd raised an eyebrow.

"So, I'll go with you on my own, honey." Chase mock-whispered.

"Now, I didn't say I wouldn't go. Did I?" Todd retorted. "I'd just like it if for once you discussed things with me before you went jumping in with both feet."

Chase waved a hand in front of his own face. "Do I ever do that?"

"No." Todd sighed. "You don't. I am wasting my breath." Then he smiled at me. "You get that bonus, darlin', and we will go on that vacation with you."

I leaped up and hugged each of them in turn. "You guys are amazing, thank you."

The pizza arrived and we sat stuffing our faces. Thankfully, Brandon was obviously too busy in bed with Tiff to notice the arrival of the high calorie delivery.

"So how long have you two been together?" I asked when we were all laid back in various places around the living room rubbing our stomachs. I was on the couch, Todd was laid across the chair, and Chase was lying across the floor.

"Two years," Todd said. "We met at work. Both had girlfriends at the time. We hit it off as buddies and went on a double-date. Not long afterwards we realized we preferred each other to our girlfriends."

"I'd had both male and female partners before," Chase added. "But Todd was straight until then."

"I'd been curious, but not done anything," Todd said. "I was confused because I really liked pussy and found women attractive. I knew you could be bisexual, but kind of didn't believe it. I thought you would be more one thing than another. That it was a confused mind rather than a perfectly normal thing."

"So, we have had a committed relationship with each other, as in no more male partners in the last eighteen months, but we have had an open relationship where pussy is concerned," Chase added.

"But that is something else we are looking to change," Todd said. "We are going to look for a woman who can complete our relationship. Become part of a committed threesome. We know it could take time and it runs a risk of things not working out, but we would like a family someday—a stable family life—and that's where we see our future. We don't want to be out seeking pussy and the other one not involved. It doesn't seem right anymore." Todd looked at me intently. "I guess this is a lot to take in, right?"

"No, it's really not. I totally get it. It's a progression of your relationship to the next level that works for you. I applaud you for making such a great choice between you. You seem to have your shit together which is a lot more than other couples I know. Can I be honest about something?" The conversation and the beer in the afternoon had loosened my tongue.

"Sure," Todd said.

"I am really surprised but I find the thought of you two together, in general, a turn on. When I was in my room before, I was curious. I looked up some MMF. Tiff had told me a little already this morning about what you were looking for, so I kinda wanted to check out what it was about."

"Your 'little death' scream was at an MMF movie?" Chase's eyes widened.

"Yeah," I said, wondering why I'd confessed that and hoping I hadn't made things awkward.

Chase leaped up. "So, we think you're hot. Do you think you might try with us? Date us, with a view to it maybe leading to something else? I am more than willing to teach you about sex."

My mouth fell open and I bet my eyes bulged with shock. I was completely speechless.

Todd put his head in his hands. "Discussion, Chase. For fuck's sake, discussion first."

"I am discussing it. What the hell else am I doing? There are words and they are being directed at Haley. Discussion."

"More like word vomit pouring from your mouth, but it's done now. So," Todd gave me that intense look again. "Do you want to date us both, Haley?"

CHAPTER FIVE

Haley

"So how about we take you out to dinner on Monday evening as a first date?" Chase asked.

"No can do. It's girls' night Mondays at Tiffs."

"Does Brandon join in with any nail painting?" he asked.

"No," I giggled. "Brandon is usually at the gym, or he goes for a beer. We used to have a girls' night every Monday when the girls both lived here. It was a tradition."

"Well, we could do something similar?"

I shrugged. "Thanks, but it wouldn't be the same.

It was chick flicks and moaning about men basically, oh and gossip from work. We will probably stop doing them soon because everyone's moving on with their lives."

"Why don't you still have them here on a Monday? We can make ourselves scarce. If we are going to be in a relationship, it would be healthy for you to have some time with your friends to be able to kick back and relax."

"Chase, we haven't even taken her on a date yet."

"Haley?" Chase came over to me and put his arm around me. "When we came for the interview, did you think to yourself, these guys will be great room-mates, or these HOT guys can move in anytime because I can perve at them all day?"

"Kinda the second one to be honest."

"I have nothing further, your honor," Chase said to Todd.

"I would love to be able to move girls' night back here if that was okay with you two. Half the time Tiff's doesn't have any clean mugs or plates. I like to prepare snacks etc. It's fun."

"That it, it's settled then. From tomorrow evening, we shall leave you to your friends and then Tuesday night we are taking you on a date. Where would you like to go?"

I sucked on my lip while in thought. "Could we go back to the Italian restaurant I went to on my first disastrous date with Malcolm? It was really nice in there. I would like to wipe my memories of being there with him and replace them with some new ones."

"Done. Call and make reservations for eight-thirty." Chase commanded. He so made me laugh.

We spent the evening ordering yet more takeout and watching game shows. I felt so comfortable with these guys, like I had known them forever. The thought of getting to know them intimately made my stomach bubble with both excitement and anxiety. The risk was that we could ruin the happy roommate situation we had going on, but then, what the hell, there were other roommates, and to be honest if this didn't work I would probably go join a convent anyway.

"Look, Todd, she's smiling, and the contestant just said she recently lost her husband. I do believe our Haley is daydreaming about our huge cocks."

"Shut up," I yelled at Chase, and picking up a cushion I whacked him with it in the chest.

"If you want to knock the wind out of me, you need to whack me with that fat ass, not a tiny cushion." Chase grabbed me and pulled me across his lap.

"Stop it, Oh my god, Chase, what are you doing?"

"I am having a feel of this lovely ass." He gave it a slap.

"Ooh, it is so bouncy. Come and have a feel, Todd."

"Leave the poor woman alone." Todd stood up. "Come on, we are off to bed."

Chase stood me back on my feet. "Remember where we left off for Tuesday." Then he winked and they left me in the living room.

AT GREEN'S the next day I couldn't help but keep smiling to myself because I had two gorgeous men taking me out the next evening, and also, I might be having some dirty, hot sex. At last!

I noted that Malcolm kept watching me with a narrowing of his eyes. I ignored him and kept tapping into my computer, making notes for a presentation I had to make tomorrow afternoon.

A colleague called me to help with the photo-copier and when I got back Malcolm was near my desk. Fortunately, I had all my documents password protected so the only thing he could have looked at was my cell laid on the top of my desk.

"Something you need, Malcolm?" I asked.

"No, not at all. I was just wondering how you were getting on with King Park. Only I have been speaking to a couple of the developers."

This didn't bother me. I knew Arthur Green, our owner, would not like Malcolm going directly to the developers. The developers went through Arthur. It was ultimately his say so. My meeting tomorrow was with Arthur and the main developer, but Malcolm didn't know that.

"Ah, that's fantastic. I also have a meeting about the development tomorrow."

"You do? Well, I'm very pleased for you. Let the best man or woman win, yes?"

"Indeed." I gave him a tight smile. "Will that be all then, Malcolm? I am very busy."

He backed away in his dark black suit looking like a retreating slug. I couldn't believe I had ever entertained the thought of dating him. I picked up my phone. I had a message from Chase.

I CALLED LEONIES. **Table for three booked for 8:30pm. Todd and I look forward to enjoyable discussions about our deal!**

.   .   .

THE MESSAGE BOX was marked as already open. I smirked to myself. If Malcolm was as pathetic as I thought he would be, my date tomorrow would be even more fun.

"HALEY, BABY. I MISSED YOU, BITCH." Kayla bent down and ruffled the top of my head.

"It has only been a week. Get off me and get in the kitchen. You can get that wine you brought with you opened."

"Yes, Miss." She saluted me.

"How are things anyway?" I asked her. Kayla looked pretty as a picture. The sun had brought out her freckles and she had a healthy glow to her usually milk-white skin. She was wearing a floral tea dress and looked stunning and I told her so.

"Why, thank you." She did a twirl. "The dress is down to a lovely little vintage unit near the gallery and the healthy glow is due to nude sunbathing in the back yard and lots of sex."

"How is the gallery?" I asked, diverting her from the subject of sex until Tiff was here too.

"Amazing. Daniel has had interest in a picture

we all did together called Submit. I think his career could be about to explode."

"That is amazing for him."

"I know. The guy works so hard. His paintings are selling so quickly right now and people are on a wait list for his works. He has been offered ridiculous amounts of money for commissioned works but refuses now to paint portraits. He wants to paint what he wants and while people are waiting to buy whatever he produces, why not?"

"Why not indeed?"

"Hi, girls." Tiff walked through the door and planted herself straight onto the couch. "I am fucked and not from Brandon. I have been all over the place today. Sold a condo in Queens and a brownstone at Upper East Side."

"Just stay away from King Park."

"You so have that in the bag."

"Not according to Malcolm."

"God, I hate that man. He does nothing but stare at my tits."

"Tiff, we all stare at your tits, darling, they're huge," Kayla added.

"Not like him. He's a slimeball."

"He will get what is coming to him. I shall make sure of it. I am a firm believer in karma," I told them.

"Right, let's eat because we have tons to gossip about."

The poor chick flick never got played that evening because we didn't come up for air. Tiff told us that she and Brandon were going to try for a baby which brought tears of joy to us all. Kayla was so obviously happy with her home life and new career helping sell art. She said she didn't miss Green's at all, mainly because there the boss didn't call her up in the middle of the day for a massive sex marathon. Tiff and I thought of old Arthur Green with his bald pate and pot belly and made a mock heave. The guy was lovely, and around sixty-two years of age.

"Well, ladies. Tomorrow evening, I have a date," I announced, followed by my breaking out into a beaming smile.

Tiff and Kayla exchanged a look.

"What was that look all about? Aren't you pleased for me?" I asked. "I haven't even told you who it's with yet."

"Haley, babes. All your recent dates have gone to shit. We are worried rather than excited."

"Well, I have high hopes for this one because I know them already."

"Well, we know it's not Malcolm, so who is it with?" Kayla asked.

"Chase and Todd."

Tiff squealed while Kayla's forehead creased. "Chase and Todd."

"Yes, I am taking a leaf out of your books, and I am going out with two men at the same time."

"Fuck me," Kayla said. "That didn't take you long."

"I am so happy," Tiff said. "I kinda set the situation up. Henry knows them."

"Ahhh, so have they been part of the club scene?"

"I think so," Tiff said. "I guess you'd know more about that than me though, Hales."

"I'll ask them tomorrow on our date." I scrunched up my nose in excitement.

"So they're okay with sharing you?" Kayla asked. "Only it can become problematic. People get jealous. We had some issues at first. Parker can get very jealous at times."

"Well, that's something we'll have to work out, but they're together, Kayla. To-ge-ther. I'd be their female."

"An MMF? You're a fucking unicorn."

I scratched my cheek. "I'm a what?"

"A unicorn. Some people don't like it being called that so don't say it out loud anywhere like the club if you go, but it's a term for when bisexual men seek a female partner to have their babies, I think. Something like that anyway."

"And they said unicorns didn't exist and yet I may become one. Can I get rainbow colored hair?"

"That's My Little Pony, not a unicorn. Now, anyway, don't get carried away. See how the date goes. No harm done if you decide to change your mind," Tiff said.

"Fuck them first," Kayla said. "Then decide."

"You are so... oh my god, so... Kayla, sometimes," Tiffany groaned.

"Well, what happened to you Tiff. 'See how the date goes'. You turned up to the condo and fucked Henry's brains out without a second thought."

"Yes, but this is our little Hales."

"Stop being shortist," I giggled. "I'm only a month younger than you and two months younger than Kayla."

"Indeed, sweetheart, listen to the voice of experience." Kayla winked.

"So, what should I wear tomorrow?" I asked them. "They already know what I look like at my best and my worst. Do I still make an effort?"

"Absolutely," they both said in unison.

"It's a date. You dress up for the date just as you

would any date. Let them know you are willing to make an effort for them," Tiff said.

"Seriously fuckable underwear underneath the dress. Lace, as see-through as possible, but no peep-holes or crotchless on a first date. Leave that for the second when they have already seen everything. Just a tease first time around."

I glanced over at Tiffany and took in her face as she looked at Kayla like she couldn't believe what she had just said. For a minute I imagined being in a room with Chase and Kayla together and I burst out laughing.

"What's so funny?"

"I just miss you ladies. I'm looking forward to a possible new future, but Monday nights have to stay forever you two. Promise me."

They both agreed to the promise and then something Kayla said earlier came to the front of my mind.

"Kayla. Earlier, you said something about a painting. That you all did it together. What do you mean? Have you become an artist too?"

"Christ, no." Kayla guffawed. "The three of us covered ourselves in paint and fucked on a canvas. Something I said gave Daniel the idea." She looked at our faces. "I know it sounds gross, but seriously, the picture is amazing. It's like our love displayed across the canvas. We did two and our other one is up on the living room wall."

"Well, look at that, Kayla might be maturing. Love displayed across the canvas," Tiff mimicked.

"Yeah, right, those are Daniel's words. I focused more on how well hung the men were than the canvas."

We rolled our eyes and laughed.

CHAPTER SIX

Haley

I'd felt strangely nervous all day. Although I'd kept telling myself I was just going out to eat with my roommates and to not think past that, I couldn't help it. I was wondering if I had made a huge mistake. Why hadn't I stuck to my original plan and gone to the club? Malcolm kept looking at me and smirking too which was pissing me off. I didn't have the energy to deal with his crap today. I was so nervous about the date tonight that my meeting with Arthur and the developer went like a dream. My presentation was immaculate.

I could tell Arthur was pleased. His face stayed relaxed throughout the meeting, and he didn't remove his jacket. If Arthur got tense, he got hot, and the jacket came off. The developer, Elias King, took me by surprise. I didn't know what I expected but it hadn't been a good-looking older man. He looked to be in his mid-forties with a sprinkling of black and gray stubble to his chin, and salt and pepper hair, spiked on the top. Most men his age wouldn't get away with that hairstyle, but he did. The pull of his shirt across his chest suggested he kept in shape. When we first met, his handshake had been firm and his hands soft, an indication that he may have started out in construction but now his business was conducted in boardrooms.

"I want someone I can work closely with on this development. Someone I can trust implicitly. I anticipate most of the properties will sell off to wealthy clients... clients who may not want others to be aware of their purchase. At this price range they could be, how can I put it, *choosy*, with their requirements."

"Haley handles many of our more exclusive residences. That's why I felt she would be a good fit for your development," Arthur commented.

I smiled. "I've dealt with many wealthy clients

and *choosy* requests. Obviously, I can't give you details as it's all entirely confidential, but I can assure you that your potential buyers will all be handled with the utmost discretion."

"Well, I'm very happy with what I've seen here today, Arthur, and I would like to accept Haley as my realtor for the development. Haley, my PA will be in touch to arrange for us to meet at the development, so I can show you around personally. I know you've visited before, but I'd like to ensure you know my vision for the place. King Park, is, in my mind, a unique development."

"Of course." I nodded. "I will wait to hear from your assistant. Thank you for allowing me to take on your development. You have my promise that your vision will be carried through. I'm looking forward to working for you."

"With me, not for me, Haley. No one I work with is my subordinate. I hate bosses who make their staff feel like they're somehow inferior."

Arthur clapped him on the back, taking me by surprise. "That's because your father brought you up right. I can't tell you how much I miss him. Haley is a superstar. You'll not have a finer realtor."

Arthur turned to me. "Thank you, Haley."

I got up to leave.

"Ah, just one more thing," Elias announced. "Can we not announce yet who is leading the development? I have another little deal happening where they might be put off if they know they haven't got this as part of the package."

"We'll leave it until you give us the go ahead," Arthur said.

"My lips are sealed," I told Elias. His mouth twitched as I said it. Surely, he wasn't flirting with me a little?

I had left the meeting and headed straight into the ladies bathroom. Checking no-one was around I'd squealed and done a little dance. I had got the development! *Fuck you, Malcolm,* I thought. I was going to have to try very hard not to do a little dance in front of his face with an accompanying smug grin.

Speaking of the devil; I hadn't even been back at my desk for ten minutes before he sidled over.

"You look nice today, Haley. Not that you usually don't, but you look extra nice today. Have you been, or are you going anywhere nice? I noticed you left your desk earlier."

"Not that it's any of your business, but Arthur wanted to check in with me about something."

His jaw tensed. "About King Park?"

"You're obsessed with that project. Not every-thing centers around it, you know? There are other properties to sell."

"Yes, but Elias King is a billionaire. To work for him could be to set yourself up for life. Word on the street is he's going to set up his own property management company, so he can keep it in-house."

"Well, I wouldn't know about that, and I am perfectly happy working here at Green's, so if that is all, I have work to do."

"Fine. Catch you later, Haley." He gave me that smirk again. I would have liked to slap it off his face.

I GOT HOME and went straight to my room to prepare for my date. I decided on a Nine West navy-blue, fit and flare dress that skimmed over my ass. It was sleeveless with a round neck and had a brown belt that cinched in my waist. I added some Michael Kor's 'Becky' dress sandals to my feet to give me some height, and grabbed my MK 'Mercer' clutch. My make-up was all smoky eyes and a red lip, and my dark hair was fixed up in a messy bun with a few stray tendrils around my face. I did the mirror shuffle where you tried to see yourself from all angles and I was pleased to see that I'd cleaned up quite well. I headed out to the living room to wait for my dates. Todd had agreed to drive us, saying that he was fine with not having a drink that evening.

"Cancel the restaurant, let's just take her to bed," Chase yelled out, jumping up and walking around me. "Fuck, Miss Martin, you look HOT."

"Chase. She is going to run back to her room in a minute," Todd scolded him.

"No, I'm not. I am totally used to him by now." I giggled. "You both look very nice yourselves. Anyone would think you were involved in property development," I winked.

"Do you really think sleaze ball will turn up tonight?" Chase asked.

"I would put money on it," I told him. "He has been smirking at me all day and he definitely read that text."

"Well, we have had an idea and we think you will love it." Todd gave me a wink back. It was nice to see Todd's more playful side. He was a lot more serious than Chase, but I just thought he took a bit longer to warm up to people. "Your carriage awaits, Mademoiselle," he added, and with that, we left the apartment and made our way to the restaurant.

Leonies was a mid-sized restaurant decorated in black and white with fifties movie posters on the walls and chandeliers hung from the ceilings. Black gloss tables had the obligatory candle on them, and the lighting was dimmed and had an orange glow to remove some of the starkness that the monotone color scheme would usually display. Todd pulled out my chair for me, a black leather cushioned back and seat alongside a silver-colored frame. Then he and Chase took their own seats opposite mine.

"Oh, it looks like we are interviewing her, I'll move," Chase said and he moved to sit to my left.

When the waiter came to take our order, I looked across at Todd. "Todd, if I ordered a half bottle of champagne would you be able to have one glass, only we are celebrating tonight."

"Yes, one would be okay." He looked at me, waiting for me to elaborate.

"Are we celebrating our threesome?" Chase asked. The waiter's eyes almost fell out of his head.

"Stop tormenting the wait staff," Todd chided. The waiter looked at us and laughed as if it was all a big joke.

I saw Chase's face tighten. I'd never seen him annoyed or angry before. The waiter took our drink order and then gave us some time to peruse the menu.

"I'm not ashamed of who we are, Todd," Chase spat out.

Todd sighed. "Neither am I, but we aren't in a threesome, Chase. We are here on a date with a beautiful lady who might be uneasy with how 'out there' you are. So just rein it in a little, okay?"

"Fine." Chase huffed. "You are a beautiful lady, Haley. What are we celebrating, darling?"

"It is totally hush-hush, but I got the King Park deal." I almost squealed the last three words, my excitement had yet to disperse.

"That is amazing," Chase said, hugging me, his previous annoyance gone in a flash.

"Congratulations, Haley. Much deserved and we look forward to that holiday," Todd added.

"Oh my goodness, yes. We can have a vacation after I've sold them all, to a place like paradise." My smile got wider than I thought was physically possible.

Our food orders were taken and we just continued with the same comfortable, cozy conversations like we had back at the apartment. The champagne made me more confident and I brought up the subject that had been on my mind and making me nervous for most of the day.

"Listen, guys, about our potential threesome situation. When we get home can we head to the bedroom? I would like to get that out of the way." I held up my hand. "I know that sounds completely unromantic but I'm nervous. You know my inexperience, and well, basically, if I can't be who you want me to be, then it's best we know straight off; you know, whether or not we are compatible."

"Ah, Hales," Chase said, adopting the nickname my friends gave me. "We will absolutely take you to bed when we get home, but do not have any worries, we are going to teach you how to do the sexy stuff until you are so good you could hire yourself out."

"Yes, Chase. Mr. Romantic there. Haley, it is not our intention to teach you how to be a prostitute. We will go back, head into the bedroom and see how it goes. Just know we are both nervous too. It is a huge step."

I breathed a sigh of relief. "Thanks, guys."

"Haley." The voice I expected came from behind me. "Imagine meeting you here."

"Malcolm. Wow, what a coincidence. What brings you here tonight?"

Malcolm's eyes flitted over the table. "I just popped in to make a reservation for a date. You know, I like this place. I was passing by, so I thought I'd book in person rather than calling." He looked at Todd and Chase. "Oh, sorry, I apologize. Am I interrupting something?"

Chase leaned over offering out his hand. "Chase Collins and this is Todd Ross."

Malcolm moved over to shake Todd's hand. "We've just invited Haley out for dinner. We're part of King enterprises. I don't know if you've heard of us? We are negotiating on behalf of Mr. King."

"Oh, absolutely." Malcolm was almost fawning. I was surprised he hadn't dropped to his knees. "Your development is one of the most exciting concepts I've seen in a long time. Haley and I have been working closely on forming the best plans in taking your development forward, haven't we, Haley?"

If this had been a real business meeting, I'm not sure what I would have done at his underhanded tactics. I was a quiet woman, and confrontation was not my thing. Malcolm had completely taken advantage of that fact.

"Really, well, would you like to join us? We have just eaten our main meal, but perhaps we could interest you in dessert and a glass of wine?" Todd asked.

Chase leaned over to me and mumbled under his breath, "He will be getting his just desserts."

Malcolm took a seat. "Oh, you have had some champagne. Were you celebrating something?"

"No," Todd lied. "I am just rather partial to the fine stuff. Shame you didn't arrive earlier, then you could have joined us in a glass."

"Not to worry, I will just stick to my usual beer," Malcolm said.

Over my dead body was he having any of my champagne anyhow.

Malcolm chatted on about his ideas for the development for a solid fifteen minutes before Todd stopped him.

"Sounds amazing, Malcolm. I'm sure we can come to some arrangement. Now can I talk candidly with you about the building? This is highly confidential and other than Haley you must not speak of it. We have taken her into our small circle and not even Arthur Green knows this."

Malcolm's eager eyes opened wide, and he shuffled closer to Todd. "Anything we talk about is strictly confidential. You have my word."

"So, part of the funding behind King enterprises comes from the adult entertainment industry."

Malcolm's jaw dropped for a split second before he quickly recovered himself.

"We are hoping that some of our wealthier investors will choose one of the King homes, and we're also going to keep one for filming high class movies. We've been speaking to Haley this evening and think it would be beneficial for you to come to our current movie set, see what we do, how we do it and then use that vision on the home Mr. King intends to keep for that purpose. You may or may not see some of the investors on that day too. I must point out that if any of this becomes public knowledge, Mr. King has advised me to do whatever is necessary to shut down the leak."

You couldn't miss the tenseness in Malcolm's shoulders at those words and when he spoke a slight tremble underlaid his voice.

"I won't say a word."

Well, who'd have thought it? Todd seemed to be rather enjoying pretending to be some kind of mob member.

"So, we will be in touch with Haley about you coming to see us. Would you be okay with attending on a Saturday, probably outside of usual office hours so that your employer isn't suspicious?"

"Of course, we will do everything necessary to assist you in this deal. Won't we, Haley?"

"Of course," I stated, and I raised my glass which was still partly full of champagne. "Here's a toast to a successful conclusion to our arrangement."

Everyone clicked glasses, with only Malcolm not privy to the double meaning of my statement.

We stayed silent on the subject until safely back in Todd's car.

"The fucking mouth on that man, Haley. I don't know why you didn't just let me and Todd beat him up at the back of the restaurant."

"Because he's not worth it," I stated. "I knew he'd show up tonight. I told you he would. He's a back-stabbing bastard. Thank you for winding him up tonight. I'll tell him it was a sham after I'm allowed to say I won the development."

"Don't say anything just yet, Haley," Todd said, winking at me through the rear-view mirror. "I'm not done with him. He's coming to the studio. I have plans to get him out of your life for good."

"You've gone all Godfather. Are you going to put a horse's head in his bed?" I laughed.

"No, but I do have plans for his head," Todd's dark eyes glistened with mischief.

"I'm seeing a totally other side to you tonight, Mr. Ross," I told him.

"You're going to see all our sides when we get home, darlin'," Chase added, and my stomach fizzled with excitement.

"Oh, she just trembled. Don't be a nervous girl, we'll be gentle," Chase said.

"I'm not nervous," I told them. "I actually can't wait."

CHAPTER SEVEN

Haley

I unlocked the door to our apartment and Chase and Todd followed me inside. As I naturally would, I headed into the living area. Todd walked over to the kitchen and took a bottle of red from the cupboard.

"Whose room would you like to go to?" he asked me.

"Let's go to mine. Mine is the largest," I replied.

"Chase, come grab some glasses," Todd commanded. It would appear Todd was totally in control of the situation, and I was happy to let him take charge.

We walked back down the hall and I opened the door to my room. I didn't know if either of the guys had had a secret peek in my room when I hadn't been around. Looking at their faces, I saw Todd taking in all the décor: my cream walls, gold satin curtains and matching bedding, along with my ornate framed mirror and ivory colored vintage style furniture. "It's like a Princess lives in here." He smiled. "Princess Haley of Dyker Heights."

"At your command," I bowed. His eyes flashed with desire. The first time I had seen a hint that he liked me in that way.

His complete opposite, Chase had flopped back on the bed like it was his own room, so there were no prizes for guessing that he'd seen my room before. "Move over," I told him. "There's more than you needs to get on the bed."

My curtains were drawn from when I had got changed earlier. I switched on my nightstand lamp and Todd switched off the main light. He sat at the other side of the bed and poured the wine into three glasses, handing one to each of us.

"Let's get more comfortable."

Todd stood and removed his jacket, hanging it over the back of my chair. Then he unbuttoned his shirt and repeated his actions. His torso was lean but muscled, with a slight smattering of dark chest hair that ran in a narrow trail down his stomach and into the waistband of his boxer briefs. He had narrow hips and a defined V and I was desperate to know what was beneath the boxers. His cock bulged underneath. He sat back on the bed and rested his head against my headboard.

"I'm too lazy to strip, Hales, you're going to have to help me," Chase said with a fake whine.

I smiled as he sat up. As usual, he'd discarded his jacket to the floor in the living area, so I helped him unbutton his shirt revealing light golden skin and a six-pack to die for. As his hair was fair it wasn't as noticeable where it ran down under the waistband of his trousers, but his abs and stomach were ripped and moved like beautiful waves on water. I had an overwhelming urge to trail my tongue all over him.

When we'd removed his shirt, he threw it down at the side of my bed. I began to unfasten the button on the waistband of his pants and then pulled down the zipper, although it was a struggle given the package underneath. Chase raised his hips up off the bed so that I could tug down his pants over his legs and off. Joining in his messy ways, I also threw his clothing on the floor. I reached over and took a sip of my wine as my mouth had gone dry.

"Now my boxers," Chase said. "I find myself incapable of doing a thing. You're going to have to do everything for me, Haley."

There was no doubt in my mind as to what he was insinuating. After my eyes saw his cock it was time to introduce my mouth. I swallowed; this was where it could all go wrong.

"Don't be nervous," Todd said gently. "We're here for you. We're not going to embarrass you or criticize you. We're all here to have a good time."

I smiled at him and then brought my focus back to Chase.

I hooked my fingers in the waistband of his boxer shorts and tugged them down, freeing his cock.

"Now take your time, Haley. We've got all night," Todd directed. "Hold it in your hand, look at it."

The cock in front of me was huge. It looked quite wide and was certainly bigger than any I'd seen before. After discarding his underwear, I held him in my hand. He was warm, and his dick hardened while in my grasp. I pulled the head back in my hand, looking at Chase for direction, and revealed a pink tip.

"Run your fingers over me, Hales." I saw a spot of pre-cum bead from the slit in the top of his head and I rubbed my finger into it and slid it around his glans.

"Just a moment. Let me grab something that will help," Todd said, and he left the room.

"See, we're not going to bite you," Chase said. He placed his hand over mine and rubbed it up and down his shaft. I found his rhythm and then he let go, letting me continue. He leaned back watching me. "Don't be afraid to go harder," he said.

Todd returned to the room clutching a tube of lube. "Strawberry flavor," he informed me. "But at first it will help your hand slide nicely down Chase's cock."

He poured a small amount into his hand and then came closer on the bed. I let go of Chase's dick and watched as Todd placed his hand around it, massaging in the lube. "Show her how hard she can go," Chase requested.

Todd gripped Chase's dick firmly in his grasp and pumped up and down with vigor.

"Wow," I said. "I would never have tried to go that hard. I'd be afraid of hurting you."

"You've done hand jobs before, right? With your old boyfriend?"

"Yes, as a prelude to the main event, but I just got him hard. I wasn't fierce like you are."

"Here, take over." Todd took his hand away and placed my fingers around Chase's cock.

Feeling more confident, I pumped my hand firmly up and down his shaft, eliciting a groan from Chase that made me stop.

"Why are you stopping?"

"I'm shocked. I never got that reaction before."

"Keep going, babe. I'm getting into it."

Chase leaned back against the pillows once again and closed his eyes, while I pumped my hand up and down his girth until my arm ached. I swear my arms burned so bad I could have cried. Todd saw my struggle.

"It is hard work, and that is why we move on to using a different body part. Now you are going to take him in your mouth, okay?"

I nodded.

"So, teeth covered, just slide him right in. You do not have to do what you have just done with your hand. Think gentle this time. The heat of the inside of your mouth is going to stimulate him, the lube will help you to slide him in and out. Feel free to wet your mouth with some wine too if you think it will help."

"I'm okay. My mouth isn't dry."

"Okay, so hold him at the base with your hand.

Now slide him into your mouth and back out, gently. That is all you are going to do at first. Get used to his size."

I did as instructed. Chase's dick filled my mouth. The taste of strawberry lube made the experience more pleasant and he did actually slide into me. I remembered Todd's words. Slide him in and slide him out. Each time I did it, I tried to take more of him in.

"Now, don't attempt to deep throat him, you will just gag. A little tip is to let the head of his cock gently hit the roof of your mouth. It feels very similar to being deep throated."

I tried to communicate with my eyes that I understood and this time when I took him into my mouth, I let the tip gently bump the roof of it. I looked over at Chase and saw his mouth was open and his breathing had hardened. My God, I must have been doing something right!

I let him slip out of me a moment. "I'll just take a drink."

"You are doing great, Haley." I found Chase staring at me. "It's hot thinking of your relatively virgin mouth around my beast."

Todd chuckled. "Are you still all right carrying on, because I can take over at any time?"

"No, I'm okay." I took a gulp of my wine. "I want to keep going. Tell me what else to do."

"Exactly what you are doing, but now suck me more. Do what they say and pretend I'm a popsicle," Chase said.

"That didn't work out so well for me with a real popsicle," I stated.

"Why was that?" Todd asked.

"I ice-burned the inside of my mouth."

Chase chuckled. "I assure you mine isn't frozen, so you'll be burn free unless I get you on your knees on that carpet."

I grasped the base of his cock once more and leaning forward I slid him into my mouth, sucking. I moved my head up and down, letting his cock bob in and out of my mouth. Then, feeling emboldened, I did what Tiff had advised me, and I took him out of my mouth and rolled my tongue gently across and around the top of his glans.

"Now, just increase the pressure of your sucking and the speed but keep to a steady rhythm. Be guided by Chase and how he thrusts inside you, okay?"

I nodded and then it was all systems go. I imagined myself to be a sophisticated seductress who had done this many times before. I placed my grasp firmly around his base and as I took him further into my mouth, I also slid my hand up and down his shaft. I sucked harder and then I increased my pace. Chase began to fuck my mouth gently and guided by him I increased my speed and pressure.

"That's it," Todd encouraged. "When Chase gets ready to come he'll tell you and you can choose to swallow or let him come out of your mouth and I'll take over at the end."

I held him out of my mouth one last time. "I want to do the whole thing."

"Okay," Todd said, and he moved to rest back against the headboard himself. He picked up his wine and settled in to watch the show.

I pumped Chase's cock and sucked. Feeling more confident with a real cock in my hand and mouth and no pressure to perform, I tried different things: swirling my tongue, sucking, cupping his balls. I figured if he didn't like any of what I was doing he would tell me. Soon Chase's rhythm appeared more focused. His breathing intensified, and his hand came toward the back of my head, guiding me to take him a little further into my mouth. The speed picked up and soon I was bobbing my head up and down for all I was worth while I sucked. My cheeks started to hurt, but I didn't care, I was seeing this through to the end.

"Oh, fuck, oh, Haley, fuck, I am gonna come."

I felt his cock tighten and his balls pull back and then with a groan he emptied his cum into me, filling my mouth. I swallowed every last drop of the salty milk and then carefully, using my hand at his base, I placed his cock against his stomach. Then I reached over and took a drink of my wine. I hoped it wasn't bad etiquette after swallowing his cum, but the taste was unusual, and my throat still felt dry.

"Bravo, Miss Martin." Chase sat back, a satisfied smirk on his face. "You did a perfect blow job. Nothing whatsoever to be ashamed of. Nothing to correct you over. You made me come and I am one highly satisfied customer."

"Chase, you're making her sound like a call girl again."

"Oh, yeah. Sorry, Hales. Tell you what, I won't pay you." He winked.

"I can't believe it. I did it. Thank you for being so patient with me." A beam set across my face and the relief that I'd performed well was as good as having had a solo orgasm.

"Can I do you too?" I asked Todd.

"I would love a blow job, Haley, but first you

need to rest your mouth, so I think it's time we took care of you."

I bit my lip, not knowing what to expect. I was still fully dressed at that point. Chase got me to stand up and he lowered the zipper at the back of my dress and pulled it up over my head, before handing it to Todd to put on the back of the chair. So he could be tidy sometimes! I stood in front of Chase facing Todd in my underwear. I'd purchased a new matching set in a silver lace with tiny crystals and sequins embroidered into the fabric, so they sparkled when they caught the light. My bra was a push-up style which held my small bust up and made it appear a little fuller than it actually was, whereas the thong let my ass cheeks out in all their glory. And that's what Chase was looking at right at this moment. His hand brushed down my right ass cheek before giving it a squeeze. "Hell, woman, your ass is delectable."

Todd leaned over toward me and offered his hands. I took them in my own and he drew me back to the bed where he laid me down facing upwards, my head resting on the pillows. I noticed his boxers bulged with his erect cock straining at the material. Todd dropped one of my bra straps off my shoulder and then the other. I lifted myself up slightly so he could unhook me. My breasts freed and my bra joining my dress, Todd looked over at Chase who came over to join us and one man sucked on one of my nipples, while the other feasted on the other. I thought I'd died and gone to heaven. I'd become so horny while I'd been sucking Chase's cock, but it was nothing on how I was now as I felt my juices soak through my panties, while I watched a blond-haired man and a brown-haired man feasting on my tits. Their hands were everywhere except *there*, trailing down my body, my thighs, up the side of my waist. Lips left my breast and kissed and sucked at my neck. Then Chase moved back and watched as Todd leaned down to my panties and pulled them down and off my legs. He eyed me greedily as he pushed my thighs apart.

"Pussy. You see as much as Chase and I love each other, we also love pussy."

He nestled between my thighs and I felt the warmth of his breath near my core. Then he took a leisurely lick up my slit which nearly had me come up off the bed.

"Oh my fucking god."

My experience of having oral sex was almost virginal. As I'd said before, Liam despised it, and to be honest he'd made me feel like it was dirty and shameful. Todd's tongue wrote an entirely different story directly on my cunt as he trailed it up my crease, teasing my clit and then went back to my crease where he stuck his tongue directly into my entrance.

I felt barely conscious, overtaken by sensations I had never experienced before. My hips rose to meet his tongue fucks until I felt a concentration of tiny, almost electric shocks, alongside a wave of complete elation. My orgasm exploded. I'd never come like that before in my life and I shook with the intensity as my juices squirted over Todd's face. He licked his lips until he'd taken in every part of my cream.

I sat up against the headboard panting. "Oh my god, I never... I never experienced anything like that before."

"He's so good with his mouth and tongue," Chase agreed. "Girl, you just had your world rocked."

"I really did." My face broke out in yet another megawatt smile. "I never knew it could feel like that."

"Well, hopefully, that's the first of many," Todd replied, moving to lie back against the headboard.

Without being prompted, I grabbed the waistband of his boxer shorts and yanked them down, displaying his cock in all its glory. It was hard as a rock, veins standing out and the head of his cock was a deeper color than Chase's, more purple than pink. His cock in itself was darker in skin tone. I marveled at the difference between their dicks. Todd's dick was also huge. I would actually say it was bigger than Chase's, but not as wide. Without hesitation, I took him in my mouth. I repeated all the things I'd done with Chase's cock, but this time I was more confident. I leaned over him, my ass high in the air while I brought him closer to climax. Chase stood at the side of the bed near the headboard, watching while he fisted his own cock a little and then he moved onto the bed where Todd took Chase's cock in his mouth. The room filled with the sounds of ecstasy. Groans, moans, sucking, licking. Todd was the first to come, erupting into my mouth. He tasted saltier than Chase, but I guessed that could have been due to the fact that we'd not used the lube. I sat back and watched as Todd's mouth bobbed up and down on Chase's cock with practiced precision. I stared, taking mental notes on how he moved his mouth around Chase's shaft. When he was about to come, he withdrew and sprayed his spunk over Todd's face. Todd licked it off his lips as it dripped down. Watching two guys really was hot.

Chase turned to me. "Well, Haley. I think that's

enough for our first evening together. We didn't want to rush you into anything too quickly, so we'd talked in advance and decided that we'd stick to oral sex tonight. Now I don't know about anyone else, but I'm satisfied, relaxed, and beat. I need my bed."

Todd stretched, leaning to grab his shirt and wiping his face. I might have been tired, but I watched those muscles as they rippled. Then he swung his legs off the bed. "I'd better go because otherwise I'm going to fall asleep right here, and as Chase says, it's too early for some things yet. Sleep well, lovely Haley. He leaned over and kissed the left side of my cheek. Chase followed suit, leaning over and kissing the right side.

They left and I didn't know whether they went to their own rooms or shared. I wasn't sure what they would do now that everything was out in the open and we were looking toward a ménage. The word made my lips curl into a smile. Two men at once. Two men all for me, well, apart from each other. Tonight I had performed two successful blow jobs! I couldn't wait to tell the girls. I quickly removed my makeup and took a shower, then I dressed in my pajamas and crawled into bed. I was exhausted and up again early in the morning. It wasn't until I was almost asleep that I realized I hadn't been kissed. My pussy lips had met Todd's mouth but I'd yet to crush lips against either Todd or Chase. I guessed that happened when intimacy deepened. I was pleased everything was going to be given time to develop, but at the same time, I couldn't wait for more.

CHAPTER EIGHT

Haley

I was pleased to discover that Malcolm was out showing properties all day and that I could go about my own day without seeing his ego-bloated face.

I was about to go show a property myself and had just grabbed my purse when the phone on my desk rang.

"Good morning, Green's Realtors, Haley Martin speaking."

"Good morning, Miss Martin, it's Alexandra Cross from King's. Mr. King has asked that I get in touch with you to arrange for him to meet you at the King Park development."

"Oh yes, of course, let me just bring up my electronic diary. I sat back at my desk and tapped on my keyboard until the main diary displayed. It was easier than trying to stare at the app on my phone, which made everything hard work.

"Okay, I'm in. When would Mr. King like to see me?"

There was a pause. "He wondered if you could meet him this afternoon at 2pm."

Of course, he did. He was a billionaire. They didn't wait for meetings. If they wanted to see you, you jumped. I looked at my itinerary for the day and hoped Tiff wasn't too busy and could fit my client in. "That would be fine. I will meet him there at 2pm." I knew I would be there by 1:45pm at the latest. Never would I leave a man of his importance waiting.

"You'll be met at the gates to the development and be given a visitor's badge and anything else you need. He looks forward to seeing you then."

"Thank you, Alexandra, please pass on my regards and tell him I look forward to meeting him too."

I put the phone down and called Tiff, passing on

my client's details for that afternoon and then I drove home as quickly as I could because although I looked smart, I didn't feel I was dressed well enough for meeting a billionaire.

AT 1:39PM I arrived at the gated development where I was given a security badge and directed to a car park. From there a man in a suit introduced himself, and handing me a hardhat took me into the main entrance of the development. The vast mansion had been separated into four, five-bedroomed residences, each with their own entrances. The only thing connecting them all was one vast marble-floored hallway. There were two apartments upstairs and two downstairs, each with their own long hallway that led down to their grand entrances. It was homes within a home.

"If you'd like to wait here, Mr. King will be with you shortly."

I thanked him and while I waited, I strolled around the vicinity. The building work appeared to be largely completed. The façade of the building was limestone clad and each apartment had its own balcony or private patio. The lawns outside were almost the size of a small park and meant that residents would maintain a degree of privacy, maybe not always from the three other owners, but at least from the general public.

"Miss Martin. Thank you for joining me at such short notice."

I startled. I was so lost in the architecture of the building, I hadn't realized the man himself had arrived.

"My apologies." He placed a hand gently on my shoulder. "I didn't mean to startle you."

My skin shivered under his touch, and I moved further away from his body, wrapping my arms around my shoulders. "It's fine. I was just admiring the beauty of this building."

"Yes, I made sure my architect knew that the outside of the building was to be maintained. It's the inside that has been modernized. Come and I'll take you into the one apartment that has been completed."

I'd only seen the completed apartment in photographs. The last time I'd visited, the front of the building had been wrapped in protective materials, there had been scaffolding everywhere and the apartments were finished in terms of the main construction but had yet to be decorated.

"If you'd like to follow me, Miss Martin."

"Please call me Haley. Miss Martin makes me sound like an old maid." Elias laughed.

"You're hardly that. How old are you if it's not too personal a question? You look around the same age as my daughter. She's twenty-one. By the way, call me Eli, that's what my friends call me and I'm sure we're bound to become them with you handling this development."

"I'm twenty-four, Eli. You have a daughter? Is she interested in joining the family business?"

He laughed again; it made his face light up. He really was an attractive man, although far too old for me. "No. No. Unfortunately, she takes after her mercenary mother, doesn't believe she needs to work for a living and likes spending my money. Are you married, Haley?"

I blushed a little. "No, I'm not."

"Don't worry, I'm not propositioning you. I just wanted to offer some advice. If you become wealthy, ensure you have a pre-nup because there are people out there who think they deserve a large part of your wealth when they didn't do a thing to contribute toward it."

"Your marriage was a success then I take it?" I quipped.

"Well, let's put it this way. I never made the same

mistake again and don't intend to. Marriage is not for me. I prefer the single life, and golf."

He opened the door to one of the downstairs apartments. It was bright and airy and had all the amenities one would expect from a luxury residence. It was beautiful.

"I can't wait to begin selling these residences. They won't be available for long, Eli."

"Well, that pleases me. If we work well together, Haley, I'd very much like Green's and yourself, in particular, to represent King's on the property front."

"Oh." My forehead creased. "A colleague of mine felt you were going to expand into the business yourself, cut out the middleman, so to speak."

"I considered it at one point, but I don't have the time. Why mess around when Arthur Green has been in the business as long as he has and knows how to sell. Would you consider being the first point of contact for my businesses? It would take you away from a large portion of the day-to-day real estate selling of Green's."

"It sounds fantastic, and I have a friend and colleague, Tiffany, who would also be a good back up for myself."

"As long as it's not that wretched man. What was his name again? Oh, Malcolm. If that man leaves a message for me one more time to speak with him directly, I'll have to speak to Arthur about him."

I smirked. "Oh, don't worry about Malcolm. I'm taking care of it."

A mischievous glint appeared in Eli's gaze.

"Really? Please do tell. I may be too old for you, but I'm not too old for a little mischief."

It would appear that Eli and I were going to get along just fine.

CHAPTER NINE

Chase

"I think last night went really well, don't you?" I asked Todd for about the thirtieth time. We'd called for lunch at a small café in Brooklyn before we headed back to the studio.

"I've already told you my answer." Todd exhaled. "It was a great night but it's extremely early."

"I already love Haley," I said. "Instalove. The minute I met her, I knew, just like I did with you."

"We dated other women for three months before we got together." Todd rolled his eyes.

"Only because I was too scared to approach the dark, brooding male, who I presumed was straight as a ruler. Had I known you were interested I'd have had your cock in my mouth within a minute of meeting you."

He'd heard this all before, but I was telling the truth. Haley was special. I felt it. We'd known her for a few months now as a friend and she was becoming more than that.

"I really hope it works out because I'm over trawling Club S for pussy," I told Todd. "I'm almost thirty. I'm getting too old."

"So, the fact I'm thirty-one means I should have stopped by now then. Put myself into sex club retirement?" Todd raised an eyebrow.

"Oh, you know what I mean. You have the stamina for things, the determination. I'm bored and over it all. We meet someone, half the time they lie about their true identity. We very rarely see them again. Sometimes one of us likes them and the other doesn't. In the meantime, people are watching and getting their rocks off while we try to enjoy ourselves. I used to find it hot, but now I'm jaded. I'm a jaded bisexual man, Todd. I want to come home at night to my man, and our woman. Maybe travel, have a family.

He clasped my hand. "It's what we both want. It will come with time. I was over Club S a long time ago. I just don't want you to scare Haley off. You know how full on you get."

"But that's who I am. There's no point me pretending to be someone else. The relationship needs honesty from the start. Well, apart from the bit where we show Malcolm around the studio." I sniggered.

"That sniveling suck-up bastard is going to get everything he deserves." Todd's voice dripped with venom, but it told me all I needed to know about Haley. He deeply cared for her too.

SATURDAY MORNING WAS the day we'd arranged for Malcolm to visit the studio. There was no way we were allowing him to come to our real place of business, so instead, we gave him the address of the brownstone we'd rented for the week to film a new set of movies. We liked to think ours were more sophisticated pornos with a storyline, though I imagined even though we spent hours making sure we had the best movie possible, most viewers probably skimmed past the whole introductory phase and went straight to the pussy shots. Our small team was already there with everything set up. The bedroom was filled with camera equipment, and the bed made. Our actors for the day Guy, Angie, and Rod (not his real name, but named for a reason) were in the kitchen, along with half the crew, enjoying a bit of breakfast before filming started. I'd had a word with Rod, told him what I had planned for Malcolm, and with the promise of a bonus he shrugged his shoulders, totally on board with the plan. I guess it was just another cock to him.

Haley had arranged to meet Malcolm for the 'studio tour', and just after eleven, I heard a cab pull up outside the house. A few minutes later the door-bell rang, and I went to answer it. The show was on the road.

"Welcome to the shoot." I shook both their hands. "Please come in. Everyone is grabbing some breakfast. I'll quickly show you around, tell you what to expect and then feel free to get a coffee and watch the action."

Haley gave me a secret wink, whereas Malcolm's eyes were wide as he took in the townhouse.

"Not what you were expecting?" I narrowed an eye at Malcolm while trying my best to keep a friendly tone.

"I honestly didn't expect movies to be filmed

somewhere so, well, nice. I kinda thought it would be in some seedy basement apartment somewhere."

"All our shoots take place in the most sumptuous surroundings and our crew and actors enjoy fantastic working conditions. We run a company with a fabulous reputation."

"Oh, yes, I wasn't insinuating—"

I cut him off. "Let me show you around as we really need to get on with the shoot. Time is money."

I walked them around the townhouse. On the parlor level, there was an enormous living room with a stained quarter sawn white oak floor throughout. Underfloor heating in every room meant our actors' feet wouldn't get cold during all the standing around. High ceilings and tall windows, along with the cream painted walls meant the house was bright, airy and perfect for filming. The bedroom we were in today was gorgeous. A large room with the bed situated at the top, with ample floor space around for all the cameras.

AFTER HALEY and Malcolm had grabbed a coffee, we went through to the bedroom to make a start. An hour later our actors were still acting out the beginning scenes of a housewife being caught in the bedroom looking out at the hunky gardener and were still fully dressed, something we expected having made so many movies, but our two guests were shuffling around on their feet appearing quite bored.

"Were you expecting things to happen a little faster?" I asked them both.

"Yes," Haley replied. "I don't know how you don't fall asleep, it's so boring."

"Haley," Malcolm scolded. "You can't say that to these businesspeople." He coughed and turned to me. "It does take longer than I anticipated, however." He adjusted his tie and preened like a peacock. "The email I received yesterday from Mr. King stated he hoped I enjoyed the experience and made the most of it."

I nodded, knowing full well that Elias King also wanted Malcolm to get what was coming to him for being such a dick. When Haley had told us he was happy to go along with our charade and would even send the email to back us up, I'd been amazed.

After a couple more hours, the actors' clothes were off and we were into the scene.

"We need the cat light. Cat light please," the director yelled.

A runner went off to the back of the room and wheeled over the massive light which was so bright you felt it could melt your eyeballs. It was set up to shine right into Angie's pussy, hence the director shouting cat light. We actually called it the pussy light but reverted to cat if we had visitors.

I watched Haley as she watched the scene acted out in front of her. It was a ménage but an MFM one. I wondered if she was getting turned on. Malcolm was, he'd moved his laptop case in front of his pants. When the scene was finished, Todd approached. "Okay, Malcolm if you stay with Chase, he'd like to talk business. Haley, are you okay to come with me and grab some lunch?"

Haley nodded and neither Todd nor I missed the look of smug satisfaction that crossed Malcolm's face and how he gave Haley a look of sheer triumph.

"So, if you'd like to follow me?"

I walked into another smaller bedroom with a double bed and a desk and a couple of chairs. I indicated for Malcolm to take a seat.

"I'm going to come right out and say it, Malcolm. You're a natural. We want to offer you a job with us."

"A job? An actual job? Not the development contract?"

"No. A full paid job. However, as I'm sure you can understand, we have a lot of enemies, and for collateral we therefore have to obtain guarantees that none of our staff give away our secrets."

"I fully understand. I'll sign any confidentiality agreements."

"It's not that simple, Malcolm. You're a man, like myself. We can make a lot of money, and when people make money it can go two ways. They can get enemies out to crush them, or they can enjoy themselves so much they can become complacent. Either way, we do something here, a little off the norm that means we, to date, have never had a problem."

"Anything. You name it."

"We need to film you sucking a man's cock."

Malcolm almost choked. "What? Are you kidding me? I can't do that. Jeez, man."

"Well, Haley is currently being offered the same deal by Todd, so I guess we'll see who wants the job more." I got up to leave.

"I'll do it," he blurted. Shaking his head as if he couldn't believe his own words. "How long do I have to do it for? Does he have to, you know, in my mouth?"

"God, no. Literally like suck on it for a minute. Just enough that we have it on film. Then it gets locked away in a security deposit box and will never be seen again."

"Okay, can I get it done with quickly? Oh my god, fuck, oh erm, sorry about that. I can't believe I'm going to do this."

"I know." I put a hand on his shoulder. "When I had to do it, I found it hard." I turned away then because I wanted to laugh at my own joke. I wished Todd and Haley had been here to hear it.

"I'm filming it on a handheld. There'll just be me, you, and Rod. So no massive audience. Now, don't worry. Rod is used to having all different people on his cock. It's not going to turn him on, you're not gay from doing it. It's just a business trans-action, okay?"

Rod entered the room completely stark naked, his massive twelve-inch cock in his hand. He stroked it, keeping it hard.

"Okay, Malcolm. On your knees, please. Time is passing quickly and we have more filming to do."

Malcolm swallowed and dropped to his knees. Then he closed his eyes and opened his mouth. Rod pushed his dick in between his lips. Neither of us said a word. We just watched as Malcolm sucked Rod's cock in and out of his mouth for about a minute.

"All done. Thanks, Rod," I shouted. Rod nodded, winked at me and left the room, taking the handheld with him. He had instructions to take it straight to Todd.

"The bathroom's down the hall if you want to freshen up," I informed a green looking Malcolm. "Then come join us for some lunch."

Malcolm nodded and then ran down the hallway looking like he was going to vomit.

I went and found Todd. "Everything good?" I asked him. "Perfect and backed up," he said. "All ready for us to wrap up this little situation for good."

Malcolm came downstairs and walked into the kitchen. He refused all offers of food, but he walked over to Haley and whispered something in her ear that made her eyes flash with fury.

"So, while it's just the four of us here. I'd like to announce that earlier I offered Malcolm a job," I announced.

Malcolm preened again.

"And if you would still like the position of the part of the wimpy computer nerd in our next production, we would be very happy to have you."

"What?" Malcolm choked. "There must be some mistake. You offered me a job at King's."

"No, I didn't," I corrected him. "I said you were a natural and we wanted to offer you a job with us, as in, the studio."

Malcolm's face drained of all color. "I sucked a man's cock."

Haley burst out laughing. "And we have it on tape, you fucking asshole."

He turned to her, looking in horror.

"That's what you get for trying to home in on my account, Malcolm, and for being one of the most unlikeable people I have ever had the misfortune to meet. You're despicable. Did you not think I'd notice that you read my private text message? Unfortunately for you, you made an incorrect assumption. I wasn't meeting business partners. I was meeting my live-in partners. Meet my lovers Todd and Chase."

Malcolm's jaw dropped. "Both of them?"

"Yes," Todd answered. "Both of us and we can assure you that she is fucking top of the class at blow jobs and sex. Your dick didn't inflate because it lives mainly on your head."

"So, this was all a fucking joke?"

"Oh no. We run a very, well-respected adult entertainment business, and if you don't want your video leaking on one of our associates' amateur channels, you'll put that cock firmly between your legs, get on with your own work at Green's and leave Haley and anyone else you annoy at Green's the fuck alone. Now get out," Todd shouted.

Malcolm didn't need to be told twice. He ran out of the brownstone. We all high-fived each other.

"Party at ours tonight," I declared. "Lots of alcohol and sexy shenanigans. We have lots to celebrate!"

CHAPTER TEN

Todd

Malcolm had gotten on my last nerve and I was pleased he ran off because I was so tempted to hold him by his lapels and beat the shit out of him. My temper rarely flared but when it did, it took a lot to get the heat to dissipate from my body.

After the shoot, we went out to eat, and with the knowledge of catching a cab home, I'd had wine with my dinner. I was satisfyingly full of food, but the burn was still there and I knew one way I could channel it that would be of benefit.

As soon as we got through the door, I pushed

Haley against the wall, parting her thighs with my knee. My mouth crushed on hers, my tongue seeking entrance into her own warm mouth. Her lips parted with a sigh and her tongue met my own.

"Come on, Chase. Go get the lube and join us." I lifted Haley up and kicked open her bedroom door. I stripped her of her clothes, Chase by now assisting, and then we stripped off our own quickly until we were all bare and ready for action. Chase leaned over Haley, placing his hand under her head and lifted it letting his mouth meet her own. I watched as they kissed.

"I can't wait tonight, Haley. Are you ready for me?" I asked her.

Chase let her mouth go and she gasped, "Yes."

I held my rigid cock in my hand and lined it up at her entrance. She was soaking wet, her juices were spilling out onto the bed. Without hestitation, I pushed inside her. Fuck, I needed that. To feel encased by the warm walls of her pussy.

She moaned.

I pulled out of her to the tip and then pushed in again. Her legs came up to wrap around me, to take me deeper. Her head was flung back.

"More. I want more," she whispered.

I gave her more. Plunging in and out of her wet

heat, the tension and rage I'd been carrying around all day went into every thrust. Chase went back to kissing her. Haley couldn't get enough. She arched to meet my thrusts and she mewled through Chase's kisses. Her hand came up to grasp his cock and I watched as she milked him. It wasn't rhythmic. Trying to co-ordinate kissing, hand-jobs and fucking wasn't some kind of orchestrated performance. It was raw. Chase broke the kiss to concentrate on the hand on his cock and her hand stopped as I rammed into her so hard she must have seen stars.

"Todd, I'm gonna—"

I flicked her clit with my fingertip as I continued to fuck her until her pussy contracted and she came all over my cock and fingers. Her pussy continued to throb against me for several seconds. I hadn't come myself yet. I wanted to wait.

"Wait for a minute," I told her, and I took Chase's hard cock into my mouth. With years of practice behind me, I placed my tongue up over the back of my throat, taking Chase into my mouth, making him feel like he was fucking the back of my throat. He grabbed my head as he guided me in a rhythm he would get off on. As I felt the giveaway signs that his come was approaching, I backed off, looking up at him and shaking my head.

"No. We fuck. Haley, move further left and turn on your side facing left."

When she'd done it, I directed Chase. "Move behind her."

I moved behind Chase. Chase brought his hand around the front of Haley and began to finger her clit, alternating with plunging digits into her pussy. "So wet, Haley, I hope you're ready for me."

She wriggled her ass at him indicating that she definitely was. "Oh that ass," Chase groaned. "Wiggle it again, baby."

He lined up his cock with her pussy and entered her slowly. This time we would take our time. I moved in behind Chase and lubing up my dick and his puckered hole, I slowly edged into him pushing through his outer ring. He moved back against me until I met the known resistance of his inner ring, waiting until it relaxed and let me push my cock in further. Chase gasped as I pushed all the way into him, my balls slapping against his ass cheeks. I held his hips as I followed his lead with my movements, mirroring my fucks to his fucking of Haley. Now we were all in perfect orchestrated motion. A trio of lovers searching for their crescendos. Leisurely strokes turned into animalistic movements and grunts as the pressure built and then Haley climaxed which set off a chain reaction. Chase spilled his load into her tight pussy and I jerked violently as my cum spurted inside Chase's ass.

We laid back against the bed spent. But this time we didn't leave. We took turns to visit Haley's bathroom, then got back in the same positions, curled up and went to sleep. My anger was no more. Malcolm was insignificant. Haley was with us and we would protect her for as long as she allowed.

CHAPTER ELEVEN

Haley

I almost asked if we could have girls' night on Sunday. I was absolutely bursting to tell the girls what had happened over the past week. So much had changed. After our date and my lesson in oral, they'd left me alone until the Saturday night. I'd been surprised. I'd kind of expected a non-stop fuck-fest. I wasn't sure whether I admired the fact they were respecting me and taking their time or whether to just go to them and demand they fucked me. I was becoming sex-crazed. Me! Little Haley Martin. The quiet girl who didn't do sex, who wasn't very good at sex, now had had two amazing experiences. I knew now that it wasn't only down to me. The lovers I'd had were useless in bed and along with my lack of confidence it had meant that I'd struggled to develop any kind of sexual skill. I also knew now that it was all about to change. Bring it on, I thought. I couldn't wait for more. Saturday had rolled around to Monday and although there'd been a lot of making out, we'd not had sex again. Instead, Todd and Chase had insisted on taking me to the movies and bowling on Sunday. They were determined to date me. They were off to the gym tonight and then had got Brandon to agree to them hanging around at his apartment, while I borrowed his wife for the evening. By the time Kayla and Tiff arrived, I was a bundle of nervous energy, had drunk half a bottle of red wine already and was feeling rather dizzy, but manic.

"Come in, come in," I'd shouted at both of them, and they'd taken a seat at the dining table while I served some spaghetti and poured the last of the red wine into their glasses.

"What the fuck is going on with you, Haley? You're like a bloody jack in a box," Kayla said.

I squeezed my ass through the gap between the table and my chair and sat down, twirling spaghetti around my fork. "I did it! I did two blow jobs and I've had sex with both Todd and Chase!" Then I squealed because I was just so damn happy and excited about the whole thing.

Tiffany high-fived me and then Kayla took her lead and did the same. Tiffany beamed at me. "I'm so happy for you. Spill it. What was it like? What did you do? Did you see them fuck again? Are two men really hot together?"

"Jesus, Tiffany. One question at a time and give the girl time to eat her spaghetti or she's going to choke on it," Kayla chided. Then she turned to me. "Haley, eat the damn spaghetti so we know what happened."

"OKAY, so the first time I just did blow jobs, but they were so kind and patient. It wasn't like they took pity on me or anything, it was still super sexy, but they gave me words of encouragement and advice, and it worked. I used some of the hints and tips you two had given me too, but it was so much better to not suck and lick a piece of hard plastic or a mushed-up banana." I made a gagging face. "Then after we set up Malcolm—I'll tell you about that in a moment —we came back here, and Todd was all masterful and pinned me to the wall. I felt like I was in a movie."

"Yeah, rewind this movie a minute. What did you do to Malcolm? I thought he'd been quiet this week," Tiff said.

"We tricked him into giving a male porn actor a blow job on camera and then told him where to go."

Kayla spat out her wine. "Holy shit! How did you pull that off?"

I filled them in on all the details of the porn shoot and how Eli King had also been part of proceedings.

"Wow, that guy really does know how to piss people off," Tiff said.

"And now he knows how to suck a dick." Kayla laughed. "That's hilarious. Are you sure you don't have a copy on hand that we can watch?"

"No, Todd actually wiped it, so it couldn't accidentally get out anywhere, but Malcolm doesn't need to know that, does he?" I giggled.

"Haley, you are becoming quite the minx. Tiffany, where's our innocent little Hales gone?"

"I think she's gone forever judging by the wide smile that's almost permanently etched onto her face. Now you know why we got so hooked on ménage. It's so decadent having two guys at once."

"Yes, but Hales has even more holy hotness

because then her guys bang each other. Mine won't cross swords, I've asked them. Parker said I could go back to sleep because I was fucking dreaming."

That made me laugh because Kayla was a force of nature, and Daniel, her older partner was a quiet man. With Parker, she'd met her match and had someone to make sure she didn't get too carried away; though I'm not sure what she could do worse than some of her past antics like being discovered having a threesome in the kitchen by her own mother and having sex on canvas. She was loud and brash and I loved her like a sister.

"Do you miss it?" I asked Tiffany.

"No. Honestly I don't. It's in here." She tapped her temple. "But I love Brandon. I cared for Henry. I thought at one time I might have loved him, but I didn't. I barely knew him, whereas as time passed Brandon and I just become closer than ever. I'm ready to start trying for a family now and Brandon himself exhausts me. That gym training gives him Olympic-level stamina. I swear sometimes I have to pretend to be asleep when he comes to me for round four in a day.

"Well, I've only seen Todd and Chase that time when I spied through their door; and then when we got together Friday night, we were in like a spoon situation, so I couldn't see them then. I'm really looking forward to actually watching them fuck each other in front of me, up close. I swear I had no idea two guys together would turn me on like it does.

"I'm so happy for you, babe. I hope it works out." Tiff leaned over and gave me a squeeze.

"Well, thank you, Tiff. Because if you hadn't spoken to Henry and engineered these two hot men into my apartment it wouldn't have happened, and I'd still be a sexual nervous wreck trying not to gag on fruit and vegetables. I had to move onto carrots. I never want to see a banana up close again as long as I live."

"To cocks in place of bananas," Kayla lifted her wine and toasted.

"To cocks in place of bananas," Tiff and I sang back.

"SO, in other news. I totally won the King development. I met the big man himself over there and I'm waiting for it to be announced to the team."

"Babe, that's amazing," Tiff said. "I knew you could do it. You deserved it with all the effort you put into the plans. Well done."

"When I met Eli, he spoke about putting more

business Green's way and having me as a contact person. I also told him about you as my back-up."

"Wow, this is so exciting."

"Sometimes I miss working for Green's," Kayla admitted. "Not the work. I actually prefer the art world, but I miss seeing you girls every day and talking about the latest gossip."

"That's why we must never let our Monday's stop. Not even when we have children. That's what fathers are for, and in mine and Kayla's case there'd be two fathers so no excuses for a lack of childcare."

"My god, are you seriously thinking of starting a family with Todd and Chase?" Tiff said.

I shook my head. "It's far too early to decide anything like that, but I want to keep a positive outlook. If things carry on as they are—and we've all lived together for several months now—then why the hell not?"

"Let's have a final toast. To friends and ménages." Tiff said. "Seeing as both things have made us all very happy."

We raised our glasses and clinked them together.

WHEN THEY LEFT, Tiff sent the men back home.

"Did you have a good time? Is your tongue worn out from all the gossip?" Chase asked.

I stuck it out at him.

"Hmmm, seems okay to me. We'll test it later though to make sure."

He sat down on the couch. "First though tell me everything. They did nothing but talk about baseball over there. Please tell me all the girly gossip. Was there sex talk? Did you tell them I had a huge cock?"

Todd came in as Chase delivered his last sentence.

"Dear God," he said, shook his head and went to grab a beer.

CHAPTER TWELVE

Haley

A week later and Eli had given the go ahead to announce the deal. Arthur and Eli came into the office having called a staff meeting. Arthur had a large bouquet of flowers in his hand and Eli a bottle of a very fine brand of champagne.

"Everyone, Mr. King has an announcement to make which is of great benefit to Green's. Please, can we have your attention for a few minutes?"

People stopped what they were doing and looked over at the impressive and commanding man standing before them.

"Thank you, Arthur. As you may or may not know, King's has expanded into the property market during the last year with a vision to develop a brand of elite housing. I am pleased to announce today that not only have we chosen a person from the team to represent the King Park development, we have also, as King's Enterprises, signed on the dotted line for another three developments which will all be coming Green's way in terms of sale and management. So, today, I'd like to formally announce that Haley Martin will be our key link person between Green's and King's."

"Congratulations, Haley," Arthur added. "And if you'd like to come forward, we would like to present you with these flowers and a bottle of champagne as a token of our appreciation."

Everyone cheered and clapped. Well, everyone except for Malcolm, who left the room. You see Green's was mainly a family-style business and although we may get a little jealous of each other's good fortune and landing of big commission deals—after all we were only human—-in the main we cheered each other on as every success meant Green's went from strength to strength and guaranteed us future employment.

I took the offered gifts and shook both Arthur and Eli's hands and then I went and sat back down.

Eli spoke again. "While we congratulate Haley today on her new role, it goes without saying that it's the team who attracted me to Green's. You are led by a fine gentleman—"

He was interrupted in his speech as everyone cheered Arthur. After the whooping and cheering calmed down, Eli carried on. "The business I intend to bring to Green's will make an impact on everyone's workload, so as a thank you for you all being so accepting and encouraging of our new business arrangements, I'm hosting a free bar tonight at my bar in Manhattan. We have the private room held for us at eight and there will be food also for you. Please come along to PlayKing's tonight and let's let loose and welcome the weekend in style."

Everyone whooped and hollered again.

"THANK YOU, Eli, for this opportunity. I promise I won't let you down."

Eli smiled. "Haley, I'm feeling like a new man lately. Obviously, I needed the new direction with the business. I was becoming jaded and then your youth and vitality must have rubbed off. I'm feeling invigorated. What happened with Malcolm?"

"He's left me alone ever since. I guess I can't ask for more than that."

"Actually, you can," Arthur interrupted, holding a piece of paper in his hand. "Malcolm just quit. He'll be gone immediately. Thank God. He was the one bad apple at Green's, a poisonous red one." He chuckled. "Now, I usually don't condone drinking at work, but I have another bottle of champagne in my office and I think we should drink to throwing out the old and bringing in the new."

And we did.

I RETURNED HOME ELATED about the new direction of my career and the disappearance of Malcolm from my life. Eli had told me to bring the guys along to PlayKing's that evening. I walked into the living room to find Chase almost bouncing off the walls.

"Haley, we have news."

"I have news too." This was probably obvious owing to the fact I had flowers and champagne in my hand, but hey, I wanted to join in with the announcements.

Todd interjected. "Haley, you go first."

"What?" Chase looked like he'd been told there was no Santa.

"Haley?" Todd prompted.

"The deal was announced today. Eli has invited us out to PlayKing's tonight for an open bar, and Malcolm quit. It's been a fucking fabulous day."

"Oh, honey, it's about to get better. We sold the business," Chase almost screamed.

"What?"

"The movie business. We were made an offer we couldn't refuse by someone who wants to take what we do and expand it. We got our retirement pot and I'm not even thirty. You know what that means, babe? The vacation is on us. Forget your bonuses, we want to take you, our treat. You pay for massages and stuff if you want to contribute."

Todd shook his head and walked over to kiss my cheek, then took the flowers and champagne from my hands and put them on the countertop. "Huge congratulations, Haley, and Malcolm is gone, really? That's the best news I heard all day." He looked over at Chase, "even better than our deal."

"You are so full of shit sometimes, Todd." Chase pouted. "Anyway, no time to waste. Let's get ourselves ready for the free bar. It's time to paarrttyyy."

AND PARTY WE DID. We let loose, we got a little wasted, and we danced the night away even though there was no dance floor in the bar. Eli came over briefly, although most of the time he was still conducting business. I met his personal assistant, Alexandra, who followed him around all night like his shadow. Eli was blissfully unaware of the look of pure longing and hero-worshiping that was on her face. I had hesitated to point it out to him in case it complicated their business relationship, but the alcohol got the better of me.

"Eli, I think your PA wants more than a business relationship with you."

Eli's eyes widened, and he gave a half-laugh. "You're mistaken. Alexandra is twenty-six, just five years older than my daughter."

"I know want when I see it and she wants you."

"Well, I'm too old for her."

"What did you say to me? I'd brought some youth and vitality to your life. She could bring some more." I winked.

"I'm going to forget we had this conversation," he said, winking back at me and he walked away.

It wasn't lost on me that as he did, he looked directly at Alexandra, who came running over to see if he needed anything. He did, and I hoped he realized that sooner, rather than later.

I turned around to see my men—yes, I realized I saw them as that now, my men—-wrapped around each other dancing.

I walked over and tapped them on the shoulders. "Is there room for one more?"

"Always," they said and let me in their circle.

A MONTH LATER, Chase and Todd had handed over the business to the new guy, Aiden Hall. They came home one evening with Chase holding a new movie in his hands.

"Are we watching your last porno tonight?" I asked him.

"Oh, we are," Chase grinned. "I think you're going to like it."

We curled up on the sofa, me in the middle of the guys, and Todd pressed the remote bringing the movie to life on screen. The story unfolded—-my story-—beginning with a woman being told she was no use in bed and leading on to her love affair with two men. I broke down in tears.

"Haley, did we make a mistake? We didn't want to hurt you. We wanted to show you how we felt you'd changed. How beautiful you are," Chase said, looking at me in alarm.

"That's why I'm crying," I replied. "I feel like I'm in a fairytale sometimes; like it's not real. You took me and made me be this confident woman I am now. You really did change a caterpillar to a butterfly."

"Except we got you to spread your legs not your wings," Chase quipped. It broke through my tears and I started to laugh.

"That you did," I said. "And I'll be forever grateful."

"Ooh, how grateful?" Chase said with a wink.

I dropped to my knees. "Let me show you."

CHAPTER THIRTEEN

Haley

Six months later

Todd and Chase had stayed on as paid consultants for a while at their newly sold business until Aiden Hall had someone trained to take over. I had sold all of King Park within the first week of the apartments being available and was working closely with Eli on a number of new developments.

But this week, we were on vacation at our dream

destination. We'd arrived in St Lucia, staying in a hotel with views of the Petit and Gros Piton mountains. Our suite was modern and well furnished with a beachfront location and 24-hour butler service. That night we had a table set out on the beach in front of our suite. It was set up underneath a wooden cabana: just a roof and four pillars, with curtains that floated in the breeze but gave us a feeling of privacy. Lanterns gave us light and kept it all very romantic.

"So, here's to our first night in St Lucia." Todd raised his glass of red wine.

"Yes, let's toast with strawberry cordial," Chase said with a wink in my direction.

"Shut up." I gave him side-eye, but then the edge of my lips curled in a tell-tale smirk. It was impossible to be mad with Chase for longer than thirty seconds.

"So, what's everyone thinking we should do tomorrow?" Todd asked.

I looked over at the other cabana directly to the right of our suite. "I'm going to have a massage."

"Oh, I'm definitely joining you on that one. What do you think, Todd?"

"I think I'm going to have a game of golf. I haven't played in a while. I'll leave you two to gossip while you're being kneaded."

We relaxed in the warm breeze. It was decadent and romantic, being spoiled as someone else cooked and brought the most delicious food to our table. The staff let us know they'd turned down the bed. There was one bedroom and a sofa bed, but we'd explained we only needed the bed. If our butler had any thoughts about our arrangement, he kept them to himself.

Thoroughly relaxed, we headed back into our suite for our first night in 'paradise', and we went through to the suite.

"That dress is beautiful," Todd said, indicating toward the maroon sundress I'd been wearing that evening. Then he walked over and flicked the thin strap off my shoulder. "But I prefer it off." He flicked off the other strap and Chase stood behind me and unzipped it, so the dress pooled at my feet. Todd pushed me back onto the couch, moved my panties to one side and slowly licked up my slit. His mouth fastened over my clit and he sucked gently, making my juices flow. His tongue continued to make leisurely trails up and down my slit, occasionally darting inside my pussy, making me moan.

Chase came up behind Todd, "My turn."

Todd left my pussy and turned on his knees to face Chase, who unbuttoned his pants and pulled down his boxers to reveal his erect cock. Pre-cum glistened on the end of his mushroom head. I watched as Todd took him in his mouth. Chase indicated for me to kneel up on the couch and I leaned over Todd, while Chase held the back of my head and kissed me, his tongue darting between my teeth. His other hand cupped my breast then caressed my nipple, while he moved in a steady rhythm inside Todd's eager mouth.

Chase withdrew his cock from Todd and told me to get on the floor on all fours.

"Todd, fuck Haley."

Todd moved behind me and positioned his cock at my entrance. Chase stood just astride my body facing Todd and again put his cock in the other man's mouth. Todd thrust inside my wet opening. I turned my head and could just make out where the men were. I wished we had mirrors in the room so I could watch our play, but instead turned back to the front, closed my eyes and lost myself to the sensations of Todd's huge cock pushing into me over and over again. Chase moved to one side of me when Todd's motions became more frenzied. I got onto my knees and Todd clutched my breast while he fucked my body hard until he came with a loud grunt, which took me over the edge. My cunt quivered as my orgasm rang out.

I turned back and rested against the sofa. "I want to watch you both," I told them.

We moved into the bedroom. Todd was soon hard again and he and Chase positioned themselves in a sixty-nine and took each other's cocks in their mouths. I found it so erotic, watching these two men, both their eyes closed as they pleasured each other, and I placed my own hand between my legs. As their fists held the other's cock at the base, I watched tongues swirl and mouths suck and listened to the slurping sounds, pops, and groans coming from the men I loved. Fuck, I realized. I did. I loved them.

My middle finger brushed against my nub gently, causing my core to drip out even more of my cream. I swept some up on my fingertip and rubbed it into my clit. It was almost like electricity was pumping through my body. Both of their dicks were otherwise engaged and I looked around quickly. I needed that feeling of fullness while I played. I wanted a cock, but there wasn't one free. I took note of the unlit candle at my bedside and reached for it. It was brand new. They changed the candles daily and it was tapered with a thicker base. I positioned it at my entrance and slowly pushed it in while I moaned, feeling it slide in comfortably thanks to my juices until it was almost the whole way in, with just enough at the base for me to grasp. I watched as I withdrew the candle from my pussy and then I pushed it back in. It was so dirty but oh so hot. Turning my gaze to the men, I watched their heads bob, their mouths working each other's cocks while I fucked the candle. I pinched my nipples with my other hand, stroking my own breasts and feeling my core quicken and pulse as if my mouth down there was frantic to reach its fruition. Chase came in Todd's mouth and without delay, Chase withdrew and concentrated on bringing his lover to his own climax, but while he did, he opened his eyes and he saw what I was doing with the candle. He didn't move his gaze. Instead, he worked Todd's dick while he watched me push the candle in and out of myself until I was fucking it hard and raising my hips off the bed. My other hand was pinching my clit. Todd opened his own eyes at this point and Chase moved him onto his side slightly so they could both have a view.

Chase's mouth frenziedly sucked on Todd's dick while they both watched as I fucked that candle like it was one of their dicks until I exploded all over it, sitting up and shaking, my breathing ragged, the candle still inside me. Todd spilled his seed into Chase's mouth, Chase swallowing it all down.

"I can think of another use for that candle," he said. "But first how about we share some more wine and catch our breath?"

Recovered, we returned to the bedroom and Chase got Todd to kneel up so that his torso rested against the wall at the top of the bed. Then he lubed himself up and pushed himself into Todd's asshole. "Now, let me enjoy the candle," he said.

I'd never been involved in any kind of anal play before, but I'd watched Chase and Todd together, so I rubbed plenty of lube onto it and then used my finger to smear some in and around Chase's anus. I let my finger push in and twist a little inside him. Chase wiggled back onto me, so I tried again with two fingers. It was a strange sensation. At first, there was a resistance but then his ass relaxed and my fingers went inside feeling the spongy insides of his inner walls. I could imagine a dick going in there and I decided that at some point in the not-too-distant future I'd like to try that too. I figured I'd let them christen my ass with their fingers first and work up to their dicks, seeing as they were so huge. If I hadn't seen them fuck each other I would never have believed such huge cocks could fit in asses. I removed my fingers and slowly pushed the candle in until it got past the tight band and slipped inside and then I slowly pumped it in and out. I matched my rhythm exactly to that of Chase's fucking of Todd and I noticed that Todd had his dick in his hand and was sliding his hand up and down his own cock to match the rhythm too. We were in perfect synchronization and as Chase sped up, so did we. I listened as his dick pumped and Todd groaned on every thrust. Todd's hand went up and down his cock so fast it almost made me dizzy and it made that slapping kinda sound as he did so. I wasn't sure how much Chase was enjoying the candle seeing as it was nowhere near the size of Todd's cock until I accidentally stopped using it for a moment, engrossed in Todd and Chase's fucking and hand jobs, and felt Chase push back against me with a definite hint to start again. Todd was the first to blow, shooting his load into his hand, his head falling forward, forehead resting against the wall. Then Chase went next, withdrawing his cock at the last minute so his cum sprayed in a jet all over Todd's rear. I removed the candle and threw it to the floor, then climbed up the bed and opening Todd's hand I licked it free of cum.

"Anyone feeling sleepy yet?" Chase asked. "Or shall we head for a skinny dip?" We all ran down to the water, cavorting and splashing each other. There was no one else in sight and it wasn't long before I felt Chase behind me, his hard dick bobbing in the water, hitting me between my legs.

"Don't tell me you're ready to go again?" I exclaimed.

"I'm always hard around you and Todd. I just can't stop. I need an anti-viagra before I have a heart attack," he said. Then he scooped me up and ran with me all the way back to our suite before unceremoniously dumping me on the bed.

"That's no way to treat our Princess," Todd declared as he walked back in, shaking the wetness from his head.

"So how should we treat her?" Chase asked.

Todd asked me to stand up and then told Chase to lie on the bed. His cock stuck straight up like a hoopla game.

"Now sit on his cock with your face facing the end of the bed, toward me," Todd directed.

"I feel like I'm being directed in one of your movies." I laughed.

"Haley, this is hotter than any movie we've made. That's fiction, this is real life."

I took hold of Chase's hard as a rock dick and raised myself above him before slowly lowering myself onto his rod. "God, that feels so good," I said. Then Todd got on the bed and began to tongue and finger my clit. "Holy fuck," I exclaimed.

The sensations from both of them were too hot for me to handle. I sank and rose on that huge cock with abandon while I clutched my tits in my hands, pinching my nipples. I could feel my ass bobbing up and down while I fucked him.

"Yes, yes, Haley, like that. Don't stop, please don't stop," Chase commanded.

I now had a hand in my own hair, holding it off my face while I rode Chase like I was at the rodeo. I almost yelled yee-haw I was enjoying myself so much.

Meanwhile, Todd's tongue and fingers continued their assault on my clitoris and labia.

"Oh, please, yes, right there, yes right there. I'm coming, oh god, I'm coming, oh, oh, oooooohh."

My juices squirted into Todd's mouth and dripped down Chase's dick. While my pussy contracted, I moved up and down on his rod as fast as I could until I sent myself dizzy through lack of oxygen. Then I felt his balls tighten and he emptied his load straight up into my pussy.

Todd knelt over me and jerked off furiously until he too let his cum flow until it mingled with ours.

After a few moments, I withdrew and collapsed back against the bed. "I can't do anymore. I'm exhausted."

"Me too," Todd said, lying at the side of me.

"Wimps," Chase quipped.

WHILE WE SAT and gathered our breath, Chase went over to the freestanding large bath positioned in the center of the suite and ran the faucet until it was full of water to which he'd added a generous amount of bath soak. "Come and join me," he yelled to us both. "No sexy stuff. I can see I've worn you both out. Let me help get you clean so we can all enjoy a good sleep afterward smelling of the scent of vanilla with undertones of caramel," he read off the label. "Oh, that makes me want to eat ice cream."

"Come on, Haley, let's get in the bath. The faster we get in, the faster Chase will be quiet and we can get back to bed and sleep."

The bath was exquisite, the warmth of the water relaxing my newly aching joints and we took it in turns to rub each other's shoulders and wash each other's hair. We soaped up each other's bodies. There was nothing sexual about it, it was sensual. As we sat, limbs entangled, leaning back against the edges of the tub, I decided to make my declaration.

"Chase and Todd, I have something I want to say." I held up my finger in front of Chase's open mouth before he could make a sound. Now was not the time.

"I want to thank you for inviting me into your relationship. I realized tonight, that well, I love you. I love you both," I told them.

"I've loved you since the minute I met you. Didn't I say that, Todd?"

"Yes, yes you did." Todd agreed, smiling.

"Haley, I love you too. We love you."

It was the perfect end to a perfect day and we dried off our bodies and lay together in the most comfortable bed I'd ever been in. We definitely needed to ask the hotel where they sourced their materials, so we could have this heaven all year round.

It had taken me a while to find out where I belonged both sexually and romantically but there was no doubt in my mind that now I had found my two true loves and I couldn't wait to see what our future held.

THE END

You can read H, Aiden, and Eli's stories in The
Billionaire Series, starting with The Billionaire and
the Virgin (H's story)
Read on for a sneak peek...

THE BILLIONAIRE AND THE VIRGIN

Chapter One.
H

June 2004

"Henry, when can I take this blindfold off? I swear I'll trip over in a minute and squash the baby."

"A few more steps, honey, and there's no way I'm going to let you do anything that will harm a hair on either yours or our son's head."

I guided her further from the car down to the driveway until Veronica faced the door.

"Ready?" I asked. "I'm going to remove the blindfold, so it might take a moment to adjust to the light."

"Hurry, Henry. I'm so goddamn excited."

I removed the blindfold and my wife gasped. In front of her was the front door of a nine-bed house in East Hampton. She took a few steps back and swung around, taking in the enormous yard, then back to the front of the house. She was yet to notice the separate three-bed annex and when we eventually walked through the house, she'd see there was a pool house to the rear.

"Henry, what is this?" she asked. My wife was always cautious. She never assumed anything. Never took anything for granted.

"This, honey," I replied, taking her in my arms and stroking her honey-blonde hair. "Is our new family home. That's if it meets your approval once we've been inside."

"But it's so huge. There's only the two of us..." She placed her hands across her stomach. "For another five months, anyhow."

I kissed the top of her forehead. "Our son is just the start. Let's see how many of the rest of the seven guest bedrooms we'll be able to fill."

She laughed at that. Her green eyes glistened with unshed tears. The baby hormones had been making her very emotional of late. "You'd better take me inside to look at it then." She moved out of my arms and grabbed my hand instead.

I took her through every room one by one. Through the living room with its vast windows that flooded the room with light, with sea-blue couches reminding us that the beach was only a few minutes away. An archway led through to a dining room, with a mirror-topped table that seated ten, and then through again to a magnificent white kitchen. But of course, what I was now desperate to show her was our master suite—a large room painted white, with floor-to-ceiling windows adjacent to patio doors that led out onto our own private balcony with a stunning view of the ocean.

"Henry, this is too much."

"Vee, we came from nothing. Built ourselves up from rock bottom, worked our asses off, and now we get to enjoy the benefits of our investments paying off."

"I guess so." She looked out at the view. "And it sure is pretty. We get WiFi here okay though, don't we?"

"Yes, my workaholic wife. You'll be able to run your property empire from whichever room in the house you decide to turn into your office."

"I like to keep busy," she said and then she

clutched her head. "Ooooh." She gripped my arm. "Wow, that hurt."

"You okay?" I led her to the edge of the bed. Vee had always suffered with tension headaches—an unfortunate side effect of the stresses of running a billion-dollar business—but the last couple of days she'd been complaining more.

"I'm going to ring Dr. Anderson later," I told her. "It could be due to your blood pressure."

"You fuss too much," she said. "I'm just going to freshen up in the bathroom. I'll be right back."

"You sure you're fine?" I asked again and was given a narrow-eyed glare. I raised my hands in surrender. "Backing off."

"Good." She smiled. "I love you, Henry Carter, but I'm an independent woman and I can splash water on my face all by myself."

"I can't wait for you to see the bathroom," I said. It was enormous, with a free-standing bath and separate steam room amongst other luxuries.

Vee had been in the bathroom for a few minutes when I called out to check she was okay. Yes, I fussed; yes, she could just get used to it. When there was no response, I hurried over to the room, fully expecting her to chastise me once again for fussing.

But she didn't.

My beautiful wife was slumped on the floor.

I'd not heard her fall because the house was so damn large.

They told me afterward that even if I had heard her, I'd have been too late. An undiagnosed brain tumor had taken my beautiful wife. Our baby boy died too inside his mother's womb at eighteen weeks old.

I lost my wife.

I lost my son.

I lost my ability to love.

My world was gone and with it went my hopes and dreams.

Instead of celebrating life, we mourned the death of a woman taken too soon, and that of my son, taken before he even had the chance to take an independent breath.

I stood at the graveside with Vee's mother, father, stepfather, and her young stepsister. Amelia was just nine years old and spent the entire funeral inconsolable, wrapped in the arms of her parents. I stood beside Vee's father, who'd never remarried after separating from her mother.

"I'll never love anyone else," I told him.

"We'll understand if you do," he said, then he looked at his ex-wife. "But I never did."

I put the house straight back on the market and sold it to the first people who offered on it. I didn't give a damn what I got for it, I just needed it gone.

I kept the business going. I owed it to my beautiful wife to work my ass off to keep our property empire growing.

Years passed.

I had needs.

I visited a sex club, and I had my needs met, with no strings.

Never again would I marry or try for a family.

I bought the club and named it Club S.

Everyone thought Club S stood for Club Sex.

It didn't.

It stood for Club Stop. It was where I called time on my life.

ROMANCE IN NYC: Double Delight

Sold
Submit
Share

ROMANCE IN NYC: The Billionaires

The Billionaire and the Virgin
The Billionaire and the Bartender
The Billionaire and the Assistant

ROMANCE IN NYC: Forbidden Bosses

Abandon

Exception

Confession

ABOUT ANGEL

Angel Devlin is the contemporary romance pen-name of paranormal rom com and suspense writer, Andie M. Long.
She lives in Sheffield with her partner, son, and a gorgeous whippet called Bella.

www.ingramcontent.com/pod-product-compliance
Lightning Source LLC
Chambersburg PA
CBHW032139050726
47591CB00001B/20